miki a *starr*
novel

by miki starr

A REIGNSTORM PUBLISHING

MINNEAPOLIS MINNESOTA

PUBLISHED BY REIGNSTORM PUBLISHING
Minneapolis, Minnesota

Printed in the United States of America

Book design by #BEINGCREATIVE Design Depot

www.mikistarr.com

For Butter & Mommy

manic-depressive illness, is a bra
isorder that causes unusual shifts
    mood, energy, and ability
function. These are not the norm
   ups and downs; the symptoms
ipolar disorder are severe. They c
sult in damaged relationships, po
ob or school performance, and ev
suicide. About 5.7 million Americ
   adults or about 2.6 percent of t
   population age 18 and older in a
   given year have bipolar disorde
ipolar disorder typically develops
late adolescence or early adulthoo
   However, some people have the
   first symptoms during childhoo
and some develop them late in lit
        Bipolar disorder is often n
recognized as an illness, and peop
        may suffer for years before it
properly diagnosed and treated. It
   a long-term illness that requir
careful management throughout t
erson's life. Bipolar disorder caus
   dramatic mood swings from over
   high and, or, irritable to sad an
opeless, and then back again, oft
   with periods of normal mood
between. Severe changes in ener
   and behavior go along with the
   changes. The periods of highs ar
   lows are called episodes of man
                and depressio

-Psychology Today, definition of Bipolar Diso

DISORDERED

day of no return.

I hate Fox Harbor.

I wasn't born here. I was born in a major city – meant to be in a major city. A big city girl through and through. Now I'm trapped in this place. Fox Harbor. Where there is no actual harbor. Eternally trapped in this back woods, *The Hills Have Eyes*, pustule on American civilization.

I'm here thanks to Marjorie's alleged split personality, Atika Dangerfield. Atika Dangerfield, what a stupid name. Yes, I said alleged, and I say alleged because I don't believe she exists. Every time my older sister Marjie does some f'kd shit, she blames Atika Dangerfield. And honestly, what real split personality would name herself Atika Dangerfield anyhow? Shit sounds made up.

So, yeah, whenever Marjie gets busted doing some

f'kd shit she claims that Atika did it. The f'kd shit that landed Mom and me in Fox Harbor? My big sister slept with my father. Yeah, real f'kd shit.

∾

Normally I wouldn't have been home in the middle of the day...y'know, school and all. Junior year and I guess I wanted to stick with it and see where it got me, but I was sick that day. That's what I told Andie at least – I mean, Mom. It wasn't a lie, not really. I was sick of school and consequently had just had a big fight with my on-again/off-again boyfriend, Javi, and really wasn't up to seeing him, or anyone else for that matter.

So I was home, just Andie and me and Andie's guilt for being a crappy parental figure. A guilt that could only be alleviated by making me soup and sandwiches every couple hours whether I was hungry or not. Dad was at work, and Marjie had already moved on to live with some kid that was supplying her with whatever she was using those days while she returned the favor with the bank between her thighs.

Needless to say, I was surprised to hear the faint sound of activity coming from the back room in our basement. I'd snuck down there to steal an ice cream bar from the deep freezer while Andie was taking a break from stalker mother duties to use the facilities.

I thought we were maybe being jacked. Not that there was anything of value in that little room but still, kids'll steal anything these days. I grazed my tongue across the metal in my lip and contemplated investigating. There was a bat leftover from my days of softball, collecting dust and cobwebbed into the corner. I grabbed it, stifling the cough that the dust was stirring up in me, and crept to the little room. The muffled banging sound got louder as I got closer. I pushed the door slowly and it opened with ease, surprisingly quiet.

I gasped, mortified. All I could see before me was big black ass. Chocolate black. Were it nighttime, I mighta missed it. A big black and naked ass that was smiling at me. Taunting. I wanted to move my eyes away but I couldn't. I could see that there were slacks resting down and around the ankles, and I tried to refocus there but I was stuck on that stupid sideways smiling face and the purplish mark, that looked like the map of some small fishing village, just below it. The bat slipped from my grasp, clinking loudly against the cement floor. I wanted to look away but I couldn't until, fortunately, it moved away from me.

"Meg! I can explain!"

My eyes finally cooperated and locked onto a pair that, despite being about three shades darker, looked just like my own. "Dad? What are you...what are you doing?" Okay, it was a stupid question but what else does one say after catching their dad with his pants literally around his ankles?

"I can explain," he said as he pushed his body off the

bed, struggling to pull his slacks up to his waist, clearing a path to reveal who he was getting on with.

"Marjie?" My eyes must've been the size of golf balls. I found it impossible to be seeing what I was seeing, except I was for sure seeing it. "What is...what are you doing? You're f'kng Dad?"

My sister didn't seem to be as anxious to conceal her infidelity as our father was. She just laid there on the old twin-sized bed of her childhood, her golden skin glistening with sweat. Hers? His? In that moment I found myself wondering who else's semen was absorbed into the fibers of that mattress.

"Oh, grow up. He's your dad, not mine."

"He raised you. He may as well be."

Marjie rolled her eyes, then rolled her nude body to the edge of the bed. My father, now concealed, approached me, reaching for my shoulders. I jerked away, disgusted.

"What are you doing? You're f'kng your own daughter?"

"Now wait a minute, Meg. You watch your language."

"You're kidding me, right?"

He took a deep breath...looked like he was trying to get his thoughts together. My eyes locked onto the tear drop of sweat on his chin that was dangerously close to crashing to the floor below. Death on impact. "Meg, honey, in all due fairness, your sister is right. Marjie's not my actual daughter. She's not my *biological* child."

My face scrunched in a combo of amazement and disdain. "Who are you, Woody Allen?"

"I don't get it."

I scoffed. "How could you do something like this? How extremely pervy of you. Sooo, what, you're gonna leave Mom now for her kid?"

My dad actually looked confused at this suggestion. "No...no, of course not. I'm not going to leave your mother. I'd never leave your mother."

Marjie jumped from the bed, slamming her bare feet to the cement floor. She pulled her t-shirt hastily over her head. *Alkaline Trio*, one of her favorite bands. She reached into the neck, flipped her full head of thick and golden, curly locks from inside. "Uhm, what? This is total news to me."

My dad turned to face my sister, his chest still bare. I swallowed bile repeatedly.

"What are you saying, Marjie? You know I'll never leave your mother."

"I did not know that, *Lyle*. That isn't what you told me."

"Oh, that's just dirty talkin'. That don't mean nothin'."

"I think I'm gonna be sick for real," I said, backing up and using the wall behind me to keep me on my feet.

"Dirty talk? Just dirty talk, huh, *Lyle*? You think you can choose Andie over me? You know she doesn't satisfy you the way that I do."

"Oh, God," I leaned over, blowing chunks all over the floor. Bye-bye soup and sandwiches. Andie's hard work for nothing.

"Disgusting, Meg," said Marjie who, mind you, was standing there with my dad's ball sweat still sticky between her thighs and who knows where else.

"Here, let me help you," I heard my dad say over the sound of my retching but I, again, jerked away. I didn't want him to touch me. I never wanted him to touch me again. "Believe me, Sweetheart, I'm not planning to leave your mother for Marjie. I wouldn't do that."

I coughed and wiped the wetness from my mouth with the back of my hand. I finally willed myself to make direct eye contact with him. "What makes you think that matters? What makes you think that she won't leave you?"

Dad looked horrified. I assumed that this expression was exactly what mine was moments earlier, and it sort of fascinated me. Everyone says how I look just like him.

"Meg...Bunny..."

"*Don't* call me that. You don't get to call me that anymore."

"Bunny, please. You're not going to tell your mother are you? You can't tell your mother."

Our eyes locked. His pleading. Mine, marking that moment as the last time that I expected to ever see my

Dad again because after an act like this, I knew I'd never want to see him again. And when I was done – *"Moooooom!!!"*

"Bunny! Bunny, please – I mean, Meg. Honey, don't this to me. I'm your father."

"MOOOOOOOMMMMM!!!"

I could hear the scurrying of my mother's footsteps pounding across the floor above and then down the stairs. She called to me, letting me know that she was coming as fast as she could while asking if everything was okay. I didn't answer. She'd learn today. I only stood there in the doorway looking at my dad and losing sixteen and a half years of respect for him, while disregarding the scent of the former contents of my stomach, rotting in a pile beside me.

My mother, hurried, paused winded beside me. Oblivious. "Honey, is everything o...kay..." Her eyes followed mine and locked onto my father. "What...what's going on here? Lyle, what are you doing home? Where is your shirt?"

I tugged at my mother's sleeve. She looked to me and I pointed past my father. Mom leaned slowly to the side while Dad did his best to continue obstructing her view. She whispered Marjie's name. Marjie, who was still naked from the waist down and suddenly, decidedly bored with the scene, was casually peeling old polish from her fingernails.

"Andie, let me explain," my dad said, stealing my

mother's focus.

"Lyle...oh, Lyle. You didn't."

"Andie, honey, just listen– "

"Marjie? But she's practically your daughter. You've raised her since she was just a little girl. She's just a child."

"But she's not a little girl anymore, Andie. She's a woman – a grown, adult woman. She looks so much like you."

Mom's face scrunched with disgust. "Who are you, Woody Allen?"

"That's what I asked him," I volunteered.

"I don't get it," he complained, flustered.

Mom and I shook our heads. Mom shoved past her husband. Grabbed his shirt from the floor and flung it in his face. "Cover yourself."

"Andie..."

"Cover yourself in front of your daughter...in front of Meg."

He continued trying to plead his case as he pushed his arms through the sleeves of his shirt.

Mom gathered Marjie's sparse clothing and shoved them at her. "You too. Have some decency, Marjorie."

"Atika."

"Excuse me?"

"Marjie's not here right now, Andie. But I'll be sure to tell her you stopped by."

Immediately angered, I cried out, "She's lying, Mom! She responded to Marjie the entire time. She suddenly becomes Atika when you show up?"

"Shut up you nosey, annoying, little shit," Atika/Marjie-Marjie/Atika spat.

"Marjorie Grace!" Mom gasped, then stopped.

I could see the trembles beginning. The bottom lip, it always began with the bottom lip. Mom began to cry. I felt as though she was always crying. Then I felt bad for being disappointed in her. She was hurt. She should have cried, but I didn't like it, not a bit. She stood there, shaking and crying and clutching her eldest child's clothing, disgusting panties included. I wanted my mother to scream and yell and hit them both and put them out of our home. But she would never do that.

"Marjie, how could you do this? To me, your own mother? Why do you hate me?"

Atika/Marjorie only rolled her eyes and snatched the clothing from our mother's hands. Finally she continued dressing. "It's Atika. Atika Dangerfield. We've met. And maybe, Andie, if you took better care of your husband we wouldn't be in this little predicament, now would we?"

"Marjie, c'mon now. Don't be like that. You don't have to talk to your momma that way," said Dad, I mean, Lyle.

"My name is Atika," she screamed at the top of her

lungs, her face a roma tomato.

Mom jumped, visibly shaken. Her hands went up and her fingers raked aggressively through her wavy red hair, her nervous habit...what she did when she was on the edge of a break. I didn't think she could handle another one. I knew I couldn't. I was afraid that if she fell apart, we'd never be able to put her back together. We don't always get along, but she deserved better than this to be her downfall. No one deserved this.

I stepped past Lyle and grabbed my mother by her forearms, pulling her hands away before she drew blood, and guided her toward the exit. Her pale, Irish skin was flushed. Her cheeks rosy red and covered in hives. She stopped in front of the man formerly known as my father.

"Andie, just let me explain myself."

"Explain?" Mom laughed cynically. "Explain how you've been sleeping with my daughter, a girl that you raised like she was your own child, this is what you wish to explain to me? Don't bother, I think it's self-explanatory. You should leave. I want you out."

"Andie, honey. C'mon, let's not be drastic."

"Drastic? I want you out!" Her fingers started en route toward her scalp again. I gently took her wrists, tried to guide her away, but she wouldn't move.

"But it's my house."

I looked at Lyle, made myself look at him and asked myself if my dad was always such an ass. Mom seemed to contemplate his words for a moment. I noticed that she'd stopped crying – and it frightened me a bit.

"You're right. You're right, it is your house. We'll leave."

"We who?" Dad – Lyle asked, wide eyed.

"Megan and me. C'mon, Meg. Go pack your things."

"Don't be silly, Andie. You're not going anywhere, you have no place to go."

"Bye, Lyle."

I hadn't realized when I packed a bag to leave that day, I wouldn't be coming back for a very long time.

day #one.

Andie was raised in the tiny, Midwestern town of Fox Harbor, although I don't think she was born there. She never spoke much about her childhood, at least not pleasantly anyhow. She never told stories about...about... hell, I don't know, baking cookies with her mom for the school fund-raiser or shopping for dresses for the school dance. Y'know, corny shit.

Corny shit that kids and their parents do on those ridiculous television shows that my friend Cam likes to watch. Corny shit shows on corny as shit stations based in small towns like the one I found myself in. The type of ridiculous shit that I imagined that the people of Fox Harbor did. Like bring casseroles to new neighbors and throw theme parties for every lame town milestone event.

Founders Day. That's a thing, right? A perfect occasion

for some high-strung, overachieving, every committee leading teenage girl to put on a show and invite the entire town, and they come because obviously they have nothing better to do. I assumed besides the roles of like, sheriff and mayor and store clerk, people in small towns who have Founder's Day celebrations, towns with such names as Fox Harbor, did nothing greater than dabbling in irrelevant drama. This includes sitting around waiting for some kid whose future consists of gas station attendant and/or teen parent finding their self-worth in prideful party planning – where irrelevant drama will inevitably unfold.

So anyway, Andie never told Marjie and me tales of picking out dresses for stupid shit like the Founder's Day Ball. Maybe television got it wrong, or she majorly missed out on the perks of being a small townie. Nor did my mother ever tell us where she was born. I suppose I never quite cared enough to ask. All I think I know is that she and my Uncle Cal, her older brother, moved to Fox Harbor from wherever they came from when she was like three or four, and there she lived until she was nineteen and, not surprisingly to me, prego.

Townies.

After that she just left – or was kicked out. That story is probably the most malleable of all Andie-Stories. How drastically it changes depends on her mood when she's recounting it. Whatever is true and whatever may be false, the one constant is that when she left her parent's home, the only thing she took with her was the baby blanket that her great-grandmother knitted for her and her mother's name, sorta. Her mom is named Margaret so Andie named her first born Marjorie, in honor of the woman she hates. Interesting concept. Name your child after the one person you like least in all the world. Maybe that explains the depth of Marjie's mental and emotional issues.

So, pregnant Andie fled her small town home when she was nineteen, not to return except for on three occasions over the span of twenty-three years. Once when her father died. I was three years old when it happened and she took me home with her. I can't remember anything about the trip, but there's one piece of photographic evidence that shows me sitting on the lap of a homely looking, overweight bleach blond with ample bosom. Until I was seven, I assumed she was my grandmother Marge. She wasn't.

The second time was when she got upset with Lyle about some f'kd shit he did to her. Until recently, he was a really awesome dad, but he's always been a pretty sucky husband. Whatever he did must've been really bad because she ran away from home. Yes. Literally. Like a child, she ran away, but that's Andie. She didn't take me with her that time. I was in the 6th grade. Got up to get ready for school and couldn't find my mother.

No one knew where she was for a week, so Dad – I mean, Lyle – called his sister Donnie and had her come by and help out with taking care of Marjie and me. About three days in she flipped out on him about not being able to deal with Marjie on top of taking care of me and her own kids. Told him that they *"need to get that girl some help 'cause something ain't right,"* and then she left, too. I didn't care, not really. Growing up with Andie for a mother and Marjie as a sister, you learn to be independent early.

The third occasion was after Lyle, her husband of seventeen years, slept with her first-born daughter from a previous relationship.

ॐ

The first thing I noticed about the woman standing in front of me on the strange porch, the woman who I was pretty certain was my maternal grandmother, wasn't the shotgun that she held aimed at my heart. It wasn't the fading red hair that I can only assume when she was much younger, perfectly matched my mother's. It wasn't even how she had the exact same green eyes as Andie, like someone 3D printed them and handed a pair to each.

The first thing I noticed about the woman standing before me on the strange porch was how differently she looked from the woman who was holding me in the photo taken someplace in this little town, thirteen years earlier.

In the middle of the night we arrived – sorry, middle of morning is a better account. Sometime after 3 a.m. I'm from a major city, meant to be in a major city with the ways and habits of a kid from a major US city. We fled to a small town with small town innocence. Better adjective, naiveté, where it would seem that a person could show up on your porch after a twenty-three year long absence and know exactly where you keep your spare key.

What I did not anticipate discovering in a small town is the penalty for tampering with said key is a slug to the chest. In my mind, slugs to chest were reserved for major city living. I survived sixteen point five years in the city without ever having a gun shoved in my chest and suddenly found myself facing the reality that I may die in Smallville because the grandmother who I never knew didn't recognize me.

"Mother! Oh dear, God, what are you doing? That's Megan, your granddaughter!"

The old lady and I locked eyes, the fading version of Andie who was holding a shotgun barrel to my chest, wrinkled her already wrinkled face and took a closer look at me before turning her gaze to meet my mom – though not moving her gun. She turned to me once more, taking a few steps closer until we were separated only by the barrel, which was now free to blow my head off if she felt so inclined.

She let out a harsh puff of air, one that smelled faintly of cigarettes and highlighted by orange juice. She took a quick step back and placed the gun at her side. It was in that moment that my life occurred to flash before my eyes. I saw my best friends, Cam and Shonie, dressed in all black, taking selfies in front of the hole the coffin that contained my body had been lowered into. I saw my on-again/off-again making out with Yaves Mendoza beneath the shade of an oak tree. Asshole.

"Mother, how could you do that? How could you pull the gun on your own granddaughter?" My mom asked this question in a way that made it seem as though our being there was no big deal, as though we were there every other weekend.

"You were gonna shoot me?" I blurted the question out without really thinking about it and the potential consequences first.

"What are ya doin' here?" the old lady asked, addressing my mom, her speech accented with the flavor of the South. Surprising.

"Visiting you, Mother. What else?" Again, as though this was no big deal.

"Don't give me that *Mother* bullshit, Andie, what are ya doing at my house–"

"Were you actually going to shoot me?" I interrupted.

"–at 3 o'clock in the gotdang mornin'?"

"Hey," I cried out in mounting hysteria, attempting to command attention that she refused to give. I knew immediately why Andie hated her. "*You actually pulled a gun on me? You were gonna shoot me?*"

Andie continued, equally unfazed. "What's the big deal, *Mother*? I'm here. Your daughter is here, what's it matter the time?"

"You need to go back to whatever hole you crawled out of and take your spawn wit'cha. I ain't got time for your nonsense, Andrea." Andie's mother turned away, turned toward her front door and reached for the screen handle.

"*Hey*," I screamed, charging forward, reaching out and grabbing her spindly arm, forcing her to face me. "You hear me talking to you. You're not *that* old!"

Andie's mother, the faded redhead best known as Marge, swiftly kicked the butt of the gun, flipping it into her palms as she took a step back to once again get a better aim at my chest – this time shoving it in good and firm. I felt my stomach bottom out and I swallowed hard, trying my best to not show how I felt. I'm from a major city – meant to be in a major city where slugs to chest is a regular occurrence. I could handle this.

Somewhere in the background Andie yelled for the lady who gave her life to put the gun down. I could hear her anger and emotion although she didn't truly sound frightened. It was that realization that served to slow my heart rate and suddenly, I wanted to laugh. I wanted to laugh at the f'kdupness of the situation. The very first time meeting my grandmother at an age I'm old enough to recall, and she threatens to murder me. Good times, good times.

"Gimme the key you took."

I wanted to be defiant, tried to be actually, but a

double-barrel shotgun to the chest is the best disciplinary tactic anyone had ever bestowed upon me. Admittedly, I would have maybe been a little less *charismatic* had Andie kept a shotgun on hand. I reasoned that it wasn't worth the trip to the morgue and dropped the key that I'd taken from the hiding space, per Andie's instructions, into her pale and deceptively fragile looking hand.

She closed frail fingers over the small gold key, dropped the gun to her side again, and turned her back to us. I was angry...beyond. Angry at that bitch for pulling a gun on me when, despite my being half-black and tan tinted, she must have recognized me as her grandchild considering I actually still look very much like Andie. Angry at Andie for bringing me to a place that she nor I were wanted.

I turned away, steam from my ears trailing me as I headed toward the car. It'd taken us seven hours of driving to get there, no way we were going home that night but maybe we could find a hotel to crash at for a few hours of recovery.

Andie didn't seem to take the hint.

"Mother," she cried out, running fast after her. "Mother, come on. You can't just leave us out here. It's the middle of the night."

"Goodbye, Andrea."

"Mother, stop. Momma, wait! Please, don't be this way. I'm your daughter, your only one. That's your grandchild."

Andie's Mom halted inside her doorway. Leaned in, set the shotgun just inside. Stepped back out, letting the screen door slam behind her. She walked toward Andie, her floor-length white gown covering her bare feet, flowing in the breeze her fast movement created in the otherwise stiff air. She stood several inches shorter than Andie, yet seemed much taller.

She pointed a finger in her daughter's face. "I ain't seen you in what, six years? Six *years*, Andie, and I barely ever hear from ya. I'd think you were dead for Cal calling me. You show up with this gal I don't know at 3 o'clock in the mornin', snooping around my stoop, and I'm just s'posed to let you in my life? No, Andie, no doing. You need to get back in ya car. Whatever done brought you here, you need to go on back home. Deal with it there. Don't bring your manure to my door."

"Fine, fine. You're right. Tomorrow. Just let us in to get some rest and we'll head back tomorrow. First thing."

"Oh no, I'm not falling for that shit. Tonight, Andrea. You go back where you come from *tonight*."

"Momma, be serious. Home for us is hours away. We're exhausted," Andie pleaded, but her momma's response was turning away, starting back to her door. "It's dangerous, you know. We could...I don't know, fall asleep behind the wheel."

Crazy Lady stopped abruptly, turned to face my mother. Her face, which had been flushed and pink, was now crimson. She rushed back to her daughter, practically running. Slapped her – hard. With every bit of strength. She slapped my mother so hard her body bent sideways. Andie's Mom stood there for a moment heaving, her faded waist-length hair covering half of her face, thin nostrils flared. Andie's hand went up to soothe her burning cheek, but her expression was unchanged. My mother, Andrea Jeanine Blakely, who cries for every reason and none at the same time, was stoic. Tears jumped into my own eyes, tears which I quickly blinked away.

Andie's Mom turned her wrath toward me and I instinctively took a step closer to the car, seeking shelter. She jerked her head a sharp left before turning away and stomping inside, but leaving the front door open behind her.

I hesitated, there was no way...no way. But realizing we were left with few options, I dreadfully reached inside the backseat and grabbed my duffle bag. Slowly, I climbed the steps and approached Andie, who had yet to budge since her mother hit her.

"We're leaving first thing in the morning," I told her at an octave that I was certain only she could hear. "There's no way I'm spending more time in this whack job's house than I have to. No wonder you never visit this place." I turned to walk away, but paused and turned back. "What was that all about, anyhow? I mean, I don't get it. Why did she slap you?"

She didn't look at me. Her eyes were fixed onto

someplace in the distance. Something unseen maybe. She swallowed hard but still did not offer any indication of her true emotion. "I told her that I could fall asleep behind the wheel."

I shrugged. "And?"

Finally, she moved her hand from her reddened cheek and started toward the car. "That's how my father died."

day #two.

Cam: OMG! Where are you? U said u were taking A day. Dude! It's been like 3 days!

Meg: Something came up. Prolly won't be back to school til Monday. Be home tonite, doe.

Shonie: Gurl! where R U? Frfr. Dat bitch Yaves already pushin up on ya boi Javi. Bruh?

Meg: Handle it. There's 2 of you. 1 of her. I'll call when I get home tonight.

Cam: You coo?

Meg: 👍

I rolled onto my back on the sofa that was actually, somehow much more comfortable than my own bed. I stared at the high ceiling inside Andie's childhood home, wondered if I'd ever been there before. Had we slept there when Andie brought us to Fox Harbor for her father's funeral?

My eyes burned. I could feel the red veins forming. I was exhausted but couldn't sleep in a foreign and hostile environment. What was the point? I may as well have been outside already anyway for all the light pouring in through the grossly overabundant number of windows. I groaned and pulled a thin blanket over my face to protect my eyes. Who in the hell needed that much light that early in the morning ever?

"May as well get up. Can't imagine ain't much more sleeping you gonna get. Not with the light."

I scrunched my face behind my hiding place. Crazy Lady wanted to chitchat. Crazy Lady Who Put Shotgun To My Chest Only A Few Hours Earlier wanted to chit chat. Crazy Lady Who Put Shotgun To Her Granddaughters Chest Only A Few Hours Earlier actually thought chit chat was something we should do. Me. I'm her granddaughter and she knew it, though she hadn't yet acknowledged it. And still she felt compelled to put a goddamned shotgun to my chest followed by attempted friendly convo at the light of day.

The smell of fresh brewed coffee cut into the home's natural floral and stale cigarette-tinged scent. It absorbed into the coverlet, invading my space and senses and turning it's little pinky finger upright, tickling my nose and attempting to lure me back into the light. I hesitated, knowing that if I did I'd have to face and possibly communicate with Crazy Lady Who Put Shotgun To My Chest, only a few hours earlier. I preferred not.

I figured I could wait it out. Had to be any moment that Andie would emerge rested and refreshed and ready to hit the road. We could hit a franchiseless coffee shop along the way. My drug of choice. When she did, I'd rise, gather my meager belongings, and we could leave the shit show in the rearview. Eat a dick, old lady.

Of course we'd have to go back home to the shit show we originally left behind...we'd have to face Lyle and the f'kd shit that he and Marjie pulled. I was not totally with that but, I supposed, anywhere beat Andie's old crib.

The sound of a screen door opening caused a reaction in me. I heard voices that I couldn't make out, but neither belonged to my mother. Then came the barking, someone visiting with a dog and I really wished they would shut it the hell up. I'd never been much of a dog person. Not much of a cat person either. Guess I didn't care much for the animals with the exception of my mini macaw, Flaca, named for my favorite character on *OINTB*. I liked Flaca, and hoped for Lyle's sake that he fed her in my absence.

Remembering Flaca, I practically jumped to a seated position, tossing the cover, reached over and grabbed my phone from the coffee table.

Thu, Jun 1, 9:03 AM

Meg: FEED FLACA

Dad:	Meg! Bunny where you giys? Are you ok. Tell you morher to snwer her phone!
Meg:	FEED
Meg:	FLACA
Meg:	!
Dad:	About to call ao puck up
Meg:	Don't call. Just FEED FLACA.
Meg:	And turn on auto correct. How many times I gotta tell you that?!
Dad:	Bunmy uiu have ro talk to me
Meg:	DON'T CALL. Turning off the phone now.

A half second later my phone rang. The screen read *Dad*. I sent it to voicemail. Hardheaded asshole. I reminded myself to remember to change his name in my Contacts. Under the circumstances it seemed more logical to list him by his government name.

The stupid barking dog continued barking, the noise getting progressively louder. A tapping sound against the hardwood floor caught my attention – albeit too late. I squealed and jumped as far back into the sofa as I could manage.

"Go away! Get!"

Cray Lady approached us in slow motion, taking her time like she could care less about the potential of my being mauled by the ridiculously oversized mongrel, whose wet nose kept nudging my toes. But then I shouldn't have been too surprised. I mean, she had put a shotgun to my chest a few hours earlier and sure as hell managed much more efficient reflexes when she was trying to kill me as opposed to save me.

She paused a few steps away, a hand on one hip...the other holding a white coffee mug with black lettering. "I think she likes you."

"Oh, God. Well, I don't like her!"

"You afraid of dogs?"

"No, I'm not afraid of dogs. Just don't like them putting their slobby f'kn tongues on my feet!"

She hesitated another wasted moment while the massive beast repositioned itself and breathed hot dog breath into my face.

"Lucy Rae. Down, girl. Down. Good girl. Go eat."

The dog responded, obediently. Cray Lady turned away, following the dog to the kitchen. Great, fully awake. Stupid mutt. I decided to just go and wake Andie so we could get out of my floral and coffee and nicotine and dog breath scented hell. Cautiously, I slid back to a proper seated position.

"Who's dog is that?" I asked, breathlessly, despite myself.

"Lucy Rae? Mine. Had her for nine years. She's a Bernese Mountain Dog."

"Well where the hell did she come from? You've had

her for nine years but obviously she wasn't here last night."

"No, she wasn't. Momma ain't raise you with good manners, huh?"

I glared at her before turning my attention to the blanket I had begun folding – because I had been raised to have good manners. "Well? Where'd she come from?"

She picked up a stool and carried it to a nearby open window. She reached over, flipped on a small fan. A cigarette seemed to materialize between her fingers from thin air. "Playdate."

I paused, looked at her like she was nuttier than I originally suspected, then regretfulness for having engaged her set in. I wanted to give her the silent treatment, prove a point. Hadn't needed her conversation in sixteen plus years, didn't need it now. It was time to go, I needed to leave. I grabbed my bag and shoved my sparse belongings inside. I sat it by the door before heading into the kitchen.

I glanced about, couldn't help myself. For all the varying shades of bright colors and dark tones, the room was white – very white. Cluttered and chaotic, but ordered. Above the countertops was just shelving attached to white tile walls. Dishes and glassware balanced on them. A large white and black trimmed strainer solely occupied the top shelf.

The uncertainty of the space aggravated me even more. Actually caused me to like her less, if that was at all possible. Her kitchen was chaos, and in her chaos was logic, and her logic felt elitist despite her reality as a hick, and likely a bigoted ethnocentric one at that.

In front of one of the windows, the one above the sink, there were two shelves, both lined with small green plants. Before the other sat a tiny, aged version of my own mother, wearing grungy denim overalls and a lightweight plaid shirt with the sleeves rolled up. Her lackluster red hair was pinned to the top of her head with a few stray strands floating about. Her abnormally small, bare feet were propped up on a dark colored counter, crossed at the ankles, and she was blowing smoke into the air which was guided to the outdoors via the fan.

Lucy Rae, the bear of a dog who attacked me, raised her head cautiously when she saw me. Andie's Mom instructed her to lay down without ever turning her way. I didn't even know how she knew the dog moved and I wanted to kick myself for feeling impressed.

"Fresh pot o' coffee if you're interested," she said, flicking gray ashes into a soda can that had been sawed in two. "Your ma couldn't function without her mornin' cup o' Joe when she was your age." She glanced back at me, gave a look of assessment, and turned back toward the window. "Well, I guess your age."

I sneered at the back of her head. "No...no thanks. I can function just fine. Where can I find And – my mother? Where can I find my mother? What room is she in?" I asked, desperately longing for a cup of the coffee that smelled so *oh-my-gawd-I-found-religion* delicious, but refusing to give her the satisfaction.

"You know she ain't comin' out. You know that dont'cha? I'm sure she ain't much changed."

I shifted uncomfortably, baffled as to why she would assume that Andie wouldn't come out and why I should also believe this. I didn't care what some stranger said; we were leaving. We would deal with Lyle and we would deal with Marjie. We would make *them* leave...somehow. We would make *them* stay away, not us. What we were *not* going to do was stay there. Not stay there with Lady Who Puts Shotgun To Legal Minor's Chest and slobbering mongrel dog.

"You don't know what you're talking about, she'll come out. Why wouldn't she? Rhetorical, by the way. Where is she?"

"That rhetorical, too?" She asked without looking at me. "Which one are you?"

I scrunched my face, unsure of what she was asking. "Excuse me?"

She blew her final lung full of smoke as she smashed her cigarette into the half can. She pulled her feet toward her chest and dropped them down, then turned on her stool, jerking her head quickly and so subtly I wasn't sure if that's what I saw happen. Loyal Lucy jumped to her feet, then sat obediently beside the stool. Cray Lady *or* Andie's Mom *or* Lady Who Put Shotgun To My Chest, scratched behind the dogs ear.

She nodded at me. "You the little one. Megan. You the one that got Cutter's name."

"Cutter?"

She raised an eyebrow at me, looked a little startled then closed her eyes and gently shook her head. I began to feel impatient.

"Look, Lady, I don't want to go wandering through your home. Y'know, good manners and all. I just want to get my mo–"

"Gene. You're Megan Gene, aint'cha?"

"Yeah, so?"

"So, Megan Gene, why are you here anyhow? Not you specifically, the two o' ya's. What happened that made my daughter bring the two of ya here? She don't never come here for no good reason."

I didn't answer. Not so much because I didn't want to – well, I mean, I didn't. She was Stranger Danger as far as I knew, and what happened in our house was none of her business. I hadn't been her business for sixteen dot five years, why should I start now? But that what happened in our house led us to her house in the middle of the night, maybe made it quasi her business. I didn't know the answer.

But if it was or was not, telling someone my dad's pervy actions...I couldn't do that. I was not ready to talk about it and especially to someone I didn't even know. Someone I didn't want to know.

"I'll find her myself." I turned away and tried to figure which direction to go in.

"Suit ya'self but if I had to venture a guess, which I s'pose I do, I suspect your no account father had something to do with it. And if that's the case, you best buckle in 'cause you ain't leavin' right yet. Least not today."

I turned to face her again. She stepped down from the stool. Ordered Lucy Rae to follow her as she headed toward her back door. My breathing sped up and I could literally feel heat permeating my skin. My cheeks, in all likeliness, resembled small apples. I had an immediate and urgent desire to lunge at her, Stranger Danger who didn't even know me, let alone my father. I wanted to wrap my hands around her tiny little, wrinkled, old lady neck and choke her until she passed out – but then I recalled that Stranger Danger was also Crazy Lady Who Put Shotgun To My Chest, and I wasn't sure how accessible firearms were in her home.

I, instead, settled on a lame and admittedly useless eye roll and turned away, hellbent on finding Andie. But not without offering an under breath, "Bitch."

"I been called worse. But good to know you really are my grandchild. Like momma, like daughter."

I paused at the bottom of the stairwell as she exited the house, closing the screen door softly behind her.

day #five.

The thick air clogged my lungs. It was barely 8 a.m. and was already so unreasonably hot. Miserable. I sat on the front porch, sulking mostly, while beads of sweat conspired along my hairline and created trails down my spine. I gathered my brown, mid-back length hair and piled it high on my head as to allow whatever bit of breeze I could manage full access to my neck.

At the sound of the yipping bark in the distance, Lucy's head popped up, then moved down before she lazily pushed her body from the bottom step. She waddled her slightly overweight frame, melting away beneath her coat, to the fence to greet the small beige dog who had the unfortunate displeasure of being named Biscuit.

Lucy Rae sniffed the excited Biscuit through the fence. About four times the smaller mutt's size, that didn't seem to stop Lusty Lucy from crushing on him. She got props for that. Biscuit's owner, Clare, an average sized woman with copper hair, tight blue eyes, and yellowed teeth, caught up to him and leaned onto the fence, somehow reasoning this as a good time for us to become better acquainted. I scowled preemptively. That didn't stop her.

"Good morning, Meg. You're up and at 'em early, as usual."

I rolled my eyes discreetly. Hadn't meant to but it annoyed me that this person spoke my name as if she knew me, and that somehow, during my brief time there, we'd become homies.

"Marge is in the back in the garden," I replied, plainly.

"How's Andie, today? She feeling any better yet?" When I didn't answer, she continued in her futile attempt at bonding. "Think you're gonna make it on the road to home today? Hope so, for your sake. Tough seeing you waiting out here all day, every day and not getting to go anywhere."

I shifted on the stoop, pressing my back into the banister, removing all possibility of eye contact. If she had any hope of befriending me, reminding me that this was the fifth day that I'd idiotically sat waiting on my ride home was a sure way to ruin it. Who was I kidding? She was the idiot for having any hope to begin with. "Sooo, yeah, Marge is in the garden."

She stood a hopeful moment longer before summoning

Biscuit and heading around to the back of the house. Lucy looked to me, then in Biscuit's direction. When I didn't budge to let her out nor acknowledge her, she trotted back to the steps, tongue dangling. Life is disappointment, the sooner she learned that lesson, the better. She trudged along, moving sluggishly past me and to a water bowl, sloppily lapping up sun-temperature agua before settling down on the stair nearest me and staring into the distance with sad eyes.

In all fairness, for me, all dogs looked sad. Guess that's part of their charm...why people who like dogs, like dogs. Human beings need to be needed, and dogs have been conditioned to need human beings. It's just that simple.

I liked Lucy Rae – sorta. I sorta liked Lucy. I think maybe it's because she was old and without options. Trapped in a ridiculously hot, boring, and barren town. Confined to being cared for by a crazy woman who thought it okay to hold a shotgun to the chest of a female minor, even after she determined that said female minor was her own flesh and blood. And I knew she was okay with this because I'd been there for nearly a week and she had yet to apologize.

I'd come to like Lucy Rae despite my better judgement, because Lucy Rae was at least genuinely kind to me. She sat with me and kept me from feeling too lonely in foreign territory...I mean, even though I didn't necessarily want her to. She didn't pry into my business nor did she pretend that I didn't exist. She didn't judge me, but rather accepted me for who I was, and it helped that she learned quickly to respect my boundaries.

I related to Lucy Rae. Maybe she'd become attached to me because she related to me too, as we were both trapped with no means of escape. Or perhaps she was using me because, though I had no immediate means, Andie was bound to snap out of her crises soon enough and we'd go home. Possibly Lucy Rae had found her freedom in what I came to represent – hope.

My cell rang and I glanced at it. The name and face of my best friend, Shashonie Marie Jackson, appeared on the screen. I looked up toward Lucy Rae who was still staring, sad-eyed. I looked at the phone again through my own sad eyes. I didn't have anything else to say to my friends. I wanted to talk to them but I couldn't be honest. I wanted to talk to them because I was bored out of my mind, but they continued to ask tough questions and push for answers. So I pushed the button to silence her before she began.

"You wanna go holler at Biscuit, don't you, girl?" She stared. I sighed and stood, walked to the gate and opened it so that she could run around to the back of the house. Fickle, just like humans. "You can do better," I yelled after her, then quickly realized that she probably couldn't.

I looked up at the window of the room that Andie was in...had been holed up in for days. I didn't want to deal with Lyle, but this was ridiculous. School was officially out in two days and I was stuck in the town of my mother's youth, missing all of the fun and all because Marjie and my dad decided to do some f'kd – no, perverse shit.

Biology or not, I had to believe that what they engaged in fell under the category of incest or child abuse, or something. That was why I had stopped answering Shonie's and Cam's calls. Because my father was an incestuous child abuser...or something like that.

They were wanting to know where we were, how come, and why we'd yet to leave. They wanted me to dish on what happened to trigger Andie's break. And what could I tell them besides a truth that was so f'ked up that she would drive me 500+ miles from home, during the school year, and then lock herself in her childhood bedroom for days? So I dodged their questions and soon after, dodged them altogether.

I stared up at the window, becoming more and more resentful. I was used to her never being fully present, never being truly whole. We didn't know what it was about because she not only refused to discuss it but she completely denied it. But suddenly it was affecting my life and I didn't want to be there.

I was bored beyond what words could accurately describe. I missed my friends. I missed my bed. I missed my bird and my stuffed rabbits. Marge had no modern conveniences worthy of keeping a teen occupied. No cable, no DIRECTV, no Apple TV, not even a damn Chromecast. She had internet but her dated PC was as old as her damn dog. Just getting operational was an event. I'd brought my own laptop but in my haste, forgot the stupid charger. Were it not for the car I wasn't licensed to drive, my celly would've been a doorstop and I would have no idea that the brief time I'd been gone was long enough for Javi to have moved on and made things official with Yaves Maldonado. Another reason I was pissed.

Me and Javi had alternated between friendship and coupledom for almost a year. If we were going to be off officially, it should've been on my terms, and that bitch Yaves shouldn't have been able to post crap on social media about *"Chillin' wit' my boo at Icon, flaggin' the middle finger at all the haters"* followed by the hashtag *javisbitch.*

A small commotion and series of barks broke me from my trance. Lucy was running after Biscuit, if one could call it that. Hobbling was a better description. Either way she was going for hers and I respected it. Clare followed, carrying an arm load of tomatoes. I turned my back.

"Oh, Meg, glad you're still out here," she said, stopping at the gate, and allowing Lucy back inside. "None of us know how long until Andie is better, but I want to tell you that my granddaughter is coming for the summer. That'll be nice, won't it? She's about your age."

I turned to face her. I wanted her to see how little I cared about her or her granddaughter. "Look, lady, no disrespect but I don't know you. Why would I care about your grandkid coming to town, another person I don't know?"

"Well, I just thought...maybe you get bored here. You're not from these parts so maybe someone your own age, who's not from here but knows the area, would be nice for you. Get you out, show you 'round."

"Thanks, but I doubt we'll be here long enough for showing me around to matter."

She stared, tight-lipped, then adjusted her tomatoes. "Well, you never know. It could be fun, y'know. And she's like you, sorta, so you already have something in common."

I looked her over, tried to figure out her meaning. "Like me? Like me how?"

"Honey, she's a mulatto, too. Oh, but she's not colored like you girls. Her daddy's a Spaniard. Port-o Rican, I think. Or a Mexican. I'm not too sure, one of 'em."

She said it in a way. Like she was proud maybe, because a biracial grandchild meant no one could call her racist ever again. Except she was a racist whether she wanted to be thought of as one or not, and I was totally taken aback. *A mulatto?* Who even used that term anymore? What kind of f'kd time warp did Andie take me through?

When I emerged from my private thoughts, I was amazed that she was still bragging about her mixed race grandkid. All for my benefit, I supposed. I cut in. "Did you just call me a mulatto?"

She paused, looked dumbfounded – or maybe just dumb. "Yes, yes I did. You and Imelia."

"Who the hell is Imelia?"

"Meg, that's my granddaughter. I just told you. I don't understand, what's the problem?"

I stepped back and covered my face with my hand. "Oh. My. God. Oh my God, where am I? Why am I here? Why can't I just go home? Oh my God, this bitch has me messed up."

"Excuse me?" Her voice was stern. From carefree innocence to believing in whippings with belts and switches pulled from trees. "Now I don't know what got into you all of a sudden. I ain't been nothing but kind to you."

"You just called me a mulatto. To my face. Why not just call me a nigger while you're at it."

She acted astounded...*acted* astounded. Astounded that I used *that* word or that I used it in her place, I couldn't tell which. Biscuit started to bark and jump around anxiously. A high-pitched bark, piercing and annoying. Lucy Rae responded by barking in return but hers was stable and grounded. She had my back. I liked her even more.

"I implied no such thing. I think you watch too much television, maybe spend too much time on the social mediums. Or maybe Andie just made a mistake raising her girls in the big, cynical city. You want to be a victim, think every white person is racist...out to get you? Won't get far in life with that attitude, young lady."

I laughed, couldn't help myself. "Now I'm playing the victim. Really, lady? You insulted me –"

"I did no such thing."

"What in the hell is going on here?" Marge yelled, her misplaced southern drawl punctuating our racial tension.

"Ask your racist bitch of a best friend," I said, turning away and charging into the house.

I couldn't handle it any longer. Andie may not have thought she was ready, but I needed her to get ready. I headed directly to the stairwell, stomping hard on the wood floors to make sure she knew I was coming. I screamed her name as I climbed the steps and walked down the carpeted hall to the bedroom that I was certain reeked of body odor and tears – the scent of depression.

"Andie! Andie," I screamed as I pounded my balled up fist hard against the door. "Come out, now! We have to go, I can't stay in this place any longer. Just take me home, please...Mom!"

I heard Marge's small feet pounding up the stairs, pursuing me, Nosey Lucy trailing. She yelled my name, but I didn't stop calling for my mother. Had I my license, I wouldn't have needed her. Were I licensed, I would've just taken the car...left her in the room that she seemed to only manage to emerge from when I was good and sound asleep, occasionally leaving behind some faint evidence of her existence. Keeping it real, were I less lazy I'd have known how to drive and I would have left her anyway, license be damned.

For two decades she hadn't wanted to be there, so I couldn't understand why she thought I would be anymore okay with it than she had been.

"Mom. Mom, please, open the door."

"Little girl." I felt my body being swung around – hard. I came to be face to face with Marge. Sort of. She was shorter than me, much shorter, but her rage and her strength made her seem as tall. I felt intimidated by her, then cursed myself for it. She was nobody. A crazy racist with crazy racist friends. When I remembered that, I felt more in charge of my emotions.

I snatched my body from her grasp – or tried to, at least. She was miniature but damn powerful.

"What the hell was that all about? Huh? You come here, a virtual stranger in my home and start callin' my friend a racist?"

"Look, I just call 'em like I see 'em."

"Why would you say some dumb shit like that?"

"Because it's true. You should know, she's your friend. Birds of a feather, right?"

Her eyes became thin green lines and her cheeks were the faded red of her hair. She set me free with a shove. "I won't dignify that. Now tell me what she say that got you so worked up."

"She called me a mulatto." Not surprisingly, she didn't react. Seemed to be that she was waiting on the rest of the story. "It's insulting. Derogatory."

Marge stepped back, took a breath. "That's the term she use what to call her own grand-babies. She always say it. Say it to them, say it to their momma. She say it to their daddy. Don't no one take to making a scene but you."

Now I was the shocked one. "Then they're idiots."

"All of 'em?"

"All of them. The granddaughter, the daughter, and the daughter's baby's daddy. Yes, all of them. You can't just let racism go unchecked like that, I don't care who it is."

I folded my arms across my chest, satisfied. I was not the one. I made my point and while at it, got from her what I needed to know. That she saw no problem with her friend, Clare, running around referring to brown children of white parents, like myself, as mulatto explained a lot.

"What do it mean?"

"What? Excuse me?"

"You heard the question. So what do it mean?" We stood looking into one another's eyes, each determined to win the staring battle we were engaged in. "You gonna go around calling people racist, you best know what you're talking about. Now go on. Tell me."

"She should already know," I countered.

"Well, I reckon she don't know. I don't know and you don't know. You tell me the word a slur, well I'll be damned. But you better educate me on why...what make it so. Now you stop making all this gotdang noise in my house. My daughter ain't changed none. Been this way her whole life. She ain't gonna come out 'til she good and damn ready."

She turned and walked away, slapping the side of her leg. Lucy jumped up and followed as commanded. I turned back to Andie's door, staring at it. Trying my best to will it open. Marge was right about one thing, this wasn't the first time Andie had done something like this – the longest stretch of time but not the first. She wouldn't come out until she was ready. I turned and pressed my back to the door, sliding down to the floor.

୬

The sound of my cell ringing startled me. I felt around the living room floor near my "bed". I shifted about, rubbing my eyes and trying to focus. The light of the phone illuminated the dark, startling my senses. I could hardly make out the image or words on the screen, but it looked like Javi. I contemplated what he may want at...uhm...2:52 am. I contemplated not finding out.

I'd been gone for a week, and he was already making out in the streets and on social media with Yaves and this was the first time he'd bothered to call me and see if I was okay. I hadn't called him either but he's the guy; if he cared he would've called sooner.

"What?" I answered in a voice that was meant to be stern but was more a strained, hoarse whisper. He didn't respond. He said my name with a question mark, and I realized he hadn't heard me. Hashtag, fail.

"Megz? Ay, Megz, you there?"

I struggled to clear the sleeping family of frogs from my throat and tried again. "Yes. Yes, I'm here. What do you want, Javi?"

"Ay, where you at? Where you been? I'm startin' to get worried. Should I be worried?"

I took the phone from my ear and looked at it like maybe it was contaminated. "What the hell? You're worried? Since when?"

"Man, what you talkin' about? Why you gonna go and say some dumb shit like that? Of course I worry, why shouldn't I be? I ain't seen or heard from you in like, a week and—" he paused, took a couple breaths. "Look, Megz, I know you was mad at me and all...I be effin' up, I know that but you know me, you know how I be...how I feel about you."

"Is that the same story you tell Yaves?"

"I...what?"

I felt the fluid trying to build it's way up to flood my eyes, angry tears that made me more angry. I didn't want to cry over a stupid boy. I deserved better than Javi, I knew that I must. He was fine, no doubt. From NYC.

Accented. Bilingual. Street, but liked to read on the low. That was what I liked most about him. My favorite author was John Grisham, and so was his. I wondered if Yaves knew about that side of him. I wondered if she'd appreciate it if she had known.

I'd never liked Yaves, but for good reason. I'd never liked that *pinche puta* Yaves because she never liked me. She never liked me because the boys at school liked me as much as they liked her. Because they thought of me as pretty, and in many cases, prettier than her. Pinche puta.

"I know, Javi. I have Facebook, pendejo. I know."

"Ay, Ma, I ain't teach you that shit so you can use it on me," he said of my swearing him in his native tongue. "What the hell are you talking about, Megz? What do you *think* you know?"

"I saw her status. How she was at the movie with her boo and shit. I saw it, so you know what, Javier? *Chingate!* Go be with your new girlfriend. I don't need this shit right now."

I pressed the End Call button and immediately envied the generation that was raised with landlines and rotary dial. How good must it have felt to be able to hang up on someone that pissed you off back in the day. What a rush it must have given.

I contemplated the next best thing, throwing my phone against the wall but thought better of it. It was my phone and even if I destroyed it, Javi wouldn't even know I did so where was the satisfaction in that? Besides, if

Andie couldn't pull herself together long enough for us to get home, it would be who knew how long before I got a replacement.

Before I fully settled on a method of action to achieve satisfaction, the phone rang again. I connected the call but didn't speak. I listened as he called my name a couple times before I disconnected. It rang once again and I immediately sent it to voicemail.

The presence of Lucy Rae sitting upright on the floor nearby startled me and I jumped. She typically slept in Andie's Mom's room. I hadn't noticed that she was even there. Hesitantly, I pat the cushion to the right of me and she immediately jumped up, offering a slobbery dog kiss. I cringed, allowing her one of my cheeks before pushing her from my face. She settled in, her large body nestled against mine....comforting me, I suppose. I stroked gently and mindlessly behind her ear while I waited to see whether Javi would try again.

I didn't like animals, especially dogs. But Lucy Rae, well, she was all I had and she was the only one that had my back in all of the bedlam. My phone indeed rang again but I decided I'd allow it to follow it's natural progression until Javi resigned, or voicemail intervened on my behalf.

I watched the screen light up with a photo of him. Light-skinned, light brown eyes, black skully cocked to the side covering his low-cut curly brown hair. Pink lips curled into a mischievous smile. I considered answering... telling him where I was and asking that he borrow a car to come get me just so I could see if Lucy would bite him if I asked her to. See how much Marge's dog really had my back. I laughed into the darkness at the thought as I gave Lucy's ears a hearty rustling.

I stopped. It wasn't a bad idea. It was a way to get back home. I could figure out how to deal with Javi, Lyle, and Marjie once I got there...stay with Shonie awhile. Javi could do it if he really wanted to. He had his license and even had a car, although it was a total beater that probably wouldn't make it past the state line without falling apart.

My phone vibrated in my hand once more. I took a deep breath, swallowed my pride, and answered.

day #six.

I was awakened by the sound of commotion. It wasn't unusual for Andie's Estranged Mom to be up early smoking, cleaning, gardening, or doing some mundane task, although she was normally pretty quiet while at it. I closed my eyes tight behind the sock that I began the practice of tying around my head before I went to bed in an effort to protect my delicate retina's from the ridiculous amount of billowing sunlight in the morning.

A cabinet door slammed, jarring me. I wondered if it was her intention to annoy me, specifically, as payback for having accused her racist friend of being a racist. Make my being there even more unbearable than it already was. Another cabinet slammed, a dish clinked against the porcelain sink, metal clanged. I sat upright and, angrily, snatched the purple and yellow striped sock from my eyes.

"Oh my *god*, could you possibly be any louder?" I screeched in a horrible, caught-off-guard, early morning voice. The house fell silent. Miraculous and immediate. I held my breath, expectant, before releasing a premature sigh of relief. An obnoxious clang rang out, piercing my ears, startling me and causing me to jump so hard that I tumbled from the sofa and bumped my head against the coffee table.

I ground my teeth, digging my palms down and pushing my body upright, clutching my now throbbing head. "What's your problem, lady?"

"One thing, missy. You *do not* use the Lord's name in vain in this house. Am I understood?"

"Excuse me? This is some joke, right? You do it all the time."

"Is that understood?"

I paused. The spot where I hit my head felt cool so I pressed harder and looked at my palm. No blood. "You're serious. Yeah, yeah, sure. Whatever."

"Don't you whatever me."

"Yeah, sure. Yes." I chuckled at the foolishness of the command as I scuffled backward and climbed onto the couch. "Wow. So now you're making up new rules just 'cause you're pissed? You can't seriously expect me to believe you're some Bible thumper after you tried to shoot me the first time you met me."

"I tried to shoot ya?" She sounded surprised. Her shoulders shook with quiet laughter. "Not yet I ain't and believe you me, if I wanted to shoot you I wouldn't need to try all that hard."

Our eyes locked. I swallowed my lump whole as discreet as I was able. I knew she was only trying to get in my head...mess with me, but I didn't know her so I didn't really know what she was capable of. What I did know was that Andie left home for a reason, a good one.

I glanced away and reached for my cell, scooting to the edge of the sofa. I flipped the phone around between my hands, rolling my eyes until they landed on the ceiling and locked there.

"Fine. I will refrain from using the Lord's name in vain while under your roof," I said through gritted teeth and under duress. I glanced her way. Her lips were pursed and she did an odd full body shrug before she turned away and opened the refrigerator.

"Respect," she spoke almost as though she was speaking to herself, like she forgot that I was in the room across from her. "Doubt she ever taught it to her girls 'cause she never learned it herself. I tried to teach her. Lord knows, I tried to teach her."

"Look, you don't want us here, I get it. I don't wanna be here. So why don't you make her come out that room and take me home? Better yet, I'll call someone to come and get me."

She chuckled, first, then Crazy Shotgun Bible Lady

laughed. The consummate redneck. I glanced around discreetly looking for signs of the Confederacy that I may have previously missed, before landing my annoyed gaze on her once again. I was unclear what I said that was funny, yet she was tickled.

"I'll get a ride," I reiterated. Little did she know, I nearly had one. Unfortunately, Bad Boyfriend Who Owns Shitty Car had a headgasket blow two days prior.

"Chile, if you could hitch a ride so easy as you say wouldn't nothin' of yourn be here 'cept your dust instead of y'stuff."

A swell of heat puffed up from my chest and warmed my throat. I tried hard to calm myself before my light-skin gave away my embarrassment and the fact that she got to me. One point for C.S.B.L.

"I can get a ride. I'll call Uncle Cal."

Her laughter vanished, her face so serious I thought I must have imagined the whole scene. She slammed the refrigerator door shut and stalked over to the stove carrying a crate of eggs.

"He ain't gonna come here for ya." Her words preceded the sound of a skillet being slammed onto the stove top.

"Oh, he'll come. Unlike you and your late husband, Uncle Cal didn't reject us because of our race."

She paused, looking at me sideways. She blew air from her nostrils while shaking her head. I swallowed hard but I didn't blink. I forced my eyes to stay open and locked on hers.

"Don't call him."

"Don't call him because you're upset that he *didn't* reject us like you did? Not everyone measures how much they love against a person's color." I mumbled that last line. After the blow up over her color-conscious girlfriend, I didn't feel comfortable speaking my mind quite as freely. She was a little scary...a bit. Maybe in that way a good grandmother should be. But she wasn't a good grandmother. She wasn't even a grandmother beyond the technicality that biology presented.

But still, she was Crazy Lady Who Put Shotgun To My Chest. She was maybe five feet tall...not even. Probably no more than 90 lbs of land muscle. Faded redhead, like dull flames pouring from her, just waiting for fuel which I'd provided. She stomped over quickly, on tiny cat feet that moved so fast that I hadn't noticed she'd moved at all until she was standing before me and snatching my phone from my hand.

"Hey," I squealed, reaching out but only catching air.

Her face was angry and contorted but her eyes seemed more innocent and pleading. An unexpected combo that I didn't know what to make of.

"You don't listen. You don't listen!" She stomped a foot and flailed her arms in a frustrated motion. For a moment she was like a small child with an old face. A kindergartner with age-inappropriate wisdom. She turned her back to me, walked away, taking my personal property along. I felt suddenly empty, like a hole had been carved from my insides. Lonely and disconnected. Technology's design.

But then I remembered that I, too, could stomp and be childlike and had more of a right to do so. I made my way to the kitchen, standing behind her as she lit a flame beneath her cast iron skillet before plopping a large spoonful of butter inside. The sizzle was the perfect emphasis to her mood – and mine.

"This what you after?" she asked, holding my phone up, taunting me with it. I reached for it but, somehow, her reflexes were better. "I give this back, you don't call my son. That's the deal."

"Why not? You want me out, Uncle Cal is my way out. Uncle Cal loves Mom and me. He wouldn't leave me stranded here and he can probably even convince Mom to go home."

She dropped the phone into the front pocket of her well-worn and beloved overalls, or coveralls as she called them. She lifted an egg between her slender fingers and delicately tapped it along the edge of her frying pan 'til she hairline fractured the side, pouring it in before picking up another and repeating the mundane process one...two...three more times.

"Why ain't'cha call Calvin before now?"

"What?"

"I ain't stutter, gal. Why ain't'cha call him before

now? Why wait until now to call him?"

"Because I didn't want to just abandon my mother when she's going through a tough time."

"But now you don't care."

"I care, of course I care but she won't come out that goddamn...she won't come out and I know she's upset about wh...what happened but I'm a kid and I miss my friends and my bed and now, thanks to her, I'm missing the last week of school. The best week of the entire school year and I'm missing it. And my friends are worried because they don't know where I am or what's going on and you obviously want me out and–"

"Who say I want you out?" She grabbed a spatula and started arranging and rearranging the breakfast food. My stomach growled loudly, betraying me completely. She glanced my way and I wondered if she'd heard it. I stepped back and took a seat on a stool, hopefully taking my belly's contribution to the convo out of earshot.

"You say. Your behavior anyway. Your attitude. Slamming things and stomping around. It's pretty apparent, don't you think."

She chuckled. Proceeded to season her eggs. "Well ain't you just a little narcissistic thang. You got me all figured out, don'tcha. My knickers in knots so you say it gotta be 'cause o' you." She ended her sentence with the business end of a spatula aimed at me and I involuntarily recoiled.

"Now you can roll your eyes all ya want," she continued, "but ain't nobody mad because you're here. I'm angry because I don't know why. Angry that my chile up there relapsed, like she ain't never growed up...like she ain't never leave this house and I don't know why."

She turned the fire off. I watched her movements from beneath the hoods of my eyes. I couldn't help myself for feeling bad. I mean, I got it. We'd been in her home for nearly a week and I refused to confess what brought us to her doorstep in the first place. And her daughter? Well she just plain refused to acknowledge anyone's existence outside her own. But for my part at least, it wasn't meant to be disrespectful. It was humiliating. It was Lyle, my dad. It was Marjie, my sister.

She glanced my way with pursed-lips. Expectant. But expecting what exactly? The truth? A little side of honesty with her egg breakfast? Or nothing at all, which is what I hoped she was expecting because that's all I had to offer.

She made a sound...a small grunt on a heavy exhale and turned away again. Put bread in the toaster. Grabbed a plate and then another and piled eggs on each one, finishing in time to grab the fresh, hot, toasted bread that popped up eager to please.

She turned my way, her arm outstretched with a plate of food heavy at the end. I hesitated, took a gulp of tasteless saliva. My stomach signaled again it's disregard for my fragile pride, and I took what was offered. A small dish with soft, room temp butter and a mini assortment of jams sat on the island counter between us. I grabbed salt and pepper and dashed each before stabbing a fork into the eggs and shoveling them into my mouth.

"Your father called here last night. He what this about, ain't he?"

I choked on yellow, fluffy protein. She nodded knowingly and smugly stuffed a forkful of egg into her mouth. I imagined jamming the fork hard into the back of her throat as my own throat closed on me. I pushed the plate away and jumped from the stool and ran to the sink, sticking my face beneath the running faucet. Choking on egg. Choking on water. Choking on anger.

Her stool scraping the tile sounded and then she was beside me, moving me out of the way and thrusting a short glass of water in front of my face. I drank quickly and pulled myself together. I smeared the wetness from my mouth with the back of my hand. Pausing and glancing around, I noticed for the first time that Lucy Rae was nowhere to be found. I was surprised at my disappointment. A kind face would have served me well in the moment.

I didn't thank her. In silence, I walked beyond the island and took a seat at the small kitchen table. I desperately wanted to eat more, but didn't.

I sighed, taking the bait. "Well...what did he say?"

"He ain't tell me nothin'. What for if you two ain't here?"

"Wait, what?" My voice was small with my surprise. I looked to her, waiting...for something. The punch line, maybe? The catch? She slid a pair of reading glasses onto her keen nose and flipped open her morning paper signaling, I supposed, that she was done with me. I wondered how old she must be. I didn't know anyone who read actual newspapers anymore. Not even my Granny Hazelle, Lyle's grandmother, and she was 96. But, then again, at that age she probably couldn't see well enough to read it even if she wanted to.

"You told him we're not here?" I asked. She nodded. "May I ask, why not?"

"I figure if you wanted him to know where ya were, you'da told him by now. Was I mistaken?"

She closed her paper and sat it firmly, turning to face me. I opened my mouth to speak. I realized that she protected us, but I wanted to know for what reason. I mean, not that we were in danger but still, she didn't know if we were or not. But I supposed that was her point...why she was upset. The unknown. No one liked the unknown. She deserved to know, though I still didn't trust her or her motives.

Her eyes moved past me and I heard the all too familiar creak of Andie's Mom's one loose floorboard. I turned, jumping from my seat in a movement so swift and coordinated it was as though I'd planned it.

"Mom," I gasped, torn between being emotional and irrationally angry.

She stood there, gazing just beyond me, unmoving and unresponsive. Andie's Mom, Crazy Lady Who Put Shotgun To My Chest and subsequently protected us from Pervy Father Figure Who Ran Us Away, moved past me quickly. This woman, who had been so strong and such a powerful force since my arrival, was suddenly a frail old lady tenderly caressing her daughters arms and trying to draw her attention. She aged 20 years before my eyes.

So had my own mother.

She'd lost weight in that room. Her face was both gaunt and swollen, a complicated combination. Dark circles were beneath her red rimmed eyes. Her pale skin was drained. I had a sudden and overwhelming urge to pinch her cheeks and smack them gingerly in that way that she always did when she was trying to "get color". I was convinced that if I did so, she'd be quasi-recognizable but I didn't have it in me to move, let alone slap some blush into her.

"Are you hungry, honey? C'mon, sit. You should eat. We have eggs and toast. Want me to fix you up a plate? Have a seat, I'll make you some eggs and toast."

"I don't wanna eat."

Her voice was a horrid gurgle that sounded as though a ball of mucus and waste was trapped inside her throat.

"You have to eat, Andrea." And like that, Andie's Mom was the Andie's mom that I'd come to know. Firm and alpha.

"You always do this!" Andie screamed the words unnecessarily. Exaggerated, like she was calling for help. The extreme shift was jarring.

"Do what? What do I *always* do?"

"Try to make me fat so no one will want me! You don't want me to be pretty. You want to be the only skinny person in the house."

"Dammit, calm down. What on earth ya yellin' for? Now that's not true and you know it. You're beautiful. My, just look at how skinny you are. I just want you to eat so you can be healthy, that's all." Andie's Mom turned to me so quickly that my already on edge heart jumped up my throat and slammed against the roof of my mouth, before falling back into place. She grabbed my forearm tight and pulled me, aggressively, aside. Her voice was low but direct. "Where does she keep her meds?"

"Her what?"

"Her meds, chile. Her medication."

"What medication? I don't know anything about any medication." I became distraught in my sudden confusion. "Why does she need...what do you think's wrong with her?"

"Oh dammit, Andie. Dammit!" She reached into her front pocket and retrieved my cell, offering it to me along with a set of instructions. Go into the kitchen and open the last drawer on the right. There I would find an address book, can't miss it. Navy blue and says *Address* in gold.

Look under V for Vanderburg aka Clare the Racist. Tell her it's an episode. Tell her to hurry.

I had no idea what was happening or what any of it meant so I jumped into action, doing as I was told as she led my mother to the stairwell.

"Megan," she called to me. I paused to catch my next directive. "I did you a favor today, now I need you to do me one. Don't call, Cal. Don't call my son."

I swallowed hard and nodded in silent agreement.

❧

I sat on the floor with my back pressed against the sofa. Lucy Rae was home and at my feet and I was relieved. The weight of her large body blanketed my toes. I wiggled them beneath her furry frame but she didn't move, just stared with her sad-looking eyes. My head dropped low and I twisted a group of wavy strands that dangled and obstructed my vision.

I was tired but not sleepy. I looked through the strands and towards Andie's Mom. She sat on the ledge of an open window blowing smoke from her lungs. Her high knot bun had slipped down and sat low on the back of her neck. She lifted a mug of black coffee to her lips and I involuntarily cringed at the combination of nicotine and caffeine.

I shifted my line of sight to Clare who sat in the rustic beige leather recliner, propped dirty feet bare, with

Biscuit sleeping soundly across her lap. Her head was tilted back, a cold brew to her lips.

Andie was asleep – finally. It'd been a long and difficult day of dealing with her and honestly, I hadn't understood why. My mom was always a little different from everyone else's mom, but this behavior? It was highly irregular.

Cam's mom was a housewife who'd opted out of the working world and instead elected to stay home tending to the needs of Cam's pops and their four kids. An active member of PTA, part-time assistant soccer coach, and the consummate chaperone who baked and volunteered in the community – basically perfection. No wonder Cam was so screwed up. Bizzy, as she insisted we call her (irony not lost), was the neighborhood mom, always trying to one-up our own mother's by doing everything better, while still making sure that we ate.

Shonie's mom was an altogether different story. An attorney at some big whig law firm and single mother of three, who worked crazy long hours and wasn't around as much. But when she was, she was the one that would take us to the places that Bizzy refused. The one that asked all the most important, yet super intrusive, questions that embarrassed Shonie but that we, on the low, appreciated.

It wasn't typical for Andie to do any of that. She was always home, but wasn't one to offer rides or cook meals. She didn't express concern about whether or not we'd eaten or how someone was doing in a particular school subject. She had no sound advice to give. She hadn't even had "the talk" with me. If I wasn't so f'kn terrified, I could lose my virginity right under Andie's nose and she probably wouldn't've even noticed.

But she was also inconsistent. There were times when she did her job like it was what she was born to do, and during those times I called her *Smother* because that's exactly what she did. But most times she was distant. Vacant. She was always there, but not always present. And it was okay 'cause you figure it's just her way. It's all you've ever known. Perhaps it's the way she was raised. And since I had Lyle, I knew I'd always have someone there who would be consistently responsible for parenting me in some form.

But now what? Now that Lyle had reduced himself from Healthy Father Figure to Perv That Sleeps With Stepdaughter and Andie was...well, I didn't know what Andie was, and that was the issue. I exhaled heavily as I tried to figure out a way to pose my questions to Clare and Andie's Mom without totally melting down.

"Those pills should keep her out awhile, but she's gonna need her medication to control her. I'm all out of anything that can help," said Clare in a voice that made you want to scratch the inside of her throat. "You know I've known your mother since she was...what? How old was she, Marge, when Zeke and me moved in next door?"

"Seven."

"Since she was seven-years old. She was a cutie pie.

So curious...so filled with life! Red hair that hung down to her elbows and she was always so dirty and messin' 'round with bugs. She wanted to be a phlebotomist when she grew up. She ever tell you that?"

My face scrunched and I shook my head slowly. "Uhm, no..."

"Not a phlebotomist, Clare." Marge's voice sounded aggravated, as though she corrected her about this often. "Entomologist. She wanted to be an entomologist."

"Enter, what? Oh well, what's the difference?"

"One studies bugs. The other don't."

I stifled a chuckle as I watched Clare search herself for a clever comeback, but clever was tough to come by with her.

She turned back to me. "She wanted to be some kinda doctor. She ever tell you anything about her home? Her past?"

I shook my head. Clare was being kind to me despite my racist accusations, and I was allowing it despite my lack of confidence that she was 100% innocent. I supposed crazy-mom-sitch trumped down low-racist-neighbor.

"She's sick, sweetheart. In her mind. Has been for a long, long time."

I shook my head, firm. She wasn't sick, couldn't be. At sixteen (and a half), if my mother were mental I'd know. Andie's Mom smashed her cigarette into the half soda can and walked, barefoot, to where Clare and I sat. She was always barefoot. Even in her garden.

"She sick," she confirmed. "But she musta got it under control at some point if you ain't know about it. That's good, but she needs to get back on her meds. My guess she ain't take 'em since she been here."

"I'm sure she hasn't," said Clare. "Last time she was here, remember? She did the same thing. Remember?"

Marge let out a frustrated sigh. "Of course I remember, what sorta question is that? She come here, no meds, blaming me for her life. Listening to those...hearing..." Her voice faded and she stood there, her eyes locked on the stairwell. For a moment I thought that Andie must be standing there but when I looked up, there was no one.

I looked back to Andie's Mo – to Marge. "But what's wrong with her?" My voice was so small that I didn't think she heard me, nor did I have the energy to repeat myself.

Marge took a seat on the sofa a respectable distance from me. "Bipolar. They say she got a touch of schizophrenia but I don't really believe that one. But they say that one what make the voices come."

"Voices?" I asked for much needed clarification. The word felt heavy on my tongue. Foreign.

"They tell her thangs...thangs about e'rybody but herself. Always thank e'rybody aimed to hurt her. They say it's voices, I think it's just attention-gettin'. She have episodes...used to anyhow. Often. Wouldn't stay on her meds. Somebody tell her we trying to poison her, she get off. She get sad and lonely. Real, real depressed."

"Suicidal?" I asked tentatively.

"Sometimes. Then she bounce back. Get all over the top. Hyper and happy."

"Manic," said Clare.

"Yeah, manic."

"Manic," I mumbled, glancing away, wondering if that explained the irregular appearances of *Smother*.

My cell vibrated. I glanced at the screen. One more of a multitude of unread messages. I caressed the sides of my phone, considered reviewing them. But I already knew what they must say. What I didn't know was how to respond. I couldn't come home because my dad was a perv and my sister was his whore. And my mom...my mom was what? I'd heard of Bipolar Disorder, who hadn't? But it was usually something said in jest, a way to make fun of someone. That my mother had been officially diagnosed with a parody disease, what did it really mean?

"Just do me the favor of not calling my son, okay," Marge said to me, cutting into my thoughts. "He dealt with this enough...dealt with this his entire life. That's what got him out there where ya at in the first place. Give up a military career for worrying about his sister. She here now. I'll deal with it til she well enough to get home."

I wasn't sure I wanted to, but I agreed.

day #ten.

Thirty-seven and fifty-three.

Thirty-seven totaled the number of unread messages. Fifty-three was the total number of missed calls, including unheard voicemails.

It was another unbearably hot day in Fox Harbor – *West* Fox Harbor I'd learned. There was a distinction, I was told, and that distinction made all the difference. Most of the residents on the west side of the town were elder in age and their families had lived there for generations. Marge, originally from Arkansas, met, married, and started a family with Gene "Cutter" Schofield who moved them to Fox Harbor because it was where he'd been raised. Once he completed his military service, there was no place else he wanted to be.

I stared through the leaves of the tree that I sat

beneath, at the clear sky, trying not to blink but losing the challenge every time. My phone chimed again stealing away my attention. An email alert. That total was now sixteen.

Since learning that my mother might be a l'il unbalanced, I shut out the world beyond the small, dusty town, completely. I'd already been distant, sure. But I had to totally close myself off in order to focus on the present and not long for home as intensely. Mom needed me, needed my help despite her not having acknowledged me since she'd sent me snooping for spare keys on strange porches. Either way, reading texts and emails from worried and nosey friends, a no-good boyfriend, and a parent that was ultimately responsible for all of it in the first place, would not be helpful.

I sat in the backyard where Andie's Mom, Marge, was fiddling around with her tomatoes or whatever veggie had her attention, Lucy Rae by my side. Lucy Rae, my new best friend. We'd found a great, shaded spot beneath an oak but still couldn't buy a breeze.

I'd become an early riser against my will. Partly because of Marge's sunrise habits and partly because the bright light of day and moderate air conditioning made it impossible to stay asleep. Somehow Andie managed, unfazed. Daily, she'd lie around in that room with the blinds drawn and the door closed. I imagined her being up to her eyeballs beneath three layers of blanket, heat be damned. That's what crazy people did, right?

She hadn't come back out of the room. Mom Who Just Revealed Self To Be Crazy would not emerge from her room and set the record straight, now would at least allow Marge inside. The door was unlocked, so I supposed anyone who wanted in was able. I couldn't bring myself to do it. I'd managed to convince myself that seeing her like that...well, that it had never actually happened. To see her like that again would make it all real.

But it was real, wasn't it? That's why I was still there. That's why I agreed to not call Uncle Cal and have him bring me home. That's why I hadn't reconsidered calling Cam or Shonie or Javi. It's precisely why I'd called Lyle and yelled at him, yet refused to tell him where we were.

There was relief in his voice when he answered. He was sure that I was calling to confess a location...tell him how terribly I missed my friends and my life and beg him to come and get us and bring us home. We would forgive him and accept his logic that the lack of shared bloodlines and DNA made what he did with his daughter – *his daughter* – forgivable.

He exhaled and in a solitary breath, regurgitated his deepest and most sincere apology, immediately followed by his rationale which could not be ignored and just had to be taken into account which, unbeknownst to him, completely negated his *deepest and most sincere apology*. It only served to make me hate him all the more.

"Did you know she was sick?" I asked.

"What? Who's sick?"

"Oh my goodness. Mom," I screamed. "Did you know she was sick?"

"Sick? What's wr– oh, you know."

I guffawed. I don't exactly know what a guffaw is but I'm pretty sure that's what I did. I wanted to hit him and had he been before me, I would have.

"Now I do and thanks to you, I learned it in thee worst possible way."

"I'm so very sorry, honey." Now *that* was an apology, deep and sincere.

"How could you guys keep something like that from me?"

"Meg, honey, we didn't want you to have to worry. We had it under control so there was no need to involve you."

I was taken aback by those words...no need to involve me. Me. Maybe I was reading into it but his specificity was curious. Not *you girls* but me. Megan. "So Marjie knows."

"Of course she knows, but that's because your mother had her *before we met*. You know..." he hesitated. I smirked cynically, disgusted by where he was headed... where he realized he was headed. "She was already exposed to it before your mom met me."

Heat wrapped around the back of my neck, little fingers digging into my flesh. "Because she was what, like five when you met her and stepped in as a *father figure*?"

"Meg...Bunny..."

"Bye, Lyle."

"Wait–"

That's the last thing I heard before I disconnected the call. My phone rang again, immediately, and three times more following. I sent all of his calls to the voicemail that I would not check.

I took a deep, thick breath, and turned, taking a quick glance toward Marge. She was kneeling in the dirt, a small shovel in one hand. She sat up fully and arched her back slightly. She wiped sweat from her brow with her forearm before putting her gloved hand on her hip and looking over her handiwork. Her freckled shoulders were red and burned from the scorching sun. If I cared, I'd have scolded her for not using sunscreen. Complained to her about the risk of skin cancer.

I twisted my body and scooted around the tree so that I was seated in the direction that she was in, flipping my cellphone around between my palms while I thought. Lucy's head popped up and her eyes fixed on me. Once she confirmed that I wasn't leaving, only readjusting, she lazily placed her heavy head back down onto the cool grass.

I opened my mouth to speak but changed my mind. I closed my eyes tight, digging around into the tiny crevices and corners on the inside that just might house the courage I needed to say the words I wanted to say. Unsure how to reference her, I settled on her government label. I mouthed her name but she didn't react. My voice had failed me.

I tried again.

There was a voice this time, albeit an insignificant one. Marge jerked slightly, as though she was lost in her own thoughts. She glanced up and about as one does when they think they may have heard their name but aren't sure. She shook her head and jabbed the little shovel into the soil again.

I rolled my eyes, the action aimed at myself, and decided to stop thinking and approach the situation head on, like ripping a band-aid off a hairy leg. "Marge."

She turned to face me. "That ya little mouse voice calling me?"

I nodded.

"Hmpf. That's the quietest I heard you since you been here."

I made a face and reconsidered letting this woman into my business.

"Well, go on now. What is it?" she asked.

I took a deep breath before I spoke. "It was my dad."

"What was your dad?"

"Why we're here...why we came here, it was because of my – because of my dad."

"Well, now I know that. Tell me something I don't know. Tell me what he done to her. Tell me what he done what set her off like this."

"He slept with..." my voice trailed off, fell into a whisper. I decided that I'd tell her, I wanted to tell her but dammit. I couldn't say the words without my eyes stinging. I wasn't used to this. I wasn't my mother, didn't cry over every glass of spilt milk. Life sucks and shit happens. Crying about it won't fix anything. You suck it up. You deal. You find a plan B, not cry like a baby. But what's a plan B for such a situation as this?

Marge pulled her gloves from her hands as she stood. She used her slender fingers to wrestle a cluster of long strands of faded flames from her face. Once victory was hers, she slapped her thighs and Lucy Rae jumped up and trotted to her side. She looked to me, jerking her head toward the house.

"C'mon, let's take a break from this heat and get some cold lemonade. I squeezed out a fresh batch last night."

I kept my eyes on the soil, shamefully wiping away any trace of my emotion. I inhaled deeply and pushed myself from the ground, following Marge inside. I took a seat on the stool, the one I mentally marked as my own. I stared at nothing really, but my eyes landed on a photo that I'd seen plenty without ever really taking enough of an interest to actually look at.

The woman in the photo looked like my mother, with a serious face and maybe, if you stared really hard, the tiniest hint of a smile. She wasn't my mother, though. It was Marge wrapped in the embrace of a burly man with a pink face and bushy gray and white beard. Although his stern expression looked cold, there was warmth in his eyes.

Marge placed a tall glass beside me, clinking ice breaking my focus, returning me to the present. I glanced up...thanked her. She nodded and took a seat across from me. We both took long, refreshing swallows and sat our glasses down. My eyes moved involuntarily back to the framed photo.

"He was good man, y'know...a good father. I think you'da liked him. More'n you like me, that's for sure."

I disregarded her thirsty reach for positive feedback. "How long were you two married?"

"Cutter and me? Shoots, nearly thirty-five years before I lost him. Only man I'd known."

I caught her meaning and tried to hide my cringe. I didn't know what more to say, what questions to ask, or even if I should say or ask anything. When someone's spouse is dead, what's the etiquette?

"So now spit it out," she said, sparing me more awkward inquiry. "What's this ya daddy, uhh, Lloyd...?"

"Lyle."

"Lyle, what he done that got you here?"

I tuned back into my drink. Put it to my lips and had the final swallow, then twirled the glass around between my palms. "He slept with Marjie." My voice was whisper quiet. She possibly hadn't even heard me. I couldn't tell because she didn't react one way or another. She drank the rest of her lemonade. Stood and took both empty glasses with her, placing them in the sink. All calm, all without reaction, and for a sec, I wondered if maybe Dad was right and I *was* overreacting.

"How long that been goin' on?" she asked without looking at me.

I shrugged my shoulders and turned in my seat. "Awhile, I'm guessing. But I don't really know."

"Sonofabitch," she said under her breath.

"I-I caught them...together," I volunteered. Now that I'd put it out there, I just wanted all of it out. It had been, like, a huge burden that I had to carry around and now I wanted someone else to have it. "I...they...they think it's okay, I think. Because they aren't actually blood related. But it's not okay...right? It's not okay because he's her dad. Period. He's been there since she was just a little kid."

"What make you think this ain't been going on the whole time?"

I was appalled, the thought was shameful. My dad was a perv but he was not some sick child molester. "What kinda shitty question is that?"

"A realistic one. What make you so sure he ain't been doing this all her life with him?"

"Because my dad's not some sicko. He wouldn't do that."

"Except he did, says you."

I slammed my palms hard against the counter and stood. "Oh, bullshit. However f'kd it is, Marjie's an adult and she wanted to...she wanted to do...what she was doing, she wanted to do it with him. She made that perfectly clear. So, no, I don't think it's been going on all of her life."

The house fell silent. I could hear nothing more than my own heartbeat, heavy breathing, and the second hand ticking. She stared at me, considering possibly. She backed down, nodded at the chair and I hesitantly sat again.

"So, she sick, too?"

"What?"

"Marjie. She got your mama affliction?"

"No." I said it vehemently, as though it were an impossibility. But the truth of the matter was, I had no idea. How could I? I hadn't even known my own mother had what Marge referred to as *an affliction*.

I took a deep breath and opened my mouth to say something but there was no sound. Instead, there was only a thought. Two. Atika. Dangerfield. But Atika wasn't real. She was just Marjie's excuse for doing the f'kd shit that Marjie did. Marjie was not crazy, not actually. She was pretty and she was first-born and she was used to having her own way. She was spoiled and despite our family not being anywhere near wealthy, she was entitled.

But she was not crazy. She was just an asshole.

"I'm certain."

"Well, so long as ya certain. Somebody woulda asked you that same question about ya momma two weeks ago, you'da been certain then, too."

We sat together in silence. I wondered how much she knew about my father. Had they met? They'd spoken, that much was clear but she was unsure of his name. Had Andie talked to her mom about her husband, her relationship? They'd been together longer than I'd been alive so it was possible. There was so much about my parents private life that I did not know.

I wondered if dishing to Andie's Mom was a betrayal to my dad. Pervy Sleeps With Stepdaughter but still my dad. He hadn't always been that guy. He'd once been Dad that showed up at softball games to cheer me on. Dad who picked me up when I accidentally got chocolate wasted on Shonie's mom's secret stash and had my lip pierced – twice, and he didn't even yell at me. He was Dad of Many Coats, not just this one thing and if Andie's Mom hadn't known him before I came to be chest to barrel on her front porch, this would be her only impression of him courtesy of my inability to keep my mouth shut.

She picked up her cigarette pack from the counter and pounded it against the base of her palm a few times. "Gonna head into town in a minute."

"What?" I asked, startled back into reality.

"Clare'll be here...oh, I don't know, in about a few more minutes or so. You're welcome to come with if ya like. Get away from the house."

My focus went to the cigarette she was pulling carefully from the pack. She took the lighter from behind the plastic and put the cancer stick between her lips. She leaned into the flame as she inhaled her carcinogen. She turned partway toward the open window, blowing smoke as she leaned over and switched the small fan on.

"He's not all bad, y'know. What he did...it was pretty f'kd – it was messed up. Royally. But he hasn't been all bad."

She nodded slowly, as though she'd already lost interest, while she played around with the smoke in her mouth. "Y'know, you don't need my approval to feel however you may feel about your father...'bout what happened."

"Of course I don't," I answered, fully offended.

She nodded again, then carefully put the flame out at the tip with calloused fingers. She exited the kitchen, aimed for the front door just before a horn triple beeped.

"So you comin' or what?"

I chewed the inside of my mouth in anger, annoyance, frustration, and wordlessly stood from the stool and followed her outdoors.

❧

My very first venture away from Andie's childhood home, first foray into the core of Fox Harbor. I trailed Marge and Clare down aisles of plants and seeds and plant food in a Menard's-style hardware and supply store. The greatest distinction being the engagement of consumers, who halted with shopping carts adorned with bald babies and blonde tykes, swapping recipes or stories about school age kids and coaches. Townie talk.

I stopped in an aisle a few feet from where Marge and Clare stood conspiring over gardening supplies. Possibly ceramic pottery or soil. Super exciting shit. My thumb hovered the keypad on my phone as I contemplated while I waited. Contemplated whether or not I should respond to the latest text from Shonie. None too pleasant by this point. Pretty pissed. Kinda concerned. Mostly slighted. Friends since grade school, even before we met Cam, and she was salty that I wasn't telling her what was up. Didn't have to read her messages to know this. She had every right.

I indeed earned her aggression and I had to tell her something sensible. I had been gone for an eternity and had not bothered to confide in anyone.

My phone rang, timed just perfect for me to answer the call instead of initiate a text. Great. I stared at my sister's face which stared back from the corner of the screen. The last face I wanted to see. The last voice I wanted to hear. I started in Marge and Clare's direction, thoughtlessly, staring at my siblings face. Perfectly gold skin with loose golden curly locs, streaked in platinum around the ends. Not dyed that way, just a natural occurrence. Same hazel eyes as mine and yet hers were somehow better...prettier. Everyone loved Marjie. They didn't know how f'kd up she was. Or, possibly they did and that's what they loved most.

I could hear her voice, small and distant, calling my name which changed from *Meg* to *f'kn bitch* when I refused to comply. So I responded with a forceful press to the END button.

Small pressure against each of my thighs startled me and I stopped walking. I looked down into the chocolatey mess of a face on the little person that was touching me. I like kids about as much as I like animals that aren't Flaca or, for that matter, Lucy Rae. I couldn't tell if she was meant to be a toddler, or just a small regular kid, or what, but she was a mess and leaving what appeared to be chocolate ice cream handprints on my cream colored shorts. F'k!

"Becca! Oh, Becca, look at what you did," said a girl with a small face and long, three-dimensional brown hair...the kind from shampoo commercials. "I am so sorry about that. She didn't mean it. She just got away. I'm so sorry. Becca, apologize to the nice lady."

My chest heaved softly in my anger and I bit the inside of my lip, hard, to avoid cursing the mother and then turning my wrath to the kid. I was not a nice lady. My eyes went from the mom that looked too young to be a mom, except she had another grubby girl clutched to her hip, then back to *Messy Becca* who smiled up at me, showing off a tiny set of teeth. I imagined this was for my benefit. This was where I was meant to be overcome with affection for this stranger's kid courtesy of her chipmunk cheeked smile and Chiclet chompers. This was the point that I was meant to say, *It's cool,* because her cute factor trumped her inability to watch where she was going.

"Hey, hey, so sorry about that. Here, maybe this'll help."

At the sound of a voice addressing me, I spared the little person my death gaze, landing it on a guy in a green smock. I discreetly looked him over. The hint of a sleeve of tatts peered from beneath his rolled cuffs. I counted four piercings in his face and what appeared to be at least 3/4" gauges in each ear (Javi only wore one and it was barely a .25"). His eyes were brown and his fair-skin was richly tanned. Despite it being hotter than Hades in August, he was true to the trend of the black beenie. Respect. An oddity in a strange land. I spied his name tag. It read, Wesley.

He addressed me again and I remembered that he was offering help. I took the damp cloth held out to me and mumbled, "Thanks."

"Hey, sorry about that, really. She's my niece. Guess she's had a little too much sugar today, right, Ness?"

My eyes returned to the one called Ness, his sister I assumed, considering they looked so much alike. I roved back and forth between the siblings, Hot Hardware Store Guy and Irresponsible Chocolate Treating Mom. Ness looked ashamed as she reached for and finally managed to grab hold of the kids messy hand.

"Sorry," she repeated as she backed away. "So sorry."

I wasn't going to give her the satisfaction of telling her it was okay, I flat out refused. It wasn't.

"My bad. That's my sister, Ness. Vanessa. She's a little in over her head."

"It's okay," I said involuntarily. I didn't feel that way, but he was really cute. "Kids, y'know."

"You new here? I never seen you before."

I laughed sarcastically. "You know everybody around here or something?"

He shrugged. "Yeah, pretty much. Small town, but it's expanding."

"Oh. Makes sense. Yeah, I'm visiting with—"

"Meg, c'mon. Let's head on out. Meet you at the register." Marge carried a bag nearly the same size as she was as she followed alongside Clare who pushed a full cart.

"You know Old Mrs. Schofield?" Wesley asked, seemingly surprised.

"Yeah, she's my...well, she's my mom's mom."

His eyes widened but he tamed them quickly. "Oh. Cool."

Disappointed, I responded, "Yup, Old Mrs. Schofield's kid dabbled in the chocolatey third of the Neapolitan ice cream bucket."

"That's not what I mean."

I nodded, knowingly. "Sure, it isn't. Hey, thanks for the towel." I threw it back at him. He caught it and stood dumbfounded as I headed off to join Marge and Clare. There was silence. Then footsteps, and soon he was upon me.

"I'm not some kinda stupid racist asshole, if that's what you're implying."

"Sounds like something a racist asshole would say."

"No. No way." He stepped ahead of me, cutting me off. "Are you kidding me? I just didn't know...well, I mean...I didn't know she had family, let alone family that would care to be around her. She's kind of a bitch. No offense."

I smiled, sincerely. First real smile in weeks. His acknowledgement of Marge as a bitch, well, it was kinda hot. "None taken. Sorry I thought you were being...y'know. It's just this town kinda..."

"It's all good as long as you know I'm not."

"Sweet." My eyes went down to my fingers and, suddenly, I felt crazy shy.

"So how long you in town for?"

"I, uhh...I'm not really sure–"

"Meg, c'mon. Let's go," Marge yelled after me, rudely disregarding that I was in the middle of a conversation with a cute boy.

"Guess you should get going," said Wesley.

"Guess so. *Old Mrs. Schofield* is gettin' kinda bitchy." I laughed, awkwardly, at my lame attempt at making a joke. "Thanks again for the towel."

He nodded, tossing it from hand to hand. He smiled at me. His smile was beautiful. "Yeah...you're welcome. Sorry Bex messed up your shorts. It was nice meeting you, though."

"Same here." Reluctantly, I turned away and headed in Marge and Clare's direction.

"Oh, hey, what's your name?" He called after me.

"Meg!"

"Meg, right...right. Hope to see you again, Meg!"

I bit down on my lip as I waved and I swear I did a full body blush. I hadn't blushed so hard since the first time Javi spit game at me. I caught up to my ride, hopeful that I would get to see Wesley again.

day #sixteen.

"Eat your food."

Marge turned away and began slamming dishes here and there, opening and closing drawers as though she forgot what she needed the moment she looked inside.

Dirty dishes that she'd just created from prepping a dinner for us of fried chicken, green beans, and packaged dinner rolls. I looked down at my plate and stabbed at the gigantic hunk of breaded breast that was cooked a little too well, fried a little too dark. Otherwise, I supposed it smelled just fine.

A loud thud from above us stole my attention. I jumped hard and looked to the ceiling. It had been like this for most of the evening but became increasingly raucous over the past hour.

Andie had barely stirred in the two weeks we had been confined to Fox Harbor. So earlier in the day when I got my first whiff of activity, hell, I was like Lucy Rae when being asked *Do you wanna go outside?* My head popped up, my ears perked and my breath caught in my throat. Had I a tail, I'd have wagged it. No shame.

Marge and me were watching a film in black and white on a local channel. I hadn't even known there was such a thing as movies sans cable but it was and I wouldn't suggest that she and I were bonding, but we were stuck together and making the best of things. The movie starred a young Kirk Douglas which made time with her tolerable, if mildly.

There was a sound...one distinct noise had my attention and I was on pins waiting, hoping that Andie would emerge, fresh-faced and freckled as she is with bag in hand, car keys jingling, smiling and saying, *Hey Bunny, get your shit and let's blow this biatch!*

Fine so she would never say that exactly but insert some Andie-ism in it's place that sent the same message, and you get my meaning.

I was no more prepared to face Marjie and Lyle than I had been after we arrived in front of Marge's shotgun, but I figured maybe Andie could convince her husband to leave the house considering he was the asshole that screwed everything up, not her. Marjie would be easy. Take her keys, change the locks, put her shit on the stoop. She was too old to constantly run home anyhow. Goodbye,

Marjorie. Goodbye, Atika.

But there was no emerging Andrea. No bag in hand. No jingling of keys. Only silence...loud, loud silence interrupted by the voice of Kirk telling us that, "Bad news sells best, because good news is no news."

No truer words, Kirk Douglas. I call that, wisdom.

Periodically throughout the duration of the day there had been similar sounds from above. Some were thuds and others were bumps, but all were taunting. At other times the sounds were hardly distinct and I questioned whether I'd heard them at all.

At a point I decided that someone should check on her and if it wasn't going to be her own mother then it would have to be me. Me. The daughter who had stuck around to be supportive even though I couldn't bear to face her once the crazy gene reared. It was as though coming into direct contact with her would cause it to dislodge itself from its hiding place, stretch open her mouth and leap free and into my own mouth agape from the sheer awe of it. It would consume me, slowly burrowing itself into my cerebral cortex.

I approached the stairwell with caution and looked up into the dismal abyss but found that I could not remember how this architecture worked. I held tightly to both banisters but couldn't move.

A hand placed on my shoulder brought me out of my trance and I looked back to face Marge who politely shook her head, wordlessly advising me to leave things be. I hadn't understood why or what the big deal was about just checking in on Andie but for whatever reason, I was actually relieved to be pulled away. I was obedient.

I tried to change the subject in my mind and find ways to distract myself from what it was that I was most curious about. But when the randomness of robust vibrations became louder and more restless and incessant, my contentment with allowing Andie private self-expression began to dissipate.

Marge insisted it would all be *just fine* and in lieu of dealing with her daughter's outbursts directly, Lady Who Put Gun To Granddaughters Chest At First Meeting took a different approach. She fried chicken.

"Someone's gotta go up there," I told Marge, pushing my plate away.

"No one's gotta do anything but let her work it out how she do. Eat." She pushed the plate to me again.

"Do you actually expect me to eat right now?" I pushed the plate away.

The sound of the back door opened. I knew who it was, who it always was.

"How's she doin'?" Clare asked. A loud triple thump was the response.

"That answer your question?" I barked. Clare's presence annoyed me. I didn't know why she was always around, always involved in what should have been a private family matter. I mean, I understood to a degree.

Understood that in Clare's eyes my mom was Little Andie Schofield, Margaret and Cutter's kid. But Little Andie Schofield had been gone for more than two decades with only three visits in between, including this one. I had not discussed any of this with anyone outside of the family dynamic, not even with Shonie who was more of a sister to me than a friend, because I understood the importance of keeping family business, family's business.

Yet here was Marge calling to Clare every time, and this relative non-relative sticking her nose where it didn't belong. Little Andie Schofield had moved on and had a life of her own that Clare, and Marge for that matter, had no involvement in, so how could they possibly know what was right or best for her?

"Someone has to go up there," I repeated the sentiment.

"Eat your food," Marge commanded.

"No. I don't want to eat," I screamed, flinging the plate across the table, sending beans to scatter about.

"You damn, ungrateful–" Marge mumbled as she began cleaning the mess I made.

I jumped from my chair, fed up with the nonsense of pretending that nothing out of the ordinary was going on. "She could hurt herself. I'm going up."

Clare rushed after me, aimed to stop me but I turned and glared a warning for her to refrain from touching me. Instead, she attempted to reason with me.

"Dear, I know this is hard to deal with, it all being so new to you but if you just let her get it out, she'll tire herself out and fall asleep. It's how this works. She doesn't want to hurt herself, she just wants some attention."

I was incredulous. I looked at Clare as though she were a plague that had sole responsibility for this disease my mother had...the cause of it's existence.

"That's how it works, huh?"

"Yes. Yes, dear, that's how it works. That's Andie's pattern."

"Let me ask you something, both of you. When did you see my mother last? Either of you? When was the last time that either of you spent any time around my mother?"

Clare looked befuddled, like she was doing mental arithmetic but was getting the order confused. She finally settled on, "It's been some years."

"Some years. How often do either of you visit her? Call her and ask how she's been, how her kids are? If she needs anything? Do you even know her? Silence, huh. So – and I say this with as much respect as I can possibly muster – what the f'k do you know?"

Her face became drawn in and her anger pumped blood to it. She had the appearance of a faded prune. Her tone changed from the polished politeness that I'd come to expect, to cold and distant. She replied in her raspy, I Smoke Too Many Cigarettes, voice, "We at least have some experience to speak of. Sixteen years and you didn't even know your mother was ill so I could maybe ask you *some* of those same questions. You wanna take your anger out on me, fine. But realize, you don't know shit."

"I'm going up there, I know that."

"I wouldn't do that."

"Good thing I didn't ask you."

"Let her go," said Marge. She leaned her back against the sink beside the open, half-filled dishwasher. Her demeanor shifted. She appeared much calmer. A hand covered the side of her face, a cigarette dangling between her fingertips.

"You sure about that, Margie?" Clare asked.

Marge coolly moved the cigarette to her lips and took a long inhale. She jutted her bottom lip forward and blew smoke into the air, not bothering to turn on a fan and aim for an open window. Her eyes went to the ceiling for a moment, then to Clare.

"She right about that. Ain't dealt with this in years. Hell, ain't wanted to. Not since she popped up on my stoop after my husband passed goin' on 'bout all the ways I wronged her. I'm here for her, ain't good enough. I stay away and it's the same, so what matter it make? Maybe I don't know how to handle her no more. Maybe you can do better, so go on. Go save her."

I nodded in agreement, pleased that she was seeing things my way for a change, and yet I didn't move immediately. The world had become quiet with the exception of the sound of an agitated Lucy Rae howling from the backyard, and the distant sound of music being played. I looked to Clare before I moved. I didn't know why. It was almost as though I wanted her blessing before ascending the stairwell.

She looked at Marge and then nodded at me, adding a shrug that said *do what you want.* Suddenly I was all nerves. I swallowed my anxiety and gripped both banisters tightly. Déjà vu. I took a deep breath and jogged up.

Music became louder. Old music. Classic rock music. I recognized it from home. The Rolling Stones. *Gimme Shelter.* She loved The Stones and she played this song most of all. A complete Keith Richards groupie, lifelong membership.

I paused at the top, then turned and headed to her door. My fist hovered for a moment, but instead I grabbed the knob and turned it. I peeked inside, pushing the door only partway open. I didn't see her.

Slowly, I pushed more and entered. The room was mostly dark with the exception of a warm glow emitting from a toppled lamp. I took a step and stumbled. I stopped and assessed the mess. Drawers had been pulled from a dresser and thrown to the floor. The contents strewn about. I took another few steps before stumbling on an overturned chair. I wobbled a bit but caught my balance.

I looked around but Andie was nowhere. The bed was stripped bare. The bureau was open, the door hanging slightly off the hinges. Maybe it had always been that way, I wouldn't know.

"Mom?" I questioned the abandoned space.

"Megan? Bunny, is that you?"

I turned at the sound of my mother's voice. I hoped the darkness of the room saved her the horror that I was certain was in my expression. She hadn't been eating and it was obvious. She stood skeletal and backlit from the glow coming from her private bathroom, wearing nothing more than a tank top and ill-fitting underwear. In the pale light and dressed as she was, she looked very much like an ailing Marjie.

"Mom," I gasped. "What's going on in here? Are you okay?"

She rushed suddenly toward me, causing me to stumble back. She placed her icy cold palms against both of my cheeks. I was chilled to my core but afraid to move her. She pressed her face to mine, her streams of tears could have easily been my own. I swallowed over and over, determined to not cry myself. She moved one hand away and wrapped her arm around my neck, her fingers working aggressively through my hair.

"It's okay...it's okay, Bunny." She whispered these words into my eardrum, consoling me as though I were the one that was sick.

I felt confused. I wasn't equipped for this, Clare and Marge had been right. Why had they allowed me to deal with this on my own? Because I insisted? A child insisted? This is where good adult supervision intervened. I wasn't equipped to deal with this because my parents thought it better to keep me ignorant about the truth, rather than filling me in and making sure that I was aware of what I may have to deal with someday. This was where good parenting was required.

My stomach knotted in my mounting rage. Lyle had caused this, Lyle and Marjorie together, but Marjie was a bitch who likely only wanted to hurt Mom's feelings. Lyle was the adult, he knew better. But this, the here-and-now, being entwined in some sick affectional embrace with my maternal figure who needed a shower and toothpaste...this helplessness that I felt was because of Andie. The affliction was hers to share so I had to believe that the decision to keep it quiet had been hers. She meant to keep me in the dark and as a result, I was stuck in a town that was foreign to me...isolated from my friends and all that was familiar with a mother that I no longer recognized and couldn't help.

I grabbed her arm and pulled it away. I struggled to detach the other that cradled my head. Finally, free of her grasp, I held her wrists, keeping her at bay as she frantically attempted to clutch me again.

"Stop it, Andie. Stop it. Just stop, okay! What is wrong with you? Why are you acting like this? Dad messed up but this...bringing us here...staying locked away in this room? Destroying it? What the hell is wrong with you?"

Her head reared back and her nostrils flared. She snatched away from my hold.

"F'k you, Megan," she spat at me.

"Excuse me?"

"You're on his side, aren't you? I knew it. Stupid little bitch. Ungrateful f'kng bitch. I do everything for you! But do you respect me? You take and take and take!...until there is nothing left for me to give and then you want to laugh at me, like I'm the pathetic one? You! You are the pathetic one!"

The tears that I had tried so hard to avoid, pushed beyond all barricades. Hot tears. I felt claustrophobic. Couldn't breathe. My own mother cursed me. I caught my breath...screamed in response. "What is wrong with *you*? F'k me? F'k you! And turn off this miserable, f'kng music and maybe you can think straight and recognize who has your back and who doesn't!"

I raged against the depressing 60's rock that followed up the at least tolerable Stones. I looked about frantically, searching for the source of the sound. I spotted the stereo in the corner of the room near a window that was covered by a thick brown curtain. I reached for it but she grabbed me by my arm, yanking me back so hard that I thought she may have it pulled out of its socket. She released me and I fell hard onto my back on the bed.

She jumped up, hovering. Her long red hair tickling the sides of my face. "I'll kill you," she screamed.

The tears that trailed from my eyes dissolved from cool sadness into red hot anger. Before this moment, my mother had never laid a hand on me with malice. Never. Not even for the sake of discipline. Even when she most certainly should have. Even when I would have understood because I had it coming.

"Aargh!" I pushed with more force than necessary to remove her from me. She stumbled backward, almost crashing to the floor but catching herself, pushed back to her feet. I jumped from the bed and attempted to stalk past her but she caught me, turning me toward her. Before I realized what was happening, I felt the sting of flesh landing hard across my face.

"Andrea!"

Marge appeared in a puff of smoke. She grabbed my mother with the strength of an eighteen-year-old man and pulled her away from me, throwing her backward to land into the nearest wall. I stood still, unable to move and unable to process what was happening. I jumped lightly at the feeling of a pair of callused hands on my forearms, guiding me backwards and to sweet freedom on the other side of the bed. As I was led from the room, it was the first time that I was happy that Clare was there.

❧

I groaned as I rolled over onto my back on the sofa, where I continued to sleep. For a moment I wished that I'd, for a night, taken Andie's Mom up on the offer of a little private space in Uncle Cal's old room. It had been a long night. My mother, who firmly disavowed corporal punishment of the variety that Lyle, on extreme occasions suggested, had hit me. And in my face. My mother had become *Crazy Lady Who*, making her mother look the part of the sane one.

My cheek had turned red and swollen. It'd throbbed to the rhythm of my heart, reminding me that my mom, Andrea Blakely, had officially lost it. So the usual sound of Marge's morning foraging through cabinets to gather utensils for the preparation of breakfast was not a welcome one. I'd only just fallen asleep.

I laid on my back with a sheet covering my face, doing little to block out the daylight. May as well get up and face the day. The sizzling scent of eggs frying was as good as any other excuse, I supposed.

Fried eggs?

I flung the sheet from me...blinked to adjust. I assumed I was seeing things when they landed on Marge, seated on the ledge with her legs propped up, feet crossed at the ankle, inhaling a cigarette. The scent of brewed coffee clinging to the air was almost an afterthought that only occurred to me after seeing the chipped, white mug that read WORLD'S BEST BOSS, resting on her lap.

Surprised to see her there, I turned toward the kitchen to see none other than my very own mother standing in place of Marge, cooking eggs the way that Andie cooked eggs – fried.

"Meg," she squealed, and I mean literally squealed. "Good morning, Bunny. Rise and shine. Brakfast'll be ready in ten. I hope you're hungry. I'm hungry. Starved actually. Feels like I haven't eaten in weeks."

"Ya haven't," Marge growled, her cigarette dangling.

"Oh, Mother. Ten minutes, guys. Meg, Bunny, go get freshened up."

"Go get freshened up?" I repeated more to myself than her, discombobulated by the unusual request.

She smiled brightly at me, behaved as though nothing happened, like everything was normal. Maybe because it was soon going to be. Andie had slapped the crap out of me just the night before, but maybe that was what she needed to experience a breakthrough. To go through crazy to return to sanity.

I pondered a moment, then smiled and ran my fingers through my hair, pushing it away from my face. Lucy Rae lazily walked to where I sat and, without thought, I scratched the space behind her ears just the way she liked it. I would miss her once we were gone.

I tossed the sheet aside and slammed my feet to the floor, watching Andie as she danced about the kitchen, catching toast seemingly in mid-air and squeezing oranges into juice. I'd never seen my mother this happy. She never danced while she cooked, never squeezed oranges.

I was pleased, but I also felt a little apprehensive

about it all. I decided that I was just still a little shook up from the night before. All was well. We would be going home. The thought excited me so much so I gave Lucy an extra snuggle. I picked up my cell and scrolled to the last group text received from Cam and Shonie.

Sat, Jun 14, 9:37 AM

Meg: Coming home soon! Should be today or tomorrow.

Cam: Realz??Do not shit me.

Meg: Realz. Sorry bout going Siberia. Complicated.

Shonie: GTFOH! So phucking pissed at you! Expecting all the low when you get back.

Meg: Yea yea. Sorry 'bout dat.

Shonie: Dead ass, Megan!

Meg: Government? Really Shashonie?

Cam: U leave no choice Megan Jean.

Meg: You too Cameron Denise?

Cam: LOL!

Shonie: Megz? Jokey jokes aside.

Meg: Ok ok. 4sho. ttyl.

So home wasn't necessarily ideal, but a start. I, with my optimistic and smiling face, turned to Andie's Mom. She looked to me, connected her grass green eyes to my hazel green ones except she didn't appear as pleased or relieved as I felt. Slowly she closed her eyes and turned her head, and when she opened them again, they were aimed at a point in the distance.

"Breakfast is ready," Andie sang. My mother, Andie, sang the words. Andie didn't sing her announcements, or instructions, or anything that wasn't meant specifically for singing. She laid around watching her soaps and judge shows and when she was in a particularly good mood, a singing mood, she sang along with the classic rock on KQRX – We Rock Radio.

"Here we go," Marge mumbled, smashing her cigarette butt into the sliced can.

I pondered what she meant by that. Pondered, but didn't inquire. She should've been happy. Her daughter was better, healed. No more Crazy Lady Who Holed Up In Old Room, and just, Andie. Just, Mom. Marge would have her home to herself once again. Just Marge and Lucy Rae, with frequent unannounced visits from Neighbor Clare. She should've been happy.

Marge and I sat at the table just as Andie set the plates before us. Eggs, pancake, and sausage, toast and orange juice. Andie took three steps back and stopped, clasping her hands before her, watching us, wide-eyed and giddy.

We watched her watching us watching her.

"Well," she opened, "try it, already."

I looked from Mom to Mom's mom to the plate. I lifted my fork and took a bite of egg. It was good. It was great. Familiar. Tasted like home.

"Andie, why don't you grab a plate for ya'self and join us?" Marge suggested.

"Oh. Oh, me? Oh, I'm fine. I'm not hungry."

"Moments ago you said you were starving. Like you hadn't eaten in weeks which, may I remind you, you basically haven't."

Andie's face fell and the look from the night before took the place of her new bubbly and bright personality.

"Well, I'm fine now, Mother."

"Mom, these eggs are really good," I said.

She turned to me quickly, almost robotic and suddenly the sun had returned. "Why, thank you, Bunny."

"Andie, honey, ya gotta eat something," Marge insisted.

"I will, Mother. When I get hungry again, I will eat."

I intervened once again. "So, Mom, you think we can head home today?"

She smiled at me. Creepy, like a Stepford Wife or something from an ep of The Twilight Zone. It was as though there was no actual emotion behind the smile. A chill ran through me. I hurried and washed it away with delicious, freshly squeezed OJ.

Finally, she spoke. "It's beautiful outside. Think I'll take old Lucy Rae for a walk. See the neighborhood. I haven't been back here in so long. Come here, Lucy."

Marge stood and held a hand up. Obediently, Lucy

Rae immediately settled back into her spot.

"No. Leave her be. She's fine."

The two stared.

I tried again for an answer. "So, Mom. We're going to go home today, right?"

I felt like I was holding my breath inside the deep end of a pool. I'd die and be reborn again in the time it took for her to respond. She just smiled at me, that creepy, empty smile.

She snapped back to focus on Marge. "It's okay, I'm going for a walk. Enjoy your breakfast. I wonder if Sarah Davenport still lives in town. She was always so nice." Barefoot, she exited the back door, closing it gently behind her.

I stood. "Mom, your shoes," I called after her, but it was too late. I looked to Marge, wide-eyed and unblinking. "What was that?"

"What that was is your mother is sick."

"But she's better. You saw her, she's better."

"I saw her and no, she ain't better. She won't be better 'til she get back on her meds."

"She was fine until you decided to go on giving her shit about eating breakfast."

"No, this the part of her sickness, she *think* she better, think she being normal but she ain't. And you ain't goin' nowhere lessen you get there ya'self, count on that."

Marge shoved her chair back and stood from the table.

"You pushed her!"

"I did what now?"

"You...you should've just left her alone. Let her do what made her happy."

Marge took a deep inhale. She was looking right at me but her expression didn't change to indicate anything that she was thinking or feeling about it all. She exhaled slowly.

"Guess you ain't learn nothin' last night. C'mon, Miss Lucy Rae. Let's go for a walk. Leave this one to come to terms with her new reality."

Lucy jumped up and trotted to catch up with Marge, following her across the kitchen and out of the house.

"F'k you, lady! F'k you," I screamed to a closing door.

day #twenty-two.

Cam: Are U close?

Meg: My bad. Not tonight.

Cam: What??! U're kidding right?

Meg: Not kidding.

Shonie: Bruh. wtf? You been gone forever, yo. You missed the last week of school. You not answering nobody's calls. Nobody know wtf is going on. I mean, realz?

Meg: ....

....

....

Cam: Spill it!

Meg: I just can't. All I can say right now. It's a lot but I'm okay.

Shonie:	Should we be worried? You need to call me and tell me wassup. I mean me and Cammie are passed that. Apparently your pops too since he asking me where you and Andie at.
Meg:	What did you tell him?!
Shonie:	What the hell could I tell him? IDK! That's the point right? Why you being all undisclosed.
Meg:	....
	....
	I guess.
Cam:	Come home! Miss u like crazy. FYI, if you care, can't keep Yaves off Javi much longer. Think they're an item now.
Meg:	He knows wassup. Thanks guys. Missing you too. G2G.

⌒

I sat on the front stoop with Marge and L to the R, sipping fresh lemonade and enjoying the breeze. It was much nicer outdoors than it had been since I arrived. I stretched my body across the porch swing, legs straight, allowing my feet to fall away and my toes to spread so that the air could weave a path through them. Marge sat on the top step, turned with her back against the banister slats. No gardening for her today, so she looked relaxed in a flowy blue cotton dress, her hair cascading freely over her shoulders.

"Oh, goddammit," she growled.

I sat upright, my hand to my heart, pretending to be aghast. "Andie's Mom!"

"Can't help it. Lord forgive me."

I turned to look in the direction she was facing. A figure in the distance. I didn't recognize the person but the way Marge's house was situated, she didn't get much foot traffic so seeing anyone new was an unusual sight. For the most part, anybody that came that way was likely doing so with intention or they were lost. I assumed the person was not lost.

"Who is that?" I asked.

"Clare's granddaughter." Marge sat her near empty glass beside her and fidgeted about in the pockets of her dress before she pulled forth her pack of cigarettes. I wondered if there was a connection between the girl and the action.

"You got a problem with Clare's grandkid?"

"Big one."

"Clare know?"

"I think it's obvious but no, I don't think she notices."

I looked back to the girl being led by Biscuit. Her head down, focused on the celly that was in her hand. She was one of those types, Walkie-Stalkie. Couldn't get to the end of the block without texting or checking her notifications.

"What's your problem with her?" I asked, suspicious. I couldn't remember her name or too many details, but I did recall Clare making a thing out of the fact that she was biracial as a means to impress me and/or get me on her team.

Marge's eyes came to me as she filled her lungs with smoke. She sat in the moment, then released both the smoke and me.

"Oh, no worries. You about to find out."

Lucy Rae, who had been taking a nap at the opposite end of the porch was suddenly alert. It was as though someone poured a fresh batch of Marge's finest arabica into her water dish. She trotted forward with tail wagging, mouth open and salivating. She stood at the edge of the step, pacing and stifling a bark.

Biscuit lost his shit as he got closer to the gate. His uber-annoying yips finally prying a solid bark or two from our anxious girl. Lucy looked toward Biscuit and back to Marge as she marched in semi-circles. Marge pursed her lips but finally nodded her approval. Lucy Rae took off, bounding down the steps and jumping about in anticipation of spending time with her bestie 4 life. Lucky.

The girl and the excited pup arrived, finally. Marge ordered Lucy to sit, which she hesitantly but ultimately obeyed, as the girl crossed over to our side of outdoors. She dropped Biscuit's leash, freeing Lucy from her command.

"Hiiii, Miss Marge," she said, excitedly in a voice that was pink and gold glitter. She was a cute girl, I supposed. Small stature with pouty lips and a nose ring. Her silky, almond cream hair divided into sections that became knotty locs at the ends, adorned by strings, shells, and clasps.

"Oh, child, you can call me Mrs. Schofield."

"Oh, sorry. How have you beeeen?" She sang her words.

"Same as always. How long you here for this time?"

She tilted her head slightly and gave a smiling look of knowing. "The youzhe. My parents just dropped me. They totally wanted to see you–"

"No they didn't."

She shifted uncomfortably, but continued, "–but Brandon's got his tournament, sooo...there's that."

"Well that is fantastic for Brandon, whoever the shit that is."

The girl giggled foolishly. "My big brother! OMG, you know that, Miss Marge – I mean, Miss Schofield."

"Oh. Yeah, guess I did." Marge's eyes were on the girl, though she didn't return an ounce of the effort the kid was putting in.

It was pretty magical an interaction to watch, considering she was one of those ditzy types who's personality was adopted from unlimited episodes of reality television. At some point she'd clearly reasoned that speaking with a languid cadence, halted tone, and the insertion of acronyms wherever possible would somehow make an otherwise annoying person more likeable. It didn't. She wasn't. And I was coming to a clear understanding of what Marge's problem was with her.

"Y'know, you really shouldn't smoke. I'm totes gonna work on Grammy Clare and Poppa Zeke over this summer. In school we're learning, like, all these bad things that can happen to the body over time. Like, you could get cancer which everyone should totally know by now, but there's other stuff like losing your foot–"

"Anybody ever tell you to shut the f–"

"Hey! Hey, hi there. Hi," I chimed in reluctantly. The girl needed saving. My good deed of the day was done.

"Oh, hi! You must be Miss Marge – Miss Schofield's granddaughter. I've heard so much about you," she said wide-eyed and toothy.

I flinched at the reference to me as Marge's granddaughter. Of course that's what I was but, that I could recall, no one had actually said those words together aloud. I glanced to Marge but she didn't seem to react one way or another. Just carried on with her cigarette despite the looming threat of losing a foot.

The girl extended her hand to me, so I shook it.

"Wow, you're much prettier than my Grammy Clare described. She said your dad is black. That's so cool."

"Excuse me?" I was taken aback, unsure if I should take offense at having my race, or rather my collab of races, discussed behind my back. The relevance eluded me. F'kng Fox Harborites.

She smiled wider, if that was even possible. She practically beamed. "It's okay, I can talk about it. I'm biracial, too. My dad, he's Cuban, Italian, and Irish. His dad is Irish and his mom was Cuban and Italian. So I'm like all of that mixed together plus my mom who is, like, I think, Scot. Or maybe Polish, not sure which. So, yeh, totes biracial."

I involuntarily looked to Marge who made a facial gesture that I interpreted as, *Told you so.* Then I swallowed my discomfort for turning to Andie's Mom for support, like she was the homie. Shrug. My eyes went to the girl again.

"Well, my dad's black and my mom's white, so yeah, guess that makes me biracial, as in *two* races."

"That's so cool. We have so much in common." And like that, I regretted saving her Marge's wrath. "I'm Amelia. And you're Megan, right?"

I double-took. "I'm sorry. Amelia? With an A? Not an I or an E and some exotic pronunciation?"

"No, just Amelia. Grammy likes to pronounce it E-mehl-ya, but really it's just Amelia."

I chuckled. Nice try, Clare. Trying to pawn your slightly multi-racial, primarily Caucasian grandkid off as one of my peeps. I nodded. "Interesting. Well, yeah, you can just call me Meg."

"Yeh, yeh, totes. Hey! Wanna do something later? You gotta feel, like, so totally abandoned out here, not knowing anyone except senior peeps, no offense. I'm rolling into town later, you can totes chill with me. I'd be thrilled to intro you to some of the local kids."

"Uhhh...," I glanced to Marge, who was pushing herself to her feet and, unfortunately, staying out of it. "I don't wanna be a burden, y'know."

"Oh no, not a burden at all. I'm pretty pops with the cool kids here. You can totally ride my coattail until you establish your own identity around these parts."

"That's...generous but I really should stick around in case my mom is ready to go when she gets back."

"Go? Where?"

"Home. I'll be going back home any day now, so I don't really need to make new friends."

Marge finally decided to chime in but in a way that was most *un*helpful. Just when you think maybe she could be okay... "Your momma ain't gonna be back until well after dark like she always do, so you might as well keep yourself busy 'til then."

"Then maybe I should stick around and help you out with, like, household stuff." I stared at her, trying my best to send her a message with my eyes. C'mon, Old Lady.

She only laughed. "What I need help with that I ain't been doing myself all these years? Go be with kids your own age. Try to have some fun while ya here."

I couldn't determine whether or not she was trying to look out for me or punish me. I wanted to kick her. Before I could counter, Amelia chimed in with, "My grandpa'll be back in about a half an hour. I'll pick you up. Wes' shift should be done by then and so should Alli's, so you can meet the whole gang."

"Wes?" Suddenly I was interested in her little adventure. "This Wes, he doesn't happen to work at the supply store, does he?"

"Totally! So you've met."

"Not really. Well, sorta." I pondered her offer for a tour and meet and greet. How badly did I care to see hardware store guy again? Enough to agree to friend Clare's fake biracial granddaugher and subject myself to an afternoon of *Logic by Amelia* and the ditzy squad of buddies she wanted to initiate me into?

Marge whistled and both dogs appeared by her side as though by magic. How could a person so adept at discipline have a child who could go so far off the rails? For three days, Andie had disappeared before the sun rose fully and returned noisy and energized, or maybe wasted, long after the sun set. I hoped this day was the day that things were different but, lo and behold, she was gone again and Marge was right, there was nothing more for me to do besides wait.

"Okay, sure. I'll go."

"Awesome! I'll be back within the hour." She bounced down the steps and, for a fleeting moment, I wondered if what was wrong with Andie, was also wrong with her. "C'mon, Biscuit. Let's go, boy."

Marge clomped up the steps with a reluctant Lucy

Rae in tow. She headed inside just as Amelia offered a, "Later, Miss Schofield. It's nice to see—"

The balance of her well-wishes were crushed in the closing door.

༞

I didn't have much to wear considering I hadn't anticipated being gone so long. I changed into the cutest outfit I had before Amelia returned. I wondered how this dingbat had gotten her drivers license while I still didn't have mine.

"...and Allison because she's so effing rave. But then there's Dob who I like to call *Dob the Slob* because he's so completely sloth. But for some reason they like to keep him around. Probably cause Maxey boned him or something. Slut. Bag. Absolute. O.M.Gawd, I love this song!"

I tried my best to tune her out but the harder I tried, the more she blabbed on about this person and that and who she liked and didn't and why and I really couldn't have given less of a shit. I reclined my seat in her grandfather's classic ride, my face aimed at the street. The breeze was nice. It was good to be away from the house, even if it did mean I had to spend an afternoon in Clare Bear's grandkids care.

There wasn't much to see. Aged homes and unremarkable storefronts. Senior couples leaving early bird specials. Three kids zipped past on boards and for a moment I felt something. Not that I was much of a skater myself but I liked to think I could be if I kept at it.

Amelia squealed and I refrained from punching her in her arm after my heart jumped into my throat. I closed my eyes and took a few deep breaths, asking myself why... why I'd agreed to this? I looked up, shaking my head, fully ready to judge – but then I saw him and remembered exactly why.

"He is so unbelievably hot. I mean, so hot. That's Wes."

"I know."

"Oh, right. You met him. How's that again?"

"Uninteresting story involving little people with chocolate ice cream covered hands."

"Oh. Well, anyways, he's gorge, right?"

I shrugged and pried my eyes away from him. My thoughts about him were none of her business. "He's okay, I guess. You into him, or something?"

"Wes? No way, we're just friends. He belongs to Alli." Amelia leaned forward, practically climbing out of the window. "Wes. Hey, Wes!"

He appeared confused for a moment as he looked from the car to the face behind the wheel, but recognition lit his eyes.

"Hey, look who's back." Wes trotted over to my side. I

sat up quickly, adjusting my clothes before I realized what I was doing. He leaned inside, looking past me as though he and I had never met. As though his niece hadn't smeared chocolate ice cream on my shorts. "Wow. Driving Big Zeke's car now? You even old enough to drive?"

Amelia giggled. "Not actually. But who in this town is gonna stop me? They know not to mess with Big Zeke's fav granddaughter."

"You're his only granddaughter."

"Shut up, right." She giggled again. She had a habit of doing that. "Headed to The Woods, you need a ride?"

"Nah, thanks. Some of us can drive legally. I'll see you there, though."

He pushed himself back from the door. His eyes came to mine but still, he said nothing. He smiled at me... maybe or maybe smiled just because. I couldn't tell. Like an idiot, I smiled in response as Amelia pulled away.

Once he disappeared from my mirror, I asked, "Exactly how old *are* you?"

"Fifteen. No worries. Got my permit."

෨

The Woods was exactly that, actual woods. It was like something out of a horror film. Something B-rated starring large-boobed blondes who tripped on nothing at the most inopportune times. In the center of it all was a cabin, dilapidated and creepy. I wasn't hardly interested in going inside, but unfortunately I was there because I was interested in seeing a guy who pretended we hadn't already met. So now it was time to dig in and do townie things with the town's kids. But these kids weren't at all what I expected. Nothing like the representations on Cam's favorite CW shows.

"What up, bitch."

Amelia's body stumbled forward from the force of the shoulder shove distributed by a tall, skinny blond that appeared from behind us. She walked lazily toward a short girl donning long pink and purple ombre hair, torn stockings with denim shorts, a tee and olive cord blazer. She took a long hit off a spliff before trading the blond for the beer can she held.

Amelia adjusted, exposing just the tiniest glimpse into her true insecurities, before jumping back into character. "What's good, bitches. Miss me? I know, I know. Is there anymore beer?"

"Not unless you brought some," Blondie responded, sardonically. She faced me, looking me over but said nothing. She pulled her gray hoodie over her head, revealing two thin and well-tatted arms.

"Who are you?" Ombre asked. She smiled wide, making her shrunken eyes even smaller. "You're f'kng gorgeous."

"Yeah, I don't know about that but, uhm, where the hell did you come from?" Blondie inquired, less kind than her friend.

I opened my mouth to speak but Amelia beat me to it. "She's my new friend. We're totes BB's in the making. Best Bitches. Our grandmother's are total besties, so it's kinda genetics."

"Oh yeah? Who's her grandmother?" Blondie asked.

"Marge Schofield, duh."

Ombre lifted her sunglasses, pushing her hair back as she settled them on the top of her head. "No shit. Schofields got a black grandkid? I've seen it all now. I thought that bitch was a Nazi."

I was rendered speechless and in that brief moment was happy that Amelia's desperate need for acceptance led her to speak on my behalf, because all I could summon were three words: Bitch. Fuck. And, you.

"Well, she does. And she's not just black, she's biracial. Like me."

Blondie and Ombre paused, glancing at each other before bursting into laughter.

"F'k no you're biracial, white girl. Her, obvi. You? F'kn poser, wanna be," Blondie said. Amelia's face crumbled. "So what's your name, new girl?"

"She's—"

"What are you two bumping cooch, or what? Can't speak for yourself, new girl? What. Is. Your. Name?" Blondie coupled her question with faux sign language and a tone implying that I was a short bus regular.

"My name is Megz, I'm not a retard, I can speak for myself, and f'k you for the implication."

"Ooooh," the two girls said in unison, looking to each other and laughing, folding into one another.

"Well, *Megz*," Ombre started, "I think you're hot. I like black girls...and black boys."

"You like everybody. You'd f'k anything, you slut," her supposed friend added.

"True that. So if you're ever interested in a little girl on girl, I'm Maxey. Wanna hit?" Ombre extended the joint in my direction. I shrugged and accepted. "This rude skunt is Alli. And those assholes—"

I turned to face the direction she pointed in.

"They're just assholes," Alli laughed, taking the weed from me.

It was good weed and the effects washed over me quickly, and before I understood what was happening, I laughed right along.

"Screw you, Alli," Wes replied as he entered, snatching the spliff before she could put it to her lips again. He took a long drag before handing it off to a guy behind him. His eyes locked onto mine as he strolled across the dusty room. Warmth blanketed my face and I prayed I wasn't blushing.

"What the f'k did you do to your hair?" A heavy kid with pink flushed cheeks and man boobs said to Amelia.

"Go to hell, Dob. Get off me. Stop it, get off me, you ass," she squealed, trying hard to keep her head out of reach while attempting snatchies on the joint.

"Ugh, ogle much," Alli barked, getting mine and Wes' attention. She stood and stomped away, collapsing onto a dusty, old sofa. "You wanna f'k new girl, do it someplace else."

"Wait, what?" I asked through my mental fog.

"Jelly much, Allison?" Wes asked, to which her response was the middle finger. He shook his head and snatched the remnant of the joint from Amelia's lips and put it to his own as hc pulled a hacky sack from his jacket pocket.

I walked to a wall and slid down, taking a seat on the floor, no longer caring about the dirt and whatever else was there. Amelia seemed to have forgotten about me and her *Best Bitch* vow completely as she followed Alli like a lost puppy. It would've all been so unbearable were I not so high.

Ombre – I mean, Maxey, took a seat at my side, a flask in hand. She offered it to me. I considered a moment, then shrugged and accepted.

"Don't worry about Alli. She isn't over Wes yet, but otherwise she's totally harmless. Well, maybe not totally."

I squinted from the unexpected burn of the alcohol. I caught my breath and took another swallow before handing the flask back. "They dated?"

"Only on and off since the 7th grade. But they've been off since he graduated and she dropped out. That's like a year and a half now. It's highly unlikely that they'll be on again anytime soon, so he's available if you're interested. And obvi you're interested. But don't tell Alli I told you that."

"I'm not—"

"Sure, you're not." Maxey turned the flask up.

I nodded. I wanted to know more, pick Maxey's brain but my own was beginning to turn to mush. Wes glanced my way as he kicked the ball toward one of the guys. I thought he smiled at me, but I wasn't sure.

☙

Marge's house was completely lit when Amelia dropped me off. The faint sound of music traveled from inside. Marge sat on the stoop, leg shaking and smoking a cigarette. Her face painted with agitation. I stumbled slightly toward her but recovered, trying my best to be normal. Tried to mimic sober behavior.

"What's happening in there?" I asked, louder than intended.

Marge eyed me strangely – at least I think she did. "Your momma home."

I perked up. "She's better?"

She sucked her teeth, mashed her cigarette and immediately lit another. "See for ya'self."

I jogged up the steps and past Marge, pushing into the house where I found Andie dancing around in front of a man I didn't know. A strange man that was sitting on Marge's couch. On my bed!

I looked from him to Andie, who hadn't yet noticed my presence. I wondered where the clothes she was wearing came from. She hadn't brought them with her. Leather mini skirts and halter tops were not part of her wardrobe at home, so where did the shit come from?

"Mom. Mom!"

She turned to face me and, at first, it was as though she didn't know who I was. A piece clicked into place finally. "Megan! Bunny, come dance with your mother."

She grabbed my hands and swayed her hips at a different tempo than the music. I snatched away. "No way. You don't even dance."

She laughed as though I'd said something that was meant as a joke. She moved about awkward and rhythmless. "Come here, Bunny, I want you to meet someone. This is Austin. He's beautiful, isn't he?" She leaned forward, running her hands through his long golden locs of hair and pushing her padded boobs closer to his face.

Sobriety washed over me at the realization of what was happening. I looked into the icy blue gaze of the unshaven intruder who was laying back much too comfortably on Andie's Mom's sofa.

"Dustin," he corrected.

"Excuse me?"

"Not Austin. My name is Dustin."

I frowned at the taste of beer and marijuana flavored bile that edged up my throat and into my mouth. "I don't give a shit what your name is. Get out."

He threw his hands up defensively. "Hey, Andrea said I could stay."

"And I ask you, asshole, what makes you think I give a shit? *Andrea* is a married mother of two and at least twice your age, so I'll say it again – get out!"

"With all due respect kid, f'k off."

I heard the click of the gun before I felt the presence of Marge. The same gun that had once been held to my chest. The same that had made my life flash before my eyes was now doing the same to this dillwad. Crazy Lady Who Puts Gun To Chest had returned full-throttle, this time aiming her weapon appropriately.

Andie, finally taking an interest in what was happening around her, cried out, "Mother, what the hell? That is no way to treat Austin. He's been very kind to me."

"Great. I'll return the favor by not shooting his dick off. You had your fun, Andie. Now get him outta my house."

"He's my friend. You have no right," she yelled and stomped her foot. She was like a child. Wearing too much makeup and too few articles of clothing, but a child nonetheless.

Dustin/Austin surrendered, placing his hands in the air above his head, sliding from the sofa and attempting to bypass my mother who clung herself to him, begging for him to stay, in perfect, humiliating fashion. He responded wisely, stating that he didn't need the aggravation as he struggled to free himself from her cat-like grasp.

Marge waved her gun toward the exit while Andie screamed and cried out her hateful diatribe. Marge closed the door firmly behind him, retiring her gun for the evening while her daughter spit venom her way. "You hate me. You've always hated me. I couldn't be perfect like your precious, precious Calvin, so you have to make *my* life hell!"

Marge's voice was pure exasperation when she spoke. "I do not hate you and you'd realize that if you would just take your damn meds!"

"Why? Huh? So you can control me? Poison my mind, make me your little puppet? Be the perfect little Andrea you want me to be?"

"Andrea, no one wants to control you unless it's to make you take your ass to bed and sleep it off. You smell like a damn brewery."

She stepped close to Marge, nearly nose to nose. Her voice was low and intense. "You will *never* control me. Do you hear me? Never."

"I don't doubt it," Marge replied, side-stepping her.

Andie looked around. She looked as though she only just realized where she was. "I'm leaving," she said matter-of-factly.

"Good riddance to bad rubbish."

I jumped in front of her, holding my hands up in surrender. "Wait, Mom. Just wait."

Andie's pink face reddened. She turned sharply and opened the door. I raced after her. Now I was the one begging for attention, pleading for her to stay. I screamed her name as she disappeared into the dark of night.

day #twenty-three.

My head pounded. My brain felt as though it was roaming about freely. Every movement caused it to relocate, changing positions likely for the sake of punishing me. I hadn't slept. Okay, I dozed off here and there while seated on the window's wide ledge. The same one that Andie's Mom liked to sit on while she had her morning coffee and evening smoke, watching the sunrise and set. This cycle repeated all night as I waited for my mother to return safely. No sleep and a hangover did not mix.

I was at a loss as to what I could do to help my mother, although I knew that I must do something. The yellow glow of the sun blended into beautiful arrays of pinks and purples of the changing morning sky. For a second, I thought I saw someone near the tree in the front yard but it was nothing more than my mind playing tricks on me.

I sat back, granting a tear permission to trail my cheek. I was too tired to care. I hoped my mother was okay. I had to believe it to be so, but the way she left the night before...

The creak of the loose wood board beneath the weight of Marge's feet demanded my attention, but I disobeyed. I kept my eyes focused. I wanted to see Andie as soon as she appeared. I needed to. The creaking halted momentarily, the patter of paws ceased shortly after.

"She ain't come home, did she?" I shook my head in response. "You sat there all night? You should try to sleep. She be alright. She used'ta do this plenty."

The creaking and pitter-patter resumed as she headed to the kitchen to start up the morning caffeine fix. I dropped my head and considered. Reluctantly, I stood and walked to the kitchen island and took a seat. We said nothing to one another. The only sound was the percolation of coffee. Marge took a seat across from me as we waited.

At the coveted beep she stood, retrieving two mugs from the cabinet. One for me, and WORLD'S BEST BOSS for herself. Poured two cups, black. We sat and drank quietly. The brew was tasty and helped to pry my eyes open just a bit wider.

Marge lifted her pack of cigarettes, flipped it over a couple of times and sat it back down. She stood and poured herself another mug. She pointed the pot in my direction. I assessed what remained and nodded, holding it out for her to top off.

She sat again, eyeing her pack. Contemplating. Finally, making a sound decision, she set her mug on the island and slipped a ciggy from the pack, flipping the small fan on so it could do its job of guiding the smoke out of the window.

She took a couple inhales and blew the smoke into the fan's path. Her shoulders relaxed as tension melted from her. She flicked her ashes into the can and looked up at me. "You gonna have to call your father."

I took a sip of coffee. "Why? Had your fill of us? Can't say I blame you."

"She getting worse."

"She doesn't want him to know where we are and I don't blame her."

"Listen to me. She getting worse. She need her medication. Now he got her right all them years ago. He maybe the only one that can."

I sat my brown mug down and pressed the base of my hand firmly against my forehead. My mother didn't want Lyle to know where we were and neither did I. I hadn't forgiven him, mainly because he hadn't the decency to even ask for it. But Marge was right. Andie seemed to only be getting worse and we weren't able to get through to her. So if Lyle could help her, I supposed I hadn't a choice.

"What's wrong with her? I mean...why is she this

way?" I heard the fragility in my voice and kinda hated it.

Marge shrugged and blew more smoke. "Bipolar disorder. I don't know if I really know what that even mean. But that's what they tell me when she was a teen. Maybe a year or so before she left home. 'Fore that, nobody know nothing what to tell me. Say it's genetic. Maybe. My husband momma had some trouble...wasn't always right in the head. They say it was due to her woman parts. Right gave her a hysterectomy. Say that'll fix it... that she'll be all better."

"Was she? Did it work?" I asked, oddly hopeful.

"Killed herself six months later so, no, I don't think so. They ain't have no fancy name for this back then...no proper treatment. They go through extremes, people with this disease. High. Low. Not much in between."

"So, basically, my mother is crazy."

Marge shook her head vehemently. "No, no, she ain't crazy. What she is, is sick. She got a disease just like people with cancer or high sugar, 'ceptin this mess with her mind. She gotta control it like any other ailment."

Marge and I jumped at the unexpected sound of the front door. I turned to see my mother entering, her face dirty and smudged with mascara stains and smeared lipstick. Dirt etched trails down each pale leg. She glanced at us dismissive as she headed to the stairwell. I opened my mouth to speak, but fearing I would send her running, stopped myself. I turned my back to her, forcing down more coffee without tasting it.

⮫

I stared at my phone. I'd taken the scenic route to my father's contact info but could only look at it, I couldn't bring myself to touch the screen. I didn't know what to say to him. *Andie needs you because you made her crazy.* It felt like asking your rapist to help your defense against him at trial.

I pressed the HOME button and watched as my icons zoomed out. I pressed again before going into my Messages app. The last text was from Javi asking whether he should just forget about me. I didn't want that, not really. I just wasn't ready for him to know my family's business. Not this type anyway. I'd typed twelve varying replies and deleted them all.

Following was a text from Cam. Seeing her name in that moment returned a memory of something that she'd once shared with us. Her favorite aunt had gotten sick and the family was worried that she couldn't take care of her own children. If memory served, her symptoms were sorta similar. Maybe...I thought, maybe I should talk to someone that knew what I was dealing with. Maybe I was altogether mistaken, but I had to ask.

Before I could talk myself out of it, I'd already pressed the DETAILS button and promptly hit call. She answered on the second ring.

"Are you with Shonie?" I asked immediately following her over-zealous greeting.

"Not at the moment. Meeting her in an hour but if you hold on a sec, I can get her on–"

"No! No, Cam. Please. I just need...I just need to talk about this to someone that can relate to what I'm dealing with, and that's you right now. Just you."

"Oh, okay. Well, what's going on? Where are you?"

"Cam, you cannot tell Shonie that I called you."

"What? Why not?"

"Because I'm asking you not to."

"Okay, okay, I won't. But you know she'll be hella pissed if she finds out."

"She won't find out if you don't say anything. I mean it, Cameron."

"I won't say anything, on my honor. Now *what* is going on?" Cam's normally high-demand and bubbly voice became low and serious.

"I think...I've been told that Andie is bipolar."

The weight began to lift from my shoulders brick-by-brick the moment I began to share info with my friend about where I was and how I had come to be there. The filthy deed my dad and my sibling had engaged in which had sent my mother spiraling into depression. And now, I didn't know who I was dealing with or what I was supposed to do. Some days she was incredibly fine – too fine. Hyper and happy, as if nothing ever happened. As if the home in Fox Harbor had always been ours together.

And then there were the other times. And though I would have never described Andrea J. Blakely as stable, nothing could have ever prepared me for those *other* times.

Cam quietly listened to me vent, and when I was done, explained her aunt's diagnoses. Cyclothemic disorder, which supposedly wasn't so bad. She'd had a rough patch but was much better. But, she informed me, the disease took many forms and as I didn't know what form Andie had, there was no way to know what Andie was dealing with and therefore capable of. One thing was certain, Cam agreed with Marge – I would have to call my father and tell him where we were.

"I'm so sorry you're going through this, Megz. But you really should talk to Shonie. She's worried about you. Can I at least tell her I spoke to you?"

I walked mindlessly to the window listening and processing. "No, sorry but you can't. I know she's worried. I'll think of something to tell her but I just don't want her to know any of this. Not now. She's too...well, she's too Shonie. I can't take the judgement on my family issues right now. She's just gonna say she already knew and make me feel stupid for not realizing it myself, you know how she is."

I squinted and stepped closer to the window while Cam rambled on about all the things that I was missing back home, moving forward as though I hadn't just confided my woes and deepest discomfiture. A car pulled in front and the door opened. I leaned closer looking at a guy walking around it who, from a distance, looked like...,"Wes?"

"What's that?" Cam asked.

"Cammie, I'm gonna have to call you back." I hung up before she could object. I pressed and held the side key to power down my phone before she could totally cock-block with a follow up phone call or ill-timed text. I headed to the front door, opening it just as Wes passed through Marge's front gate.

He froze, looking up at me. "Stalker much?"

"Says, Guy Who Shows Up Unannounced."

"Who says I didn't come here looking for your grandmother?"

"Did you come here looking for my grandmother?" I asked, trying not to openly cringe.

"No."

"So you must be here for Lucy Rae."

"Who?"

I chuckled. "You're here because..."

"I'm off today. It's beautiful out and I thought you might want to get out the house. Figure you could use a friend that's not Amelia."

I laughed. "I could definitely use a friend that's not Amelia."

He smiled at me, white teeth, mostly even. He jerked

his head toward the vehicle. I felt myself blush as I stepped toward him, then paused, remembering something vital. I held a finger up to indicate I needed another moment and re-entered the empty house, closing the door behind me. I powered my phone back up and went to my messages, typing a simple text to my dad that read: At Andie's moms. Need meds. Come now.

I powered down the phone again and stuck it in my back pocket. I closed my eyes and took a few deep and cleansing breaths, shaking my troubles off. I reached back, easing the black binder down and shook my hair free, tossing it about over my shoulders before smiling into a nearby glossy framed photo and making sure my teeth were clean. Satisfied, I exited the house and joined Wes on the walkway.

≈

I didn't actually consider Amelia to be a friend. She was more like a cancer. Your defenses shut down, she latches on and starts growing on you, and before you know it – she's metastasized and you're kinda stuck with her until...y'know. So I began to tolerate her, sorta like I'd done with Clare. Like grandmother, like granddaughter.

A couple days after I'd reached out to my father, as my cancer and I were returning from a little hang time in The Woods, I spotted Lyle's car parked directly behind Andie's immobile one. "I gotta go," I said, jumping out and taking off before Amelia could ask any silly questions or offer unnecessary companionship. I took the steps two at a time and ran into the house. There he was, Lyle Alexander Blakely aka my father, bka Pervy Sleeps With Daughter Just Cause They're Not Blood Related.

He faced me, looking nothing at all like the monster he'd metamorphosed into in my mind. His salt and pepper hair was freshly cut, like he wanted to make a good impression. The stubble on his face was not, like he forgot the impression he was trying to make. His eyes were the same kind eyes he had always looked at me with. His full brown face was slimmer; he had lost weight. He didn't look scary or threatening or any of the ways in which I had made him out to be when I thought of him. He just looked like...Dad.

I softened. I didn't want to but it happened. I tried my best to fight against it, remember the way he was the last time I saw him. Recall his pants around his ankles and the lax way he dismissed his engagement with Marjie, a child he'd raised. Try as I might, I couldn't recall it exactly as it was. Maybe it wasn't as bad as I thought. Maybe I'd embellished. He was just my dad standing before me and, though I hadn't realized it until that moment, I missed my dad.

But then I remembered my mom. I couldn't have embellished that. What she was going through and how his actions had triggered it was all too real. That was the trick. I was sufficiently angry all over again.

"Bunny," he sighed, taking a step toward me as I took

a step back.

"Lyle," I replied, working up to my previous venomous state. "Tell me that you've taken care of Flaca while I've been gone. That's all you really need to say to me."

"Oh, yes, yes, of course I have. When you get home you'll see. We'll leave as soon as Mom gets here."

I looked to Marge who sat quietly on the ledge smoking and, I imagined, keeping an eye out for her own daughter. I looked back to Lyle.

"How long have you been waiting?"

"A couple hours now."

"How come no one called me?"

"Figured there was no rush. Not until she showed at least. I drove off, got something to eat. Just got back. If you made friends here, I didn't want to take you from them prematurely."

"How considerate," I grumbled. "Well, why didn't you tell me you were coming?"

"Well, you know I tried but you don't answer my calls, so..."

I rolled my eyes back, shaking my head as I moved to take a seat. My dad looked nervous, standing awkwardly, holding his nearly empty glass of water. His eyes darted about, as though he didn't know where they should settle.

The phone rang louder than ever. Marge smashed her cigarette, rising and heading toward the kitchen to answer it. She spoke softly into the receiver a few moments before hanging up. I was pretty certain it was nosey Clare Bear trying to find out what was going on after her gossipy grandkid told her how I ran off when I saw the strange car out front.

A bark from Lucy preceded the sound of the back door opening. Two conspiratorial voices entered ahead of the people speaking. I stood. Marge ordered Lucy Rae to stand down with a gesture.

My mom stumbled forward, laughing with a man who was trailing her, his hand on her waist, holding her up or, prepping to lay her down. He saw us before she did. The man straightened, his expression becoming more serious. He released his grasp on my mother. Andie tumbled forward, catching herself on the edge of the island counter.

"Miss Marge," he said a little too loudly, nodding in her direction before offering my father and me our own acknowledgement.

"Pat. What'cha doin' here with my daughter?"

"I, ummm...she uhhh...well, I wanted to make sure she got home okay." He nodded irrationally, like he was agreeing with a voice we couldn't hear. He appeared nervous under Marge's steely gaze. He opened his arms wide, then closed his hands together a few times. Looked as though he was prepping to give a presidential debate speech. Finally, he ran his fingers through his shaggy brown hair, tossing it from his sweaty face. He approached my dad with his hand extended, paused, and wiped sweat onto the front of dirt-caked jeans, then tried again. "Hi, I'm Pat. I went to high school with Pandy."

"Excuse me?"

"Pandy. Oh, sorry. It's what we called her back then. Andie-Pandy, heh." His hand remained extended, waiting for my father to accept.

"Well, *Pat*, I'm Pandy's husband and this is her youngest child and I'm here to take her home. Sorry if I stepped on your plans for gettin' laid tonight."

Pat shrank into himself, holding his hands up defensively, promising he didn't want any trouble...was only being a good friend. He looked about, fidgeting. "Well, I guess I'll just head on out. Nice meeting ya. Miss Marge. I'll tell my momma you said hi."

"No, I didn't." Marge glared, her arms folded across her chest.

Pat nodded for no real reason, smiling a goofy, nervous smile and waving incessantly as he walked to the front door. A mixture of a wail and a growl erupted and the lot of us turned in time to see Andie running at top speed toward Lyle, led by kitchen scissors held high above her head.

I screamed her name. I hadn't seen Pat move, only saw when he appeared between my parents, gripping Andie's wrists tightly and pushing her back with force. Lyle's hand moved to touch his ear. A horrified look covered his face when he saw the red on his fingertips.

"Andie...Andie-Pandy, it's me. It's Pat. Gimme the scissors, okay," Pat reasoned. "Don't do this, Pandy-Bear, okay?"

Mom's face was contorted and hardly recognizable. Her eyes were deadlocked on my dad. I tried to speak, to say her name but my words were stuck somewhere in the back of my throat. Marge approached and tried reasoning, and when that failed, demanding until finally she simply overpowered Mom and pried the scissors away from her. Andie jerked her arms violently until Pat released her, backing away cautiously.

"Mom." My voice, hardly above a whisper, jarred me.

I immediately regretted making my presence known when her wrath redirected to me. "You did this!" She charged my way, squinty eyed and nostrils flared. Her overdone makeup would have been comical had she not looked so menacing and un-Andie-like.

"I didn't..."

"You called him, didn't you? *Didn't you?* You brought him here after I told you I did not want to see him!"

I felt the sting before she finished her sentence. It was worse this time, worse than the first time. Quick and masterful, as though she slapped people all the time. My eyes watered instantly from the force and my hurt feelings. I stumbled back, nearly loosing my footing. The effort on my mother's part would have been impressive had tiny little Marge not manifested between us, landing her own open palm blow across Andie's cheek so hard that my mother landed squarely on her ass, body twisted sideways.

"You ain't gonna keep hitting this girl, Andrea. Lucy Rae, shut up!"

Lucy's bark died to a whimper as she paced anxiously in circles. My dad rushed to my side, checking to be sure I was okay. I insisted I was. A thin trail of blood trickled down his ear. Pat grabbed my mother beneath her arms, trying to help her to her feet.

"I told her to call him," Marge continued, her voice raised. "I made her do it 'cause you need help and I can't help you here. It's time for you to go home. Time to get back to your life...whatever worked for you before ya come here."

Andie sat, arms folded across her breasts, refusing to give any aid to Pat's efforts. Her face curled into a snarl, pointed down like her head was too heavy on her neck but her eyes aimed up. A child that wanted its way. Her voice was low and cold when she spoke. "F'k you, Momma. I don't know what Daddy ever saw in you, you bitter...old... bag. I hate you. I hate you!"

Though she did not react, Marge looked deflated. Her pale skin became ashen. To my surprise, I felt bad for her.

Marge said, "Get her outta here, Pat."

Pat struggled to remove my mother who's voice grew

incrementally louder as she spit the most vile insults at her own mother. I wondered whether it was her disease that generated such hatred, or if it was personal. Finally, Pat made progress, removing Andie-Pandy, kicking and screaming, from the premises.

Marge stared blankly at the back door, while thoughtlessly caressing the top of Lucy's head, calming both their nerves, I'm sure.

"How long has she been this way?" Lyle spit at a stunned Marge.

I answered on her behalf, "A couple weeks...maybe."

"And you just now call?" My dad paced angrily, touching his finger to his bleeding ear. I offered to get a bandage but he refused, insisting he was okay, it was a flesh wound. Finally, his pacing ceased and he addressed Marge once again. "I'm sorry but I can't take her, not like that."

Marge spun on her heels, facing him. "What you mean, you *can't* take her?"

"Dad," I cut in.

"She's too far gone. You really should have called me sooner."

"You mean you *won't* take her."

"You chose to harbor her...keep her this way."

"She was far gone when you met her. And you dealt. God bless, you got her right, and now she need you again."

"I was a much younger man back then. I'm sixty-three years old now. No. That's your child out there, you fix her this time. I'll take mine, you tend to yours."

Marge moved fast toward Lyle, pointing a bony finger. "That's your wife out there."

Lyle's expression changed. He looked suddenly nervous. His eyes shot to me and then back to Marge. "No. No, she isn't."

"Excuse me," I commanded, stepping closer. "Yes, she is."

"No...no, honey, she's not. We were never married."

"I saw the pictures."

"We had a commitment ceremony, that's all. I'm... well, I'm twice divorced and I promised myself I'd never get married again. So no, no Andie is not my wife."

I collapsed into the recliner. In a matter of a few weeks, my entire world was being turned upside down – hashtag, chaos – and summer had barely begun.

"Well ain't this just the biggest pile of horse shit if I ever seen one. You been with my daughter twenty-years of her life and you done with her just like that? Just 'cause ya ain't legally married? Why, you one selfish son of a bitch."

"Marge, I love Andie, I do. But you waited too long to call me. She's welcome home whenever she's ready. As soon as she's better." The two stared at the other, neither backing from their stance on the subject. Finally, Lyle stepped back and re-directed his focus to me. "Megan, get your things. Let's hit the road. We have a long drive ahead of us."

Stunned and uncertain, I watched Marge. Tiny and aged but strong. She stepped away, retrieved another cancer stick and lit it right there in her living room. After the bombshell my father dropped, I didn't blame her. I wanted one myself.

I pushed myself to standing and walked in slow motion to where my partially packed bag sat. Finally, I could go home and leave this forsaken place in the rearview. Escape early mornings in a hot house with no satellite TV or WiFi. Trade in Amelia for my actual friends, for Cameron and Shashonie Marie Jackson. I lifted the bag to my shoulder and remembered my bird Flaca, much less needy than Lucy Rae. My stuffed rabbit collection, the very reason for my epithet.

But Andie wouldn't be coming with us and it forced me to ask myself what home truly was? Material items and history? Friends and familiarity? Marjorie and Lyle had changed the dynamics of my world, destroying the sanctity of my home. Was it still home without my mother?

I sighed. Dropped the bag to my feet. "I'm not going."

"Of course you're going. I'm not leaving you in your mother's care another day. Now pick up your bag and let's go."

"No. I'm not...I'm not going with you."

"Bunny—"

"Dad, no. If my mother isn't welcome, then neither am I."

"This isn't a democracy. Your mom is sick—"

"Yes, she is and who is to blame for that?" I stepped closer to my dad, angry and hurt and betrayed. "You created this problem and now you want to just dump her here."

"It isn't like that. I'm an old man now—"

"I'm sorry, you're an old man? Marge is like twice your age so what is your point?"

Marge stepped in, "Watch it. I ain't that damn old. Look, Meg, don't worry about me. Gone home. Probably the trouble I earned for letting my sick child go out into the world alone with a baby all those years ago. You ain't happy here no way, so just go on home and be a kid. Enjoy your summer."

"No, not without my mother. We don't often get along but still...she's my mother. I can't just leave her. Not like this."

The room fell into a silent standoff. Marge sat, stroking behind Lucy Rae's ears. Andie's muffled complaints created ambient sound. I watched my dad, watched the wheels of his mind turning. The loud sound of glass shattering disrupted those thoughts. A large rock from Marge's garden landed on the kitchen island, skid across, and crashed onto the floor.

Lucy Rae backed up to safety, then went crazy. Pat cried out an apology from the backyard and promised that he had things under control. Marge swore loud and repeatedly as she struggled to calm Lucy once again.

Lyle grabbed my arm firmly with one hand and my bag with the other, pulling me hard toward the front door. "Let's go, Megan. The time for nobility has passed, you're going home."

I jerked hard, screaming at the top of my lungs. "No. No! Let go of me. I'm not leaving her. Marge shouldn't be forced to do this alone when she doesn't have to."

My father, upset, released me. I snatched my duffle from his grasp. He placed his palms against his waist. "Fine. Fine! But if she hurts you—"

"She could never hurt me as much as you already have." I chewed the inside of my lip and swallowed the tears that were trying to push free. I wouldn't give him the satisfaction.

Lyle reached inside his jacket pocket and pulled out two pill bottles, slamming them hard on the nearest end table. He looked at me, his eyes pleaded once more before he turned sharply and exited Marge's home.

I stood, listening to his fading footsteps. The sound of the engine coming alive caused my body to convulse. My breathing became unsteady. I focused on my exhales as a way to calm myself, while tears flowed down my face and congregated around my chin.

"You didn't need to do that," Marge said, soothing a shaken Lucy Rae.

I swallowed hard, immediately re-thinking my decision. I rushed past Marge and toward the backyard. "I didn't do it for you."

Andie sat, curled in a ball in the middle of the yard, crying into Pat's lap. I tapped him out and took over, hoping to convince her that I wasn't going to abandon her the way everyone else, at some point, had. I assured her that Lyle was gone and wouldn't be coming back. Although the thought pained me, I did my very best to convince her, and myself, that everything was going to be alright.

day #thirty-six.

I stomped noisily up the stairwell, aimed for Andie's room. A week had passed since my dad showed up in Marge's living room offering me the opportunity to go home. Home. To my own bed, in my own room, with my own photos, posters, and drawings on my own wall...with my own pet. My own life.

Home. Where my friends were and where I had a boyfriend...if I still had a boyfriend. Where everything made sense – everything except that very thing that brought us to Fox Harbor in the first place.

Home.

But I rejected that invitation in order to stand by Andie's side. To be there for her, I declined an opportunity to leave with Pervy Father Who Sleeps With Stepdaughter aka Asshole Who Lies To Actual Daugher And Abandons Common Law Wife, in order to show Mentally Ill Parental Figure that she had a reason to heal.

How my sacrifice was repaid was through the empty pill bottles I held in my hands – the empty pill bottle labeled Lithium and the empty bottle labeled Zyprexa. Tossed down the drain, or maybe flushed down the toilet. Flaunting her outright disregard in my face.

I turned the knob, and in full dramatic form, kicked the door open. She needed to understand how angry I was, how disappointed. I had been there for her but she was the mother, it was time for her to be there for me.

The room was dark, the curtains drawn. The air was thick. The outline of her body laid still beneath a sheet decorated with tiny embroidered flowers. She didn't move. Didn't jump, didn't budge.

Her back was to me. I felt, suddenly, intrusive. Like an inconsiderate child who wanted to play the television loud while her mom was trying to take a well-earned nap. I crept around to the other side of the bed, surprised and, honestly, startled to see her eyes wide open. I watched, waiting for her to blink to confirm that she was even alive.

"What do you want?" Her voice came to me before she managed the blink I sought. It was thick and gravely. There was no emotion present in her eyes, in her face, or in her voice. No life whatsoever.

I lost my nerve for a moment but remembered the empty pill bottles – one Lithium, one Zyprexa – that had been practically full when Lyle slammed them onto the end table before he left me behind to care for my mother, the woman that I thought was his wife.

"Why did you do this?" I yelled, holding up the bottles.

"Stop yelling. My head is killing me."

"Why did you dump your pills?"

"Why not?"

"That's not an answer, Mom."

"I don't want them, why do you think? And you're supposed to be the smart one." Her voice remained completely even, completely devoid of emotion.

"I stayed here for you, to help you–"

"Lower your voice."

"–but you have to help yourself."

She rolled onto her back, groaning along the way. She pushed the sheet from her upper body, stared up at the ceiling. Her expression was annoyance, like I was the problem. She grumbled, "I don't need your help."

I looked up at the sound of footsteps clomping down the hall. Marge entered the room, demanding to know what was going on...what all of the fuss was about. I held up the two empty pill bottles, then turned them upside down.

Marge wrapped a skinny, muscular arm around her waist. The other, she moved up so that she could plant her face into her palm. Her head shook gently side to side. "Why, Andrea? Why would you do something so foolish?"

"I hate those pills, Mother."

"You need them to get well."

"You imply that something is wrong with me. If you two would just let me be–"

"Andrea, you sick."

Mom sprouted up, grabbing the pillow from behind her and swinging with all her might, flinging it across the cluttered bedroom.

"I hate those f'kng pills, Momma, I hate them," she screamed, spit flying from between her lips.

"Calm down, alright. Now just calm yourself."

"No, I will not f'kng calm down! I *was* calm but you two nosey bitches won't leave me the hell alone! You're trying to poison me with that shit. I know it. You know it. It's a conspiracy and you're just upset that I'm not dumb enough to fall for it any longer!"

"Whose conspiring against you?" Marge asked as though it were a legitimate question.

Andie flung the sheet from her legs for no apparent reason. Didn't get up, just sat there in her underwear, topless.

"All of you! You. Lyle. *Her.* Those stupid, f'king doctors. Every last one of you. I'm not sick but you continue to say that I am so that I will be. To fit your agenda. To control me."

"How many times I gotta tell you, ain't nobody tryna control you. We only want you well."

"Those goddamn, f'kng pills drain me of everything. They suck the life from me. What's the point of living if you're not alive?"

She was breathing heavily. Her small, saggy tits rising and falling. I began to seethe. How dare she? *How dare she?!* I sacrificed for her, sacrificed *everything* that was important to me in the moment and for what purpose? And besides, was *this* living? Being holed up in a hot room, lonely and depressed? I held both bottles up high so she could see them, then chucked them at her one at a time.

"F'k you, Mom," I said, as I stalked past Marge and out of the room.

"Don't be mad because I beat you at your own little game," she screamed after me.

"F'k you!"

I was done, through with my mother. Through with Psycho Bitch Who Refused Treatment. I'd made a mistake not leaving with Lyle, but I wouldn't tell him that. I wasn't ready for him to be right about anything when he was wrong about everything.

I paced the living room, anxious and biting my nails. Marge could deal with her. Dad was right, she was her problem. Marge was right, it was her payback for letting her go all those years earlier. I was the child, this was not my responsibility.

I spotted Andie's large, black, knockoff Coach bag sitting on a chair beside the kitchen table. I went to it without thinking. Opened it up and dug through until I found her wallet. I flipped through her cards until I located the AmEx. It was the one with the highest limit and most likely to have enough on it for what I wanted.

But what I needed first was WiFi and a reliable computer, something Andie's cheap ass mom did not have, but good ol' Clare Bear did. I left the house, jogging down the steps. Lucy Rae trotted after me, looking sad as always.

"Sorry, girl," I muttered as I exited the gate, aimed for Clare's house a half a block up.

My fist hovered the door. I'd never been to Clare's. It felt awkward. I didn't know what to expect. I spied the doorbell and decided to ring it. Standing anxiously, waiting, I looked about wondering if anyone was home. I turned and was just about to buzz again when the door swung open and I was face to barrel chest with a bear of a man in red flannel and old man jeans.

He glared down at me through beady, rat-like eyes that looked even smaller courtesy of the overhang of skin above them. His lips were a thin line peering through a burst of gray and silver hair covering the skin beneath his nose, to the space underneath his broad chin. He said nothing, only glared.

My pits moistened and I felt myself panic slightly. I had no idea what we were doing and how to put an end to it. So I spoke. "H-hi. I'm Megan, Marge's – Andie's daughter. I'm looking–"

Rudely, the man turned away in the middle of my very respectful intro, edging the door toward close. My eyes widened in protest but my mouth didn't cooperate. Clare popped into view, catching my gaze and rushed toward me.

"Clare, you best deal with this n–"

The door nearly closed on me, muffling the balance of his sentence but I was sure I'd heard all I needed. Clare caught it in time for it not to slam in my face, purposely speaking loud enough that I would not catch the entirety of the man's statement.

"Meg, what're ya doing here? Everything okay at the house?" she asked through a plastered on smile.

"Did he just call me a–"

"Noise. When he's home he hates noise so he wants me to deal with it. And, you rang the bell. Most don't ring the bell. How can I help you, dear?"

I eyed her curiously but opted to let it go. "I was just looking for Amelia."

"Oh, honey, she took her Papa's car and gone into town with Maxey and Jojo. Something I can help with?"

I shook my head, frustrated. "No, thanks."

I walked away without another utterance, leaving Clare to stammer awkwardly with irrelevant and unnecessary parting words.

Slowly I walked toward the house, unfocused, figuring out where my next step should lead. I hadn't bothered to store Amelia's number, so I couldn't call her. I'd have to go into town to find her and seek her help. They called it *going into town* but in reality it was merely a twenty minute walk which I could manage just fine. I made walks like that frequently and easily back home. I only hoped I'd find her there.

≈

I turned onto Grand Street, the center of town and the pride and joy of the Fox Harborites. This was where the magic happened. Groceries, clothing, toiletries, gardening supplies, were all purchased there. What seemed to be the sole gas station in town was just across the street. And beside it was a Greyhound station. It was housed in a tiny, dated building that resembled something straight out of an episode of any 1950's black and white sitcom.

I noticed it off-hand the last time I was in the area with Amelia on a special trip to Armie's Garden Supply and Candy Store, two things that didn't match. It was hardly recognizable and I might have missed it were it not for the bus gassing up next door.

At the time I didn't think much of it. But now... I approached the block were Armie's was located, hopeful that the girls went there for ice cream. If they weren't there, I could think of only two other places to check.

"Hey, Meg, what you doing around these parts solo?"

I recognized the voice and smiled. I turned to face Wes, approaching in white shirt, slacks, beenie, and smock that let me know that he was on the clock.

"Hi." I could feel the outbreak of goofy on my face and blushed from embarrassment, which only made things worse.

He kept coming until he was right on me. He wrapped his arm around me, hugging me into his chest which aligned with my face. I took in the faint scent of a body spray mixed with mild sweat-inspired musk.

"You here with Old Lady Schofield?"

The goofy refused a courteous exit and I, momentarily, forgot how to answer, or even how to speak. Amelia, for as much of an idiot as I believed her to be, had been right about one thing – Wes, slender with all his tattoos and piercings – was *effing hawt!* He said my name and I snapped back to reality.

"Huh? Who? Oh, no. I walked. Looking for Amelia. Have you seen her?"

Wes eyed me like I'd surely lost it. One tolerates Amelia, but one never seeks her out.

"Why?"

"I need to buy – I just need to borrow something of

hers. I went by her grandparents but Clare said she left with Maxey and some Joe somebody."

"Jojo, Maxey's little sis."

"Oh." I felt myself becoming lost in his eyes as he stared at me. Quickly, I found a new topic. "Some bear-looking dude answered the door. Her grandad I suppose."

"Yeah, that would be the infamous, Big Zeke."

"Yeah, well, I'm almost certain Big Zeke referred to me as a—" I paused and scanned Wes' face before continuing, "the n-word."

He laughed. He had the audacity to laugh. My blood boiled instantly, only seconds from inferno level. His hotness was diminishing fast. I supposed he read my expression because he threw his palms up defensively, backing slowly away.

"My bad. You know I'm not laughing 'cause I think it's funny. I'm laughing because...well, he did. If you think Big Zeke said it, Big Zeke said it. So f'king predictable. He's such an asshole."

Predictable. I knew it, I'd known it all along. So why did hearing it from someone else cause hurt feelings?

"So...a lot of people here...that's how they see me?" A tear stuck in my throat. Suddenly I wanted to punch something or someone other than my mother. I cleared the emotion away.

Wes jerked his head and I followed his lead. We headed toward his store and turned along the side, taking a seat on a huge, rusty metal structure.

"People from The Skirts, they're old school, y'know. They don't care much for change. Where you're staying, out there with Old Lady Schofield, you're sorta in the heart of The Skirts–"

"The Skirts?"

"Outskirts...what we call the outskirts of town."

"Great." I dropped my head low, shaking it side to side. I felt the warm firmness of Wes' hand take hold of my own. I admired the subtle contrast in our colors. His fingers caressed mine, sending chills through me.

"Hey, hey." With his other hand, he used a finger to gently press my chin up until our eyes met. "Everyone isn't that way. It's...it's part of the culture, but people are changing. A lot of 'em, they want to change with the times. And the more the African Americans cross The Line–"

"Cross the line?" I repeated, horrified.

"The Line, another Harborism. Crossover from their historic side of town to this one. The more that happens, the easier it gets...the more progression there is. It takes time though. Curse of the small town, I'spose."

I pondered the information. "So what about your friends? Alli and Maxey and those guys?"

Wes chuckled. "They're all assholes, but they're equal opportunity assholes. But you do get kids around here that think like Big Zeke on occasion. Mostly ones from

The Skirts though."

"And you? Where are you from?"

Wes chuckled awkwardly and looked away shyly. "The Skirts. East side."

I didn't want to press any further because I didn't want to learn anything about Wes that would disappoint me. But, I couldn't help myself. "And what do you think about all of this?"

His brown eyes returned to my hazel ones. My breathing was suddenly shallow as he eyed me seriously. His lids lowered as he leaned in toward me. His lips were soft when they pressed into mine. With his tongue, he pushed my lips apart so that he could enter. My heart raced as he slid closer to me, our bodies pressed together. His hand grasped the back of my neck, easing up, his fingers creating paths through my loose, wavy hair.

"Ahem."

I jumped harshly at the unexpected sound of someone clearing their throat. I adjusted my clothing, though I didn't know why. I was disappointed to see Amelia eyeing me, judging. I brushed it off, jumped down onto the concrete.

Maxey giggled idiotically as her eyes passed from Wes to me, to Wes and back. She put a joint to her lips and inhaled, speaking in a thick voice before the smoke exited her mouth.

"Nice, Wes, pushing up on the new girl before she

gets to see what a dick you really are. Wonder what Alli is gonna say when she hears about this?"

Wes snatched the joint and hit it. "What I do concerns Al about as much as it concerns you." He walked away, claiming her weed as his own.

"Give it back," Maxey whined. "Give it back you dickwad. Fine, I won't say anything."

Wes flashed his sexy smirk, holding her drug just out of reach. I was struggling with what I should be feeling as I assessed the interaction.

"So...you like him now, huh?" Amelia inquired, expressionless.

"Do you?" I asked.

"No. God. Of course not."

"So why do you care?"

Wes finally returned the joint to Maxey, nearly half gone. He walked back to me, placing an arm around my shoulder. He nodded at Amelia who only scowled in return. He leaned into me, his lips nearly touching my ear. He whispered words to me, personal, that only I could hear. I smiled.

"I gotta get back," he said, standing upright. He turned my face to his and stole a quick peck. "See you later?"

And like that I recalled why I was even there to begin. I felt my smile fall away in slow motion. I lied, "Y-yeah.

Yeah, sure."

Wes turned away and jogged into the large store. I watched until he disappeared behind the doors. I turned to see that Amelia was still eyeballing me, as though I had somehow wronged her.

"So you guys a couple now or what?" Maxey asked, a devilish grin on her face. She offered me the joint. I declined, so she handed it to Amelia who only then looked away. "I hope so. You two would make a f'king hot couple."

I ignored her. "Amelia, you heading back anytime soon? I was actually looking for you."

Amelia low-key rolled her eyes. "Yeh, I could totally tell."

"Seriously. I went by Clare's looking and she said you were out here. Your granddad was none too pleased with me being there."

She looked embarrassed, though I couldn't tell if I was simply projecting what I wanted her to feel. She eyed me from head to foot before returning Maxey's nearly disintegrated joint. An emo brunette with blonde highlights bounded the corner.

"C'mon," said Amelia, stalking ahead like I brought word that she was grounded or something.

"Hey, you're out?" the girl asked.

"Yep. Gotta help a *friend*," she answered sarcastically, throwing a look my way.

I rolled my eyes but said nothing. After today I would never need to see her again so why should I have given two shits about her jealousy. If she wanted to pursue Wes, she was free to do so once I was out of the picture. She'd fail, but maybe that's why she always pretended that she saw him as nothing more than a friend. Because she already knew she'd fail, or rather, she'd already failed.

"So what do you want?" she asked as we approached our designated block in The Skirts.

"A favor or two that I'm pretty sure you'll be happy to oblige." I explained my intent to purchase a Greyhound ticket homeward-bound and my hope that she could have access to her grandfather's car that night to drop me off. No way I was gonna make the pitch black walk, especially after learning what I'd learned.

She stopped the car outside of Clare's, keeping it in drive with her foot on the brake. She adjusted in her seat for a better look at me, I presumed.

"Sooo, you're just gonna go AWOL on Wes? Did you even tell him?"

"Amelia, I don't know why you care. You act like you're P.O.'d that I kissed him—"

"I'm not."

"—now I'm trying to leave, so you should be pleased."

We watched each other, waiting for the other to make the next move. She re-adjusted, using her small muscles to push the lever at the top of the steering wheel into

PARK. She turned the ignition off, taking the keys out. I did a double-take. It was the first time I noticed the small confederate flag keychain mixed in with the others.

Noticing me noticing, she, red from actual embarrassment, gathered the key ring tightly into her palm. "I'll get my laptop and meet you on the stoop."

"So you'll take me?"

She looked surprisingly sad when she responded, "Yeh, I guess."

day #thirty-seven.

I'd never run away from home before and I wasn't even sure if this counted considering Fox Harbor was absolutely not home. Still, I supposed my actions would've had me labeled a runaway given that I was a legal minor in my mother's custody and I left without her authority or knowledge.

But to be fair my mother hadn't been my mother for weeks. She wasn't present at all. And based on her outburst, she wanted me gone. One of the last things she said to me was that she wanted me to leave her alone. So I did as instructed, being the obedient child that I am. I left her – alone.

I used her card online and ordered my departure ticket for the very next morning. No use in wasting time. Rip it off, like a band-aid.

Getting out wasn't difficult. Andie remained in hibernation, while Marge had taken Lucy Rae and gone down to visit with Clare Bear and her hubby, the Imperial Wizard of Fox Harbor. But as a precaution, I instructed Amelia to meet me a little ways from the house. Better to be safe than stuck in this dump for another couple weeks, at least. I spent the night at the station but left Amelia to believe I was taking a 10pm bus just in case she decided to rat. Didn't need her Nosey Nana trying to be helpful and bringing me back.

The only difficulty I faced was the phone call that I got from Wes while I waited for the Thelma to my Louise. I watched my cell ring with my thumb hovering ACCEPT. But what would I have said? Sorry, my mom was just revealed to be a psycho, and a quasi-slutty, quasi-violent one at that. Couple that with the big reveal about my spending my summer in the midst of The *Real* Mayberry. I had to escape before the lynchings kicked up. He called a second time but hung up before I could make up my mind.

I sat in a back seat on the 7:20 a.m. bus, staring at the latest text from Wes asking for my whereabouts and plans for the day, including how disappointed he was that he hadn't gotten to see me the night before.

I closed my eyes as the large, mostly empty bus rolled along, thinking back to the kiss we'd shared. I smelled his scent on my shirt and almost felt the actual sensation that moved through me when his palm gripped the back of my neck and his slim fingers cut through my hair and massaged the base of my head.

I missed him. Part of me regretted my decision to leave so soon without seeing where things could go. But what would be the point? Whatever happened with Andie, I would not stay in Fox Harbor. No matter, I would have left him anyway, eventually. I supposed if it was bound to happen, best it did before feelings settled in any deeper.

Halfway through my nine-hour trip, I called Shonie. It was my third attempt at reaching her. I thought to call Cam to find out what was up, but realized my battery was way too low and dammit, in my hurry to get the hell outta dodge, I completely forgot my charger. First my laptop and now... As a result, I had to be cautious with usage so texting and web surfing was out as well. My negligence made for a rather boring trip so, I slept as much as I could manage.

∂

I hadn't realized that having been awake and watching my back all night at the Greyhound Station had me incredibly worn out. After our lunch break stop off at Mickey D's, I slept the rest of the way, waking up just as the bus pulled into the city limits, about twenty miles outside of our downtown, much more impressive than Fox Harbor's. Take that, Smallville.

I stretched long and lithe, matching my body to the smile that spread across my face. I looked about, taking it all in like a dreamy teen seeking riches and fame in the big city.

HOME.

I was a kid on her way to Disney World for the very first time. Away from Fox Harbor. Away from Crazy Ladies Parts 1 And 2, Clare Bear and her racially-addled grandkid, along with a multitude of low and high key racists that I was sure were as happy to see me go as I was to be gone. The only part of Fox Harbor I'd miss was Wes.

The bus finally pulled into the depot. I was anxious and excited. I'd see my friends soon. It felt like years had gone by rather than weeks. I powered my phone up, fully expecting to see a multitude of new voicemails and missed calls. There were a couple from Marge and my dad, one from Amelia likely confessing that she'd blabbed, but none from Shonie.

She'd been calling or texting me almost daily for weeks, but now that I wanted to reach her, nothing. There were a few missed texts, but Shonie was the sender of none of those either. Wes' name appeared highlighted by a blue dot to its left. I pushed aside the emotion brewing. I took a deep breath and shrugged it off before I touched the screen.

Thu, Jul 4, 2:32 PM

Wes: You coulda told me

My heart sank. I turned responses over in my mind but settled on –

Meg:	I'm sorry :(
Wes:	...

I watched as the three dots appeared on my screen, watched and waited until they disappeared. I swore silently and tried Shonie once again. It rang only once before I got her voice saying, "What's good? You reached the voicemail of Shashonie Marie Jackson. I ain't got time for ya right now but you know I got love for ya. Leave a message. Peace!"

"F'k," I blurted out. Those closest to me on the bus glanced back with shamed stares. I reciprocated with a look that dared them to question me. I grabbed my duffle and stumbled along, following the rest of the passengers down the aisle, bumping into the back of the seats along the way.

I stepped down, took in a deep and cleansing breath – the sweet stench of home. A mix between freshwater and stale urine.

I glanced about trying to figure where to go. Sure, I was home, but I'd never had cause to go Greyhound before and so I'd never been to the depot. I walked to the street to find a clue as to where in the city I was, while everyone else went inside. A small group of older black men, grungy and passing a cigarette between them, argued about nothing important.

"Ay, sexy redbone. Hey! Hey, gurl, what choo is, with yo' fine self. Got that *good* hair – ooh wee! And pretty...

pretty as you wanna be."

"Bird, check it out, she got some pretty eyes, too. 'Mind me o' yo sista, Dessa. Gal could kill a nigga wit dem eyes, ha!"

"Yeah, but Odessa ugly as a skunk's butt at the bottom of a tractor."

Two of the men cackled and slapped palms at the insult. Normally I would've been disgusted...old men hitting on school girls. But given the unique circumstances, I smiled while I gave them the finger.

"Why 'on't choo come on ova here, young thang. I got someplace for you to stick that finger. I bet choo taste just *like* caramel candy. Mm! Fine self." The group doubled over, more cackles and high fives. Argument over, problem solved.

I pulled my phone from my jacket pocket as I turned the corner. The red charge symbol illustrated the catastrophically diminishing levels of battery life. I took my chances and dialed up Cam. She answered on the second ring.

"What up, bitch?"

"Cam, you know I hate being called that."

"Grow up. I can't believe you're actually calling me back after hanging up on me, what...a week ago."

"Something came up but I'm glad you picked up. Listen–"

"Hang on."

"Cam, what? No–"

She put me on hold. I screamed her name into the phone as she yelled at one of her sisters in the background. I began to pace, pounding my fist against my leg, trying to mentally will her back to the phone. I looked at my screen – 2%.

Finally, she returned, albeit unfocused. "Whatever my ass, Brit! I'm telling mom, don't worry! Ugh. Megz, you there?"

"Yeah, barely. Anyway, I'm calling to see if – hello? Cam? Hello?" I snatched my cell from my ear and looked at the screen in time to see the spinny *your phone is now a paperweight thingy* before blackout.

I screamed. Loud. Top of my lungs scream. Screamed the scream that makes people within your scream radius hover the 9 on their phone before they realize that there is no actual danger. A woman passing by with her son glared in my direction.

"The f'k are you looking at?" I spat.

She covered the boy's ears and rushed him past, like I'd actually said something he hadn't heard before. Probably even from her. I turned back toward the depot, eyeing the long row of yellow cabs. I was quite a ways from my hood, I didn't have enough cash, and since nobody knew I was coming, public transpo was going to have to cut it.

❧

The block. The neighborhood of my youth. I was so happy I wanted to salsa all the way to my Maple Ave home, but I wasn't ready to be there, not yet. I wasn't yet prepared to be left alone with Lyle. I mean, what if he and Marjie were still... Andie's presence hadn't stopped them before, so what motivation was there for them to be moral now that she was long gone and sans her mind?

I walked past the houses on Sherman Street lugging my duffel which, by now, felt like I was hauling bricks. My feet hurt in my flat canvas gym shoes. I was tired and thirsty, hot and in need of a shower and hoping to God that Shonie was at least home.

I plastered a smile on and waved at familiar faces who greeted me as I passed. The block was busy with some kids playing while others were scurried in for dinner. I hadn't realized before just how much I'd missed the noise and activity.

I passed through the gate and jogged up the steps of the brick duplex that Shonie's family resided, and rang the doorbell. Commotion could be heard on the other side, voices and feet, so I knew at least someone was home. I sighed, relieved, imagining a hot shower and Shonie's queen-sized bed.

The door swung open and I came to be face-to-face with Shonie's older sister LaTavia. Tay-Vee, home visiting from college, smiled brightly and pulled me in for a hug.

"Megan? Girl, what you doing here? Ooh, you look a mess."

I stepped away and glanced down at myself as though I forgot what I looked like. I chuckled. "Long trip."

"Yeah, Sho-Sho said you was outta town. Said you left randomly and nobody knew where you was. Everything okay?"

"I did. I was. It is. I'm back." I smiled awkwardly, opening my arms wide in presentation and providing a clear view of my oversized travel bag. "Is Shonie here?"

"Naw, her and Cam went to a kickback at Lonnie Jessup's crib, I think. A fourth of July thing."

I swore and looked in the distance in the direction to Lonnie's. I'd totally forgotten it was a holiday. Goodness, I did *not* want to walk any longer. I turned back to face Tay-Vee. "I just...I tried to reach her to tell her I was coming...my phone died. I'm tired. Can I just...stay here til she gets back?"

Latavia's face took on an odd expression. Only then did it occur to me that I was talking to her through the open door. The sister of the friend I'd had since the 2nd grade, Tay-Vee was as much my sister as Shonie's and yet she was talking to me through a half-opened door like I was a Jehovah's Witness trying to sell her on religion.

She sighed. "I don't know, Megz. I don't think it's a good idea."

My eyes watered and I rapidly blinked them dry.

Exhaustion had me emotional. "Why not?"

"You should really talk to Sho-Sho. I can't get involved in my sister business. I mean, you know how she get."

I really wanted to cry. Something was wrong and I wasn't certain I knew what. I was exhausted, I was hot, I was thirsty and hungry, and now... I just wanted to cry, but I didn't.

"Can I at least just leave my bag. That's a six block walk and it's heavy."

She offered me a pity smile and nodded, taking my bag from my shoulder and placing it just inside. She mouthed the words, *I'm sorry*, as she closed the door in my face.

❧

It maybe started as a simple holiday kickback but, like most gatherings at Lonnie Jessup's, it had grown. Kids loitered shamelessly in front of his moms house. While she was likely off doing a double or triple at the hospital, an indiscriminate number of wanna be's and hoodrats partied in and around her home. I knew most since most were raised within a 6-block radius of me.

Black wrappers, beer bottles, and cigarette butts littered the walkway. I cringed, feeling bad for Ms. Jessup, when someone poured out a little liquor on her rosebed. I had a flash of Marge kneeling in soil with Lucy Rae by her side, but quickly shoved it out of my brain.

"'Sup, Meggy-Megz." That was Brother Cass. He was like the big brother of the neighborhood, the one that rejected adulthood. No matter how old we got and how many of us moved on, Cass was there to usher in the new generation. "How you been, gurl? I ain't seen choo in a minute. Ay, wanna hit this smoochie? Dis shit fire."

"Hey, Brother Cass. Nah, I'm good on all counts."

"You lookin' fo' yo homegirls, aint'cha?"

"Yeah, as a matter of fact."

He rolled weed smoke around in his mouth a couple beats before reaching back and passing the gutted and reloaded Black to the next in line. Cass closed his eyes a moment, savoring the effect. He opened them slowly as he blew the smoke in my direction. He looked surprised to see me then, as though he suddenly recalled that he'd only a moment before been speaking to me, jerked his head toward the house.

I walked up past him and went inside, scanning the crowd. Loud, profane rap music surrounded me, the music of my generation. I wasn't a huge fan but I reflexively bobbed my head anyhow, trying to distract myself. I paused when I spotted my childhood friend across the room nursing a wine cooler, pretending to indulge.

No one ever seemed to notice that Shonie never actually drank or smoked anything, no one but me. She held whatever vice was passed her way, talked and laughed and passed it along, but never actually put it to her lips. This was but one secret she and I shared. I doubt Cam even knew. She was a loud, abrasive smack talker, who was secretly a goody-two-shoes that managed to always be the sober life of every party.

She didn't see me. Her thick, back-length braids were gathered high on her head, appearing to be too heavy for her slender neck. She looked cute as always in a black spaghetti strap tank and no bra, and cutoff denims with peek-a-boo pockets and classic 5th gen Jordans on her feet. Her mocha brown skin was tanned, serving as a reminder of all I'd missed out on.

Ayesha, the girl she was kicking up with, gently tapped her hand, the one with the poser bottle. Shonie turned to face me. That devious smile, the one that made her look so mysterious...like she knew something about you that you didn't want her to know, vanished.

She pointed her bottle and charged at me. "F'k off, Meg," she said, and kept it moving.

She was pissed. I racked my brain as I followed her fast pace but drew a blank. I mean, sure, I hadn't been very communicative but I wouldn't think that would cause her to have such a grandiose piss fit.

"Shonie, what the hell? I'm sorry I left without telling you. It wasn't my choice, Andie made me and everything got out of hand–"

She stopped abruptly, spinning on her heels, her ropes of hair nearly smacking me in the face. She paused, all her weight on one foot as she leaned, tilting her head to the side. The small gold nameplate glistened as she twirled her neck at me.

"That's what you think this is? Well, ain't you just a cocky l'il bitch. Contrary to what you may think, a sista *can* have a life sans you." She turned and continued out the front door with me on her heels.

"Okay, so you're mad that I didn't tell you what was up."

"Gettin' warmer."

"I didn't tell anybody, bro. It wasn't personal, it's just...I didn't really know how to talk about it. I was gonna to tell you tonight, I plan to tell you everything. You won't even believe–"

Shonie stopped again and I nearly crashed into her backside. She looked into the distance toward a giggling and wasted Cam stumbling into the yard, hanging off Marcus Price. Shonie's eyes went from Cam and landed on me. Meaningfully, she folded her arms over her breasts and in a mocking tone repeated, "I ain't tell nobody, bro."

My entire body tensed as the picture came into focus. She continued forward and I ran down the steps after her. "I can explain–"

"Don't bother. Ten year friendship versus four, and when shit gets real for you *she's* your go-to. She's my homegirl too, but bruh. C'mon. But I get it. Ya'll got more in common than we do." She grazed her fingers across her rich brown skin when she said it pointing out the stark contrast in our color...implying that I turned to Cam because we're both white.

"You know that's not—"

"And by the way," she cut in, "whatever shit you left with Tay-Vee, it'll be on the porch whenever you're ready to come get it. I heard it's s'posed to rain tonight so you might wanna hurry." She tossed the bottle and deuces before turning away and stalking off, sashaying her hips extra hard like she does when she believes to have satisfactorily checked someone.

"Sho, you're leaving? But the party's just starting," Cam slurred, her arms wrapped loosely around Marcus' neck. "Meg? Is that you? Oh my god, you're back! When did you get back?"

She pried her weight from Marcus' grasp and attempted to throw it onto me in a friendly embrace but I, angrily, shoved her away.

"What...*the f'k*," I yelled. Heads turned casually and ears perked up, paying closer attention in the event my rant led to blows being thrown. "What the f'k, Cam? I told you not to say anything to her. I was *very* clear. *I* wanted to be the one tell her. I only called you for advice and now she's...and I have no place to...what the f'k?"

Cam looked startled. Deer in headlights. Suddenly sobered. "My bad. I was drunk that night and I thought..."

My eyes closed tightly, trying hard to keep my emotions at bay. My head pounded, stomach turned upside down. "Mmmmmarrgh! Stop drinking. God!"

I stomped past Cam, letting my shoulder bump her hard. She called after me, started toward me but the look in my eyes warned her to stand down.

"Where are you going? Can we just talk about it? I'm sorry," she yelled. "I'm coming with you."

I turned to face her. She froze. "No, Cam, no! Leave me alone, okay. Just leave me the hell alone. You've done enough."

I needed to get away. I couldn't handle Cam's excuses for her betrayal. My world had been turned inside out and my one constant had been made unstable. I didn't make it very far before I found myself face-to-face with Yaves and crew. Welcome home, Meg, welcome home.

"Aye, look who's back in the city. Come to claim your precious little Javi?"

"I don't want Javi. I don't give a shit about you throwing your used up cunt at Javi," I retorted, but didn't mean it. I did care, lots.

"Me?" She laughed and looked around at the faces of her tickled friends. "Puta, please. You can have that madre chingado. I don't want him. Go get him. He's right over there."

She pushed past me, laughing. I looked back, watching them while wondering what changed. I turned around and walked slowly to the end of the fence. Javi was there, halfway up the driveway with his tongue so deep inside some girls mouth and hand so far up between her thighs, I swear the two were going to meet in the middle. He looked my way casually, then appeared startled.

Rage filled me. Mom, Dad, Marjie, Cam, and Shonie... it was all just too much. I picked up a nearby half empty beer bottle, reeled back and chucked it. I aimed for his head but it whizzed by, shattering on the concrete.

"F'kn bitch," the girl screamed, aiming her body at me but was restrained by Javier. He laughed while she tossed insults at me in Spanish. I offered both my middle finger before rushing off to safely determine my next move.

❧

I sat in the passenger's seat working on my emotions. I wanted to be angry but couldn't force it, though I gave it the old college try. Besides, it was no ones fault but my own that I wound up in Uncle Cal's F150 en route back to Fox Harbor. No one's but my own.

I just couldn't bring myself to go home and face Lyle at the scene of his crime. Couldn't bear to look at Marjie. My re-entry plan was ruined thanks to Cam. I meant to make my way home gradually with the support of my best friends. But Shonie wasn't forgiving me any time soon, as evidenced by my duffel being left on her porch as she said it would be.

I had betrayed Shonie and Cam betrayed me. And although I had good reason for doing as I did, my sister-slash-friend Shashonie was not above a good grudge. Without her by my side I couldn't walk through my door. Instead, I took a bus across town and knocked on Uncle Cal's in the middle of night, filling him in on all that was happening with his family.

He was livid – with everyone. Mom for not taking her meds when she knew she needed them. Marge for keeping it secret. Me for the same infraction but, mostly, for abandoning my mother when she needed me. Above all, my father for being a complete douchey, pervy, a-hole. Because of that, my uncle refused to return me to his care. I fought against his decision, the obligatory teenage tantrum, though not so much as to sway him.

Marge greeted us much differently than when I first arrived with Andie. She hugged her son, held him close. He towered above her. My uncle, Officer Calvin Miller Schofield, with his red hair and freckles, looked like a ginger bear cuddling a chew toy.

I expressed my love to Lucy Rae. I'd missed her during my hiatus.

"Well, hope you got it outta ya system," Marge said, giving me a stern look, "'cause we got bigger issues now."

Uncle Cal and I glanced to each other like one of us knew something the other didn't.

"What is it, Mom? What's going on?" Uncle Cal asked.

"Andie's pregnant."

day #forty-five.

I gave my uncle my word that I would not leave again. Promised to stick for the summer and be there for his sister, in his place. He hoped my presence would help to bring her back faster than if she were to be left alone with their mother. I promised to stay and he promised that if I did and she failed to come around by summer's end, he would bring me home and let me stay with him and my Aunt Julia, assuming I didn't want to go home to Lyle – which he was dead against.

To sweeten the deal, he took me shopping, adding much needed variety to my summer Fox Harbor wardrobe, in addition to purchasing me a new charger for my laptop and installing a Wi-Fi router. At least I could watch Netflix and Hulu in my downtime which was exactly what my sixteenth summer had become. Downtime.

Uncle Cal's presence made things feel less horrid, if slightly more normal. I supposed it was because he remained as the one constant in my life. But he was an officer of the law and was needed on the city streets. He had a wife and three fair-haired boys. He couldn't stay.

I stretched out on my back across the sofa that was now just that since my uncle convinced me that I should take his room for the duration of my stay. The clamor in the front yard that was Clare and her beloved Biscuit bounding the stairs, grew nearer. The pair entered without prompt. Clare smiled at me in that overly-pleased manner that made me distrust her motives, more since meeting her husband. She opened her mouth to speak. I pointed at the phone by my ear to imply I was too busy to chat, despite having been on hold nearly five entire minutes.

"Okay, I'm back," Cam said from her end, curiously breathless. "Sorry I took so long. Marcus stopped by so a brief make-out sesh was in order."

"Aren't you grounded?"

"That's why it was brief."

I'd forgiven Cam her major friend faux pas, despite that she was completely foul for having outright betrayed my trust. I had directly forbade her to say anything to Shonie about what I'd shared, partly because I wasn't emotionally ready to deal with her Judge Judy, but more important, because it needed to come from me. Something so intimate couldn't dare be shared third party.

But I had to ask myself, was it really all Cam's fault? I entrusted her with a secret that, per the friendship honor code, I should have shared with my closest friend first. Add to that Cam's budding alcohol abuse that was becoming seemingly, increasingly worse as the school years passed, and I should have suspected that a summer juice-fest would have her regurgitating info in the same manner she would the contents of her stomach the very next day.

So all said, it wasn't really Cam's fault, was it? It was mine. And keeping it real, were I to begrudge Cam in the way Shonie was me, who else would I have to lean on? Amelia was avoiding me. Although she was one I did not wish to miss, boredom could be a bitch. And regardless of what I wanted, *that* bitch was not seeing me. One could only assume she was still salts about my liplock with Wes, but post my decision to ditch quietly, I needed the little Walkie-Stalkie back on my team as an in to get me back on his. In the meantime, Cam was all I had.

"...but she never showed," Cam concluded.

"Wait – Shonie's igging you, too?"

"Earth to Megz. Duh, yeh. I mean, I get why she's p.o.'d with you, my bad for being insensitive. But why is she avoiding me? Yes, I was the bearer of borrowed news but I was merely the unintentional bearer, not the owner."

I twisted my lips into a pout, reflecting on all I knew about Shashonie Marie Jackson over a decade of friendship. "I know but it's not about you, it's about me."

"Makes no sense, you effing weirdos."

"Makes perfect sense. Don't worry, she'll come around and much faster with you than with me."

"Mayyybe...maybe not."

"What's that supposed to mean?"

"She's been hanging a lot with that Ayesha chic *and* the Kim G's."

I sat upright. "Kim Garnett and Kimesha Gabbardi?"

"You know some other Kim G's in the hood? They've been tight. Quiet as kept, Meggy Megz, there may not be a me, you, and she-some when this summer is done. As we both know, our girl is thee Grudge Queen, straight up."

"Yeah..."

"Yeah..."

Clare and Marge sat together in the kitchen, clucking like the hens they were. I heard their voices but wasn't focused on the content, nor could I any longer hear what Cam was saying in my ear. I could only focus on the irony of Lyle's infidelity, the place where I'd unwittingly taken my lead. In a way, I was guilty of the same – cheating on my wife (Shonie) with her kid (Cam). My own f'kd shit.

My mother's small voice startled me. She must have developed some serious ninja skills because I hadn't even heard her descend the steps. Maybe I was too deep in my own thoughts. One moment there was the sound of the activity of people leading their every day lives, the next — holding their breath in wait, wondering which Andie it was today.

I watched her but said nothing, only observed. Andie stood halfway between me and where Marge was arranging flowers she'd picked from her garden. She wore the most clothing I'd seen her in at once in weeks, maroon sweats and matching hoody with cracked lettering that was partially missing.

"I'm sorry, wanna repeat that," Marge said, pausing mid flower fluff.

Mom looked like an oversized child waiting to be reprimanded, all folded into herself as she was. She swayed ever so gently as a boat floating in the middle of the ocean. Watching her was almost nauseating.

"Will you take me to see Dr. Van Aalsburg?"

Marge nodded. "Of course. When you wanna go?"

Tears spilled from Andie's eyes, seemingly unprompted.

"Let me call you later," I mumbled to Cam. "It's my mom," I added, not wanting to leave her hanging this time.

Clare was at my mother's side before I could make it off the couch. Andie slipped away to the floor with Clare following her lead, holding her against her breasts. I looked to Marge but she had moved on to flipping through her address book with the phone poised in one hand.

I stood, feeling every bit of an incompetent imbecile, not knowing what my part in all of this should be. Clare's eyes came to meet mine. It was as though she took control of my being. I found myself taking careful paces forward until I was on the other side of my mother. I sat, taking her thin, translucent hand in mine and caressed gently.

❧

They argued the entire ride home, my mother and her mother. I smiled...on the inside at least. Mother That Hid Mental Illness Unjustly From Child had seen a doctor, finally, and by her own choice. Not for her sickness, but for confirmation of the growth of a seed inside of her. For me this was a start. For the first time in weeks I had hope that there would be an end to the drama and depression. She and I would go home together and possibly even before summer's end.

I had hope! After all that Andie had put Marge and me through, I could see a light at the end of a very dark tunnel. And if my diagnosed, unmedicated, bipolar mother could see the err in her ways, maybe Shashonie would see how grudging me, her very best and dearest friend, was wrong.

Cam was wrong. At the end of summer there would be an Us. She'd phase out Ayesha and the Kim G's because they were merely placeholders. She used them to fill a void created by the absence of *Us*, and if Stubborn Andie could come to see she needed to see a doc, then of course Shonie would come to see she needed...Us.

But ahead of the light was still a very dark tunnel and one where a positive pregnancy test existed. My forty-plus year old madre was preggers and it wasn't her fake-husband's kid either. It was the spawn of some 8th grade educated hick from The Skirts, and if she refused to see that termination was her best and only option, I could be tied to Fox Harbor for the rest of my youth.

This is what the argument was about, Andie's options. That and the fact that she should've taken the doc up on his offer and advisement of weaning herself back onto medication, especially now that she had altered hormones to contend with.

"Mom, you know you can't keep it," I volunteered. She glared in my direction. I didn't give her the satisfaction of reacting.

She returned her icy gaze to the back of the passenger seat and spoke in a cracked voice, "I'm tired. I don't wish to discuss this any further."

"Oh, *you* don't wish to discuss this?" Marge said. "Well la di da."

"Momma, please. I said I'm tired, can we just drop it already?"

Marge adjusted in her seat, staring dead ahead and I gambled, mentally willing herself to keep silent. Clare had barely eased the car to a halt before Andie was nudging Marge's seat forward, forcing her to hurry and jump out, so that her pregnant and bitchy kid could retreat to her dungeon, effectively blocking us from her thoughts and decision-making.

I shook my head but refused to allow Andie's brand of insanity to get to me – not today at least. I followed Clare out of the vehicle and headed toward the house but steps from the gate I peeped Amelia on the approach. She'd seen me many times since my return and hadn't stopped by or spoken once. I, assuming she was looking for Clare, looked away and kept forward.

"Meg," Amelia called, walking faster to catch up to me. Clare smiled as she passed me by, pleased that maybe Marge's grandkid and hers had some hope of becoming the future them after all. Never. I paused mid-stride and looked at her but said nothing. "Hey, you're back."

I rolled my eyes and kept moving. "I've been back, but you knew that."

"Yeh...wait, just wait. I knew but – look, you didn't bother to tell me you were back yourself so..."

"Well, I didn't really wanna come by your grandparents place. You know how much your grandpa hates *nnnnoise*."

She made a confused face which quickly morphed into one of revelation as she decoded my statement into her best guess of my meaning.

"I was just wondering if you, like, wanna hit the town? You gotta be totes bored and I'm meeting up with Maxey in like, an hour for a little free-range shopping, and her kid sis Jojo – you met Jojo, I think...right? But anyhow, she's coming with and I totes need a third wheel to balance the maturity factor in this equation."

"Free-range shopping?"

"Yeh. Oh my god, you never – shoplifting."

"What the hell, Amelia? You want me to go stealing with you and your frenemies?"

"Oh GTFOH, Megz, right?" She shrugged like it was no big deal, then stared at me in awe. I stared back unblinking. "Fine, f'k. You don't need to come in with. My accessorizing is on the downslide and I saw a couple items to bring me on the upswing. We are totally corporate with this shit, in and out and off to Nik Lake for clothing optional aquatics and general chill time with the crew. *If* you're interested, and not too much of a pussy, of course, you're welcome to come."

My eyes went to the house. I could see it's going-on's like I had x-ray vision. Clare and Marge were seated across from one another at the small round table, sipping coffee while alternately discussing how best to get Andie to kill her fetus, how to convince her to get back on her medication, and the latest in gardening and local politics. While Lucy Rae would be half asleep at Marge's feet, and Mentally Disordered You Know Who was holed up in her bedroom buried under covers, with little to no clothes on and curtains drawn. Exciting stuff.

Amelia's offer of lifting a little merch in the interest of

fashion increased greatly in its appeal. And for as much as I'd tried to convince myself that I didn't care, there was a thrill at the possibility of seeing Wes. I, personally, found the clothing option to be my preference, but I could be persuaded to shed an item or two if required and it got me on Wes' good side again.

I took a quasi-reluctant step back in Amelia's direction. "An hour?"

She nodded. I nodded.

❧

Although I could feel his brown eyes on my moderately melanated skin for most of the evening, Wes had yet to speak to me. I tried with every bit of me to not look his way. Instead, I watched Amelia dance around in her sky blue matching bra and underwear, showing off the new belly chain she'd acquired earlier in the day, like it was no big deal.

She and the Jojo that she hated so much, held hands and laughed as they danced in a circle around the water's edge, off the beat of the blue grass music that played through a speaker in the sand. Beyond the dancing duo, a smashed and topless (and I assumed bottomless) Maxey could just barely be made out making out with the oversized Dob. Picture of a walrus screwing a raccoon came to mind. I visualized his perpetual apple red cheeks had become candied apples.

I shook my nearly empty beer can and contemplated getting a fresh one for something to do and...well, as a legit excuse to satiate my intense desire to look in Wes' direction while not exactly looking at him.

I glanced about somewhat casually. Darkness was descending upon us as the sun sank beyond the horizon. If Wes and I had been on good terms, it could've made for a perfect romantic experience, sans the teenage lust-f'k in session in the lake beyond us. I wondered if they did shit like that on Cam's small town CW shows.

I chugged the last of my drink and pushed myself to standing, intentionally keeping my eyes to the sand as I trudged to the cooler. A fresh can appeared with no effort from me. I looked up and my eyes landed just below his, fearful of making direct contact.

"Thanks."

I looked away but didn't walk away. I watched Amelia chase Clarke, screaming, her hands attempting to conceal the bounce of her heavy boobs, as he teased her by twirling her stolen bra above his head.

I sucked in the evening air and held it as the heat of Wes' presence began to consume me. He stood so close that his bare arm ghost touched mine. He swigged his beer. Nervously, I followed his lead.

"Why'd you come back?" he inquired without facing me.

I glanced to him, then quickly away. I nodded toward

the activity. "Cause I missed this so much," I answered with an awkward chuckle.

"Okay, why'd you really come back?" This time he looked at me. I could feel his eyes planted on the side of my head.

"What? You don't think it's possible that Fox Harbor fun time has been the highlight of my life?" Finally, I worked up the nerve to look him in the eye. I shrugged. "I wasn't ready to be back home. Things didn't really...it wasn't the way I left it."

He watched me in silence, scanning my face. The rapid darkness making it difficult to read his expression. My heart felt as though it was creeping up my throat, interfering with my air supply.

He broke our connection after what felt like forever. "I'm glad you came back."

I fought against the smile attempting to break free and tuned back into the action on the waters. The three, Clarke, Amelia, and Jojo were now swimming together, their clothes in a pile at the shore.

"What the hell is this?"

I jumped guiltily, startled out of my personal and age-inappropriate thoughts, and turned at the sound of the familiar voice. Alli approached with another girl. I instinctively took a small step away from Wes, then cursed myself for having done it.

"Who listens to motherf'kng Dave Matthews Band

anymore?" Alli continued as she approached, walking past me as though I didn't exist, and straight to Wes, snatching his beer and chugging it.

"Anyone with good taste in music," Wes replied, taking his drink back.

Alli scoffed as she reached into the cooler. She tossed an ice cold brew to her compadre, a tall, van-sized girl, with heavy brown hair that hung to her waist. The girl scowled down at me as she held a cigarette to her lips.

"Who're you?" she asked, snarling.

"Who are you?" I answered in kind.

"That," Alli began, pointing my way, "is that f'king dimwit Amelia Davenport's little groupie friend. I heard she ran away from her psycho bitch of a mom, but look... she's returned."

"What did you just say?" I asked, taking a step closer.

"Please. Everyone in The Harbor knows everyone else's business. You think no one knows your mom's a loon? She's f'kng historic around here, which is more than I can say for you. Guess you realized that you have no life of your own in whatever *hood* you come from, so you ran back to try and fit in with us."

"Cut it out, Alli, okay," Wes said, trying to move her away from me.

"Wow," I said, feigning shock at the unprompted and unwarranted insult. "And all of this from a desperate, drop-out addict, whose solitary life goal is getting her ex to fit into that worn out slash between her thighs. You thought that little gotcha was gonna hurt my feelings? You're nobody to me. Nothing. What's your future look like, Alli? Gas station attendant or fat mistress? Why would I ever try to fit in with you?"

Alli balked at the insult before shooting a murderous look to her friend for daring to see the humor. "You don't even know me, you little bitch."

"Call it bitches intuition."

The venom in her blue-gray eyes bore into me so deeply, I could feel it. I swallowed the hint of fear rising and steeled myself, clenching my fist, just in case she decided to take it there. Her eyes moved past me, became a squint.

"What the hell? Is that Maxey f'king motherf'king Dob? And you're just letting this happen? Come help me get your fat f'k of a friend off of her! Eww," Alli cried, grabbing Wes and pulling him along.

He winked at me as he followed her lead, making me thankful that the night hid the blush I felt spreading across my cheeks.

day #forty-eight.

My very first ever encounter with Andie's mother was having the business end of a shotgun pointed at my chest. Since, she'd accomplished incredible feats of discipline, like wordlessly commanding a dog and slapping a woman twice her size and maybe half her age so hard she practically kissed the floor. By my assessment, this made Marge an OG. I wondered if that was terminology she was familiar with.

But if those exploits were not enough to warrant the label, finding Clare and myself standing nervously on either side of her as she confronted a woman who was, at worst, two and a half times Marge's size, at best, three times – in her own home! – certainly did.

"You gonna come to my house, tellin' me 'bout my

son? Well you sure got a lotta nerve."

"When ya son's action impact my daughter, hell yes. Now, Lou, he in there or not? You gonna answer me or I'mma find out on my own."

The woman called Lou appeared dazed for a moment, then smiled smugly, looking Marge over. "You ain't fixin' to come up in my house."

"If that's what I gotta do."

Lou's blue eyes rounded out and bounced in her head. She was a large woman. Broad shoulders and shaped like a rectangle. Marge couldn't have been more than 5'2" and 100 lbs soaking wet, and here she was ready to come to blows with this structure of a woman, and on her territory.

Clare Bear was visibly shaken by the encounter, evidenced by her suggestion of, "Let's just go."

I caught the sight of the mitt that disguised itself as Lou's hand. Sure, I understood Clare's apprehension, but I still shook my head in disappointment. What sorta Ride-or-Die was she? By no stretch of the imagination had Marge and I bonded, and likely we never would, but I respected what she was trying to do. Maybe her interest in Andie's life was too little too late, but the intent and effort and willingness to put one's self in harms way was appreciated.

Besides, coming to Loubelle Higgins' home was by no means anyone's idea of step one. Andie was stonewalling. No matter how many times or ways Marge or I broached the subject of doing what was best for the developing fetus, she shut down. So Marge tried a different tactic – figure out the potential baby daddy options and convince them to talk some sense into her. Shouldn't be difficult, who would want to have a rando kid with a nut job born out of a booty call?

It was a stretch but worth a try, and most of Marge's ear-to-the-street queries led back to this Pat character. So that brought us to the weather-worn, attention-deficit of a home three doors down from the bar that, during her manic times, my madre frequented.

Marge's head remained angled up, facing Big Lou, unblinking but addressing her sidekick. "I ain't goin' nowhere til I talk to Pat or this bear of a broad tell me where I can find 'im."

"Ya pushin' it, Margie. I could crush you between my pinky fingers." Lou illustrated the point by holding up the smallest of her thick, pink, sausage fingers.

I shivered. Marge chuckled. "Oh, Lou. You mess around and have a heart attack tryna catch me. Ain't nobody worried about you."

Lou placed her hands firm against her invisible waist. "Why you lil ol' ornery bitch."

"You big ol' fat ass bitch."

While the two dead-locked and I took mental bets on things like, who would hit first and which bitch would actually come out victorious, a loud noise emitted from the rear of the house catching all of us off guard.

"There he is," Clare called out, pointing.

I stepped out far enough to see the familiar frame of the man who had saved my father's ear that day. For that I was grateful, but not the possibility of his parenting the seedling taking residency in Andrea's womb.

"Pat! You get your scrawny ass back here and talk to me," Marge yelled. She turned sharply to face me, her faintly red braid whipping. "You young. Go after him."

My eyebrows shot up and I pointed at my feet which were loosely protected by a cheap pair of salmon colored flip flops. She rolled her eyes back into the distance Pat was disappearing into.

"I'm sorry, Marge. You just missed 'im," Lou said over her own raucous laughter. "Maybe you can catch up to him. Well, go on now. He ain't got on too far."

Marge turned calmly – at first. Her face contorted and I sensed a flame light beneath her. "You got-dang wildebeest–"

"Ohhkay," I interrupted, "I think Clare's right. Pat isn't here so maybe we should just go."

"You best listen to ya quadroon grandbaby, if ya know what's best. It's clear Pat ain't done nothin' wit' Andie seein' as she only let monkeys climb her tree."

Appalled, I stepped away from Marge with a feeling like someone had poured hot coffee over my head, slowly. Ignoring my swift mental calculation resulting in me being hospitalized awaiting the shutdown of vital organs if I dared to attack Pat's mom, I went for it anyway only to be blocked – or possibly saved – by Clare Bear.

The door slammed hard and the vibration shook us. I snatched aggressively from Clare's grasp. I could hear some words of consolation coming from her mouth, but I couldn't make them out nor did I care to try.

"I knew it," I spit at Marge's back. She stood stock still, staring at Loubelle's closed door like she was broken-hearted or something. "I knew this town was filled with cross-burning racists. Why did you bring me with you? Did you know she'd say some f'kd shit like that? Huh? Maybe...maybe you wanted her to. Wanted her to say what you've been thinking since I got here."

Marge didn't move, she didn't react, just kept standing there stuck on pause. I stared at her still frame, my chest heaving, face warm. Clare stepped around me blocking my line of sight.

"That absolutely isn't true and I think you know it."

"Says the racist best friend."

"Now you just stop that, Megan. You know that ain't true. You know my own granddaughter is a–"

My eyes went to Clare's. I waited for her to say the word. I watched her fumble mentally for a synonym for mulatto. "Is what, Clare? Your granddaughter is a what? A white girl? A Caucasian with trace amounts of Hispanic blood?"

"She's a biracial just like you."

"She isn't a *biracial* just like me. Do you two even know what that word means? She's a white girl, plain and ordinary. And you are a racist, plain and ordinary."

Horror streaked Clare's face and her pale cheeks gradiated from pink to red. "You take that back. I have been nothing but kind to you."

"I know, I know. Like that time you tried to spare my feelings when your husband called me a nigger practically to my face! That *was* thoughtful of you to try to make me believe I'd misheard."

Clare tripped over and stumbled around words but was unable to come up with a coherent defense. Beyond her, Marge finally moved. She walked pointedly toward the house.

"Nothing, huh," I ranted, addressing Marge. "No denial, no agreement. Ambiguity, what kinda f'kd shit is that? Just say it. Tell the truth about why you disowned my mother when Marjie was born."

It was as though I was speaking from behind soundproof glass. Instead of answering to me, she sifted around the dirt outside the home until she stood bringing a large rock with her. Before I was able to process the fact that Marge was taking a page out of Andie's book of tantrums, the mini-boulder had been launched and crashed through one of the home's windows.

"Margie, what have you done?" Clare cried out,

rushing to her side, attempting to pull her away.

My eyes bugged out of my head so far, for a split second I really thought they would get stuck. I could feel the color raining away as I watched Marge standing there, waiting. For what? Feedback? The locks were undone and the huge woman emerged, her eyes going from the shattered window to Marge's defiance. Her girth shadowed the entryway and I nearly expected a blue ox to amble out from behind her.

A flash of fear and sadness shot through me. I'd only just met my maternal grandmother, and now she was going to die in brutal fashion. But Lou didn't leave her doorway. Behind the anger, I was certain I saw a modicum of a fear of her own.

"I'm gone have to insist that you apologize," Marge commanded.

"You broke mah window!"

"I'mma need you to apologize, right now."

"You know you one crazy bitch. No wonder that kid of yourn ain't got all her marbles."

"So I been told, but we still gone need that apology."

Anger finally began to cover the landscape of the woman's pig-like face, though she remained, surprisingly, a safe distance away.

"Fine. I'm sorry I called your grandchild a octoroon–"

"Actually you said quadroon," I cut in. "You right,

semantics. Carry on."

She rolled her eyes from me and back to Marge. "Anyhow, I ain't apologizing for you. I probably shouldn'ta brought a child into it, so I'm 'pologizing for that. Now if you don't mind, I'm gone need you to get the hell off mah property 'fore I get the sheriff out here."

Satisfied, Marge faced us, Clare and me. "C'mon, y'all. Let's get on," she said as though nothing out of the ordinary had happened.

"You paying for this, Margie Schofield!" Piggy Lou yelled after us.

Marge stopped walking and grabbed my arm, snatching me around to face her. "Never again, y'hear me? Don't wanna hear no mo' 'bout it ever again."

I swallowed hard and nodded my acceptance of her terms. She gave a quick, curt nod in return and headed to the car, flipping Lou the bird along the way.

෴

We rode in silence. I couldn't shake the vision of Marge throwing a rock through a woman's window, shattering it and making *her* say *she* was sorry! This was done possibly for my honor...possibly for her own, I didn't know which it was but whatever the reason, I admired it.

I'd accused Clare of being racist, and in many respects I was sure that was true. But that woman...Lou...she had been intentionally mean and hurtful in her word selection.

Her apology meant nothing. Clare was right, she had been nothing but annoyingly kind. Although her hubby had unapologetically referred to me as the n-word, and it was likely that Clare had used the word just as casually, possibly even in reference to me – she had never treated me like one.

"Sorry," I mumbled, barely audible. I didn't want to say it, but I felt I should. No need to make a production out of it.

"You say something back there?" Clare asked.

I closed my eyes and my lips clenched. I took in a tight breath and exhaled another, "Sorry."

She nodded. "I know. Heard you the first time." Her eyes caught mine in the mirror. I chuckled lightly, shaking my head and looking away. I deserved that.

A pink dirt bike sat propped against Marge's fence. Amelia. I wondered why she would be at Andie's Mom's house if I nor her grandmother were there. Andie was wide awake when we entered, the exact opposite of her state when we'd left. Upon our return she resembled something of an actual human being.

Andie sat at the small table, entertaining. Her cheeks were pink and shiny, appearing freshly scrubbed. Her cleansed hair rested damp over her shoulders, the fragrant scent of shampoo clung to the air. Between her palms she held a yellow ceramic flower mug. Across from her sat Amelia, giggly and giddy as ever, holding a mug in one hand as she used the other to pop a forkful of pie into her mouth.

"What's going on here?" I asked apprehensively, maybe a tad envious that Andie appeared to have emerged from the confines of her dark soul at Amelia's behest rather than mine, her own daughter.

Amelia stood and sat her mug on the island counter, turning toward me with her cheerleader vibe. "Hi! You're back! Ohmagawd, like, I totally had no clue that your mom was so boss. Bomb to the maximum."

I shook my head, mouthing that last line and asking myself, who says shit like that? Andie shifted in her seat before siting her own mug down and rising to join to me.

She smiled down at me while rubbing her hand over my hair. "Bunny, I love your new friend. She's so funny and sweet. You need more friends like Amelia." She hugged me uncomfortably and kissed my cheek.

I glanced between the two, the goofy grin on Amelia's face and the spacey look in Andie's eyes and immediately knew the appeal – they were both bat shit. Certifiable. Except Mom had a legitimate excuse.

"Amelia, sweetheart, let's go." That was Clare speaking from just inside the doorway. Marge entered after, halting abruptly, then walking past Andie and me, responding to the barking at the back door. She answered, allowing Lucy Rae access.

"Why? Me and Andie were having thee best convo," Oblivious Amelia inquired.

"Yes, we were," Andie agreed.

Repulsed, I eased from my mother's grasp and took a seat at the breakfast table.

"C'mon," Clare repeated. "You promised to help Poppa in the yard, remember?"

Amelia made a pouty face that I could only assume was the tool that she used to get her way. Realizing this wouldn't be one of those times, she complied sharing parting air kisses with my mom.

I growled, rising to the close the door firmly behind the pair. The air in the room became frigid. Marge and Andie stood staring on opposite sides of the island, like they were in a good ol' western standoff. I nearly expected a bale of tumbleweed to pass through.

"I saw Lou today," Marge opened.

Andie's gaze dropped. She turned away and focused on clearing her and Amelia's tea time snacks.

"Why?" she asked, amazingly calm.

"You need to have an abortion and y'know it, but you draggin' ya feet."

Andie chuckled cynically. "And you thought *Lou* was going to help you convince me?"

"No. What I thought maybe Pat the daddy and he could. Any chance Pat the daddy?"

Andie didn't respond. She covered the pie and placed it on the island.

"Mom," I said in a pleading tone as I approached.

She laughed. "The two of you? Such an unlikely pair. You know she put me out when your sister was born."

"Now that ain't the truth and I wish ya stop tellin' people that."

"Yes, she did. But you go ahead and follow her lead. You know her real worry? If it isn't Pat's, then who? Could it be yet *another* black man?" Mom's voice stayed calm. She smiled like we were discussing a new shopping mall that opened, or the latest townie gossip.

My eyes shot to Marge, assessing her reaction and feeling only mildly guilty for having done it. Marge massaged her temples aggressively. She dropped her arms to her sides and stood a moment before jerking open a drawer, pulling forth her cigarette pack. She snatched one out and lit it, taking a long drag, her tense shoulders falling.

Marge asked, "Who else you slept with, Andrea? If it ain't Pat, do you even know whose it is? What about that boy I put outta here at gunpoint? It belong to him?"

"That isn't any of your business, *Mother*."

"It is so long as you in my house."

"Then maybe I should leave."

"Andrea."

Andie answered by shoving the yellow ceramic mug to crash to the floor as she stalked toward the back door.

Sunshine colored chunks and spilled cold coffee created angry artwork and startled Lucy Rae.

"You are such a child." Marge shook her head. Disappointed, she turned away, blowing smoke toward the window.

I ran after my mother, calling her name which merely bounced off her back and rolled back to me. I stopped. Watched her reach the edge of the property and contemplate which way she wanted to go. I realized an awful truth – I was always chasing after her. Calling her name. Being ignored. Well, this was the last time.

"You know what, I agree with her...I agree with your mom. I may not like her and she may not like me, but she's right. How do you expect to raise another baby when you yourself are behaving like one?"

She halted. Turned her head partially in my direction. I waited. Hoped she would come back prepared to continue the discussion...be an adult about things. Instead, she turned away, standing in place for the briefest of moments, before deciding on a direction and disappearing into the distance.

❧

I didn't expect Andie to come back anytime soon. That hadn't been part of her M.O. When she felt the need to escape, once she left, she was gone. She stayed out for days, usually two...three at a time.

Needless to say I was surprised and startled at the sound of the knob turning and door opening. I paused the series episode I was catching up on and turned to see what version of my mother was going to walk through the door. She jumped when she noticed me sitting in the darkness, my face illuminated by the light of my laptop. It was just past 1 a.m. which certainly made it an early night for her.

"What the hell?" she complained, turning on a nearby lamp. "Why are you sitting in the dark?"

"Watching *Game of Lies*."

"Oh," she said, intrigued. "What season?"

"Newest. You're back...early."

She shrugged, staring toward the empty kitchen. I followed her gaze, almost expecting someone to be standing there. She snapped out of her daze and looked to me, smiling sadly before taking a seat on the sofa beside me. She took my hand into hers, squeezing it and bouncing it up and down.

"You like it here?" she asked, finally breaking our uncomfortable silence.

I looked at her as though she'd surely lost her mind. The irony was not lost on me. "Uhm, no."

"You don't?"

"It's not a secret, Mom. I don't belong here."

"So you'd rather be with Dad."

I paused and looked over her face, trying to determine if we were having an actual, normal conversation, or if she would flip at any moment. "If I wanted to be with Dad, I'd be with Dad. I only want you to get better."

"Better. What does that even mean?" She reclaimed her hand but continued smiling like all was right with the world.

"C'mon, Mom."

"This is about my baby."

"Your fetus. Your medication. Mom, you can't have the baby, you know that right? You're just doing this to give your mom shit for not being there for you when Marjie was born. It's okay, I get it. I'm still a kid, y'know, it makes sense. But you're not. You gotta concede this one."

Andie held her smile, taking my hand once again. Her other hand came to my face, gently caressing my cheek as she gazed into my eyes.

"You know, I hadn't really paid attention before, but you look a lot like my father." Her eyes shifted about, I assume assessing my features. My almond eyes, my nose and full lips...pouty lips as Javi always described them.

She moved my hair, wavy like hers and hanging loose down my arms...tucked a few strands behind my ear.

"Mom," I said softly. "Just tell me if this is your way of sticking it to Marge for awhile. I promise, I won't say anything. In case you haven't noticed, I have your back."

My mother's answer was kissing my forehead. She leaned back and looked me over once more.

"Goodnight, Bunny." She rose and headed for the stairs.

"Mom," I pleaded. "Mom."

She jogged lightly up the steps without a response.

⸙

I shot upright in the darkness, the only light being from the full moon that shone outside of Uncle Cal's childhood window. I felt like someone had tried to strangle me and was struggling to catch my breath. The sound of my heart pounded in my ears, practically drowning out the sound of heavy and muffled baselines coming to me from outdoors.

I took several deep breaths and calmed. I'd had a nightmare, no big deal. I looked about, still in Fox Harbor. Still in Uncle Cal's room. It was only a dream...it was only a – oh shit!

...*heavy and muffled baselines coming to me from outdoors*... I sprang from the bed, stumbling into the dark hallway a moment after Marge passed by, fuming and grumbling loudly.

I cursed while smacking my face to encourage myself to awaken fully and faster. There was something majorly wrong with this scenario. First, we were in what Wes had referenced as *The Skirts* or what Shonie would call *West*

Bumblef'k. Absolutely no one banged beats in the middle of the night, or at any point for that matter, in this part of West Bumblef'k!

More frightening than any nightmare was recognizing the music as part of the death metal genre, and I knew but one person that would be so disrespectful as to blast it in a residential neighborhood, subs and all, in the literal middle of night.

I ran quickly down the steps behind Marge, losing my footing and nearly busting my ass in my effort to catch her before she answered the incessant pounding on the front door.

"No! No, don't open it. Don't open it."

"What? Don't tell me you know who out here bangin' on my door and disturbin' my neighbors with that devil music?" Her hand was poised to grab the shotgun and, for a selfish moment, I considered backing off. Then I remembered who it was and if Marge pulled a gun on her, she might have to use it.

"No. I mean, yes. I mean, let me handle this."

Marge eyed me curiously but made Lucy heel and stepped away from the firearm. I inhaled deeply, held it there for a moment, then exhaled as I opened the door.

"Go away," was my greeting.

"Well, f'k you too, baby sister."

"What do you want, Marjie? You've caused enough trouble, don't you think? Now please, go back where you came from."

Marjie looked me up and down. Marge approached, grabbing the door and opening it wider.

"So this the original one," Marge said in reference to her namesake.

Marjie smiled at her. "Grandmother," she cried out, shoving me aside and throwing herself around Marge who, cautiously, accepted the embrace. After allowing a respectable amount of time to pass, an uncomfortable Marge slipped free.

I addressed my sibling. "Okay, you've effectively caused a scene, now go."

Marjie smiled down at me. "So you get to spend time getting to know our grandmother but I don't? F'k that. I'm not going anywhere, baby sister."

My eyes went to Marge, pleading silently for her to back me up. We had enough to handle with Andie, we couldn't add Marjie to the mix. She was a huge part of all of our troubles and I knew without a doubt, she would only make matters worse.

Marge sighed. Message received – and disregarded. "C'mon."

Marjie cut her eyes, offering a suspicious smirk before turning and giving the thumbs up to whoever was in the drivers side of the noisy vehicle, but quickly held up her palm to stall him.

"Unless, he can stay the night. It was a long drive–"

Marjie reasoned.

"No," Marge answered.

Marjie rolled her eyes and waved. The guy, getting her meaning and driving off, added a double beep for good noise law violating measure.

Marjie bit her lip seductively as she watched after him. "F'k, he was hot."

"You make that the last time you bring all that noise to my door, y'hear," scolded Marge.

Marjie looked confused and offended at once. She wasn't used to being told what she could and could not do. It felt good to witness. If Marge was good for something it was discipline. Marjie nodded and half-smiled as she entered fully. I shoved the door closed behind her for lack of any other way to express my anger.

"Nope. No way. She cannot stay here." Andie stood at the bottom of the stairwell clutching her still flat abdomen.

"Mommy! Did'ja miss me?"

"Get out," Andie screamed, charging toward Marjie but stopping short, as though she were suddenly frightened. "Get out! Get out! Get out!"

"Andrea," Marge pleaded. "I need you to relax."

"If you want me to relax then you make her leave."

"That's your daughter."

Marjie beamed. "That's right, Mom, numero f'kn uno."

"I can handle this on my own, thank you very much." Marge turned back to her own disrespectful child. "It is way too late and we already done sent off her ride. Now, we all gone go on and get some sleep and sort this in the mornin'. Understood? Andrea?"

Mom's eyes formed into thin emerald lines across her face. Her teeth gritted as she spoke, "Daughter or not, I want her gone in the morning."

Marjie shook her head. "You're not getting rid of me, Mother. Get over it."

Marge and I locked eyes briefly before she guided Mom back upstairs. "Meg, grab some linens and set your sister up on the sofa."

Marjie faced me. I snarled. "Where do you sleep?" she asked.

"No, Marjie. You heard her. You get the couch."

She pointed toward the ceiling, a mischievous smile creeping up. "Up there?"

"The couch. I'll get you a blanket."

"F'k that. You've been here long enough. Get yourself a blanket."

"Hell no," I screamed at her, trying to pass her by but she shoved me – hard. Malicious.

"Goodnight, little sister," she said, waving her fingers as she headed toward the discovery of Uncle Cal's room, with her own duffle bag in tow.

day #fifty-one.

Lucy Rae lay stretched out, a fur coat in the cool shade, collapsed sideways offering an open invitation to whomever was willing to accept. Too lazy to roll fully onto her back, this angle would have to do. Hell, she was old. Amelia did the honors. She knelt beside the old girl, caressing her partially exposed lady bits. Lucy's head lolled to the side, her tongue dangling. She looked to be in heaven, and Wes, Clarke, and I laughed.

I savored this moment of peace. It was what I needed since my older sister's arrival had come along and reversed all progress. Andie retreated back into herself, rarely emerging from her room. She refused to be coaxed out so long as her eldest child was present and had even returned to the practice of locking her door. I couldn't say I much blamed her for that. It was likely more about keeping Marjie out than not letting anyone else in.

As for me, my official notice of eviction from Uncle Cal's former boudoir came in the form of finding all of my belongings strewn about in the upstairs hallway, and yet another door locked on me. I contemplated confronting my sibling but what would be the point. She'd win, she always won.

To my dismay, I truly began to empathize with Marge. This absentee family arrives on her doorstep ritualistically uninvited and unannounced in the middle of night, bringing nothing but headache and tension. So, maybe she deserved to deal with Andie's shit, but Marjie and her spoiled brattitude and bullshit alter was more than anyone deserved.

"So are Maxey and Dob like, an official item now?" Amelia asked, scrunching her face as she looked between the boys.

"F'k no," Clarke answered, easing onto an old swing that hung from the tree. He looked to me for permission to sit. I shrugged. I'd never used it. Didn't trust it.

"So why does she keep boning him? It's gross."

"Der. It's cause he's a fat ass."

I threw a questioning look his way. "What does that have to do with anything? Shouldn't that be a reason *not* to bone him?"

"God, you girls are clueless."

"Screw you," Amelia laughed.

"Enlighten us," I offered.

"You know what they say about fat dudes, right?"

We all laughed and shook our heads.

"No one says anything about fat dudes," I said. "Other than they're fat and they need to lose weight."

"Besides that." Clarke eased carefully into the swing, supporting his weight on one foot. "They say they got fat dicks."

I stared at him, stunned, then fell into hysterics. Amelia and I disagreed, waving him off.

Amelia added, "Yeah, *short* fat dicks."

"I'm telling you guys. Dob's packin'."

"Like you'd know."

"Of course I know. That's like, my brother. Right, Wes?"

Wes blushed but nodded.

"Eww, gross. I can't believe you guys go around looking at each other's dicks." Amelia abandoned Lucy's belly and crawled to where Clarke partially sat on the swing. I wondered if her all-fours, ass in air commute was for Clarke's benefit, or Wes'. Wes brought his eyes to mine, moved them to Amelia's ass and made a face. I laughed quietly as she slithered her body between Clarke's thighs. Speaking of dicks... "Can I try on your glasses?"

Wes slid in beside me, so close I could smell the scent of fresh squeezed lemonade on his breath. A cool breeze passed through me.

"Those two might be next," he said, picking petals from a dandelion.

"What? No way. I think she'd rather sleep with you." I nervously glanced his way, assessing his reaction. There was none.

He watched Amelia who laughed a little too intensely at something Clark said. "Probably. She'd be too freaked out about what Alli would do to her if she ever went for it."

My face fell at the thought of Wes with either girl but I quickly perked it back up when he looked in my direction. We sat together, catching up, joking around...sharing. Enjoying the afternoon.

Clarke moved fast and sudden past Amelia, nearly knocking her backwards as he scrambled to me. His voice was low and deliberate when he spoke. "Who...is that? She is so f'kn hot."

Our eyes followed the trail of lust that colored a path of red across the yard to the back door where Marjie stood wearing practically nothing but sexuality. She was dressed in a long black shirt that had been thoroughly shredded through the shoulders and entire bodice, revealing the swell of her small breasts and her ridiculously firm golden brown abdomen. Her denim shorts were practically underwear, and considering she likely wasn't wearing any actual underwear, the shorts probably served as just that.

She was crossbred, gazelle and lioness, her mane wild and untamed, in need of water but still f'kng gorgeous. Typical Marjie. She appeared to stare at the sky from behind dark glasses, a cigarette between her lips. In actuality she was watching us, I was sure of it. Ever the attention-whore, she was watching us to make sure we were watching her.

"She kinda looks like you, Megz," Amelia observed. "Prettier though."

"Yeah, like you Meg, if you were hot," Clarke added. Amelia smacked his arm. I rolled my eyes at them both.

Wes asked, "That your sister?"

I nodded, reluctant to publicly acknowledge that awful truth. I hated Marjie. And not because she was screwing my father. I hated her long before that. And not in the Big Sister Slash Little Sister Healthy Rivalry way like Cam and her sisters. There was nothing healthy about Marjie's and my relationship. She was toxic. She was Satan.

"Hey guys, you wanna get out of here?" I asked hopeful.

"And go where?" Wes asked.

"Does it matter? Anywhere but here."

"Oh, shit," Clarke said excitedly, rubbing his palms together and scrambling to his feet. "She's coming this way. How do I look?"

Wes answered, laughing, "Like the piece of shit you are."

I jumped up, taking Wes' hand in mine, trying my best to urge him forward. Too late. Before I could get him fully to his feet, a barefoot Marjie was upon us.

"Going somewhere, little sis?"

"As a matter of fact–"

"Rude. You're just going to go and not introduce me to your new friends."

I paused, glancing around at their faces and taking note of the special desperation in Amelia's and especially Clarke's, feeling sorta bad knowing he didn't stand a chance. Marjie would crush him.

I sighed heavily. "Wes, Amelia, Clarke. That's Marjie. Now, can we go?"

Clarke's ocean-blue eyes waved behind his dark eyeglass frames. "Marjie. So, like, you're named after your grandmother."

I shook my head gently at his epic fail. Marjie's smile dropped off and her eyes cut through him. I wondered if he could feel the cold steel of her hazel-green gaze tearing his soul from his body. I assumed so when he stumbled limply and adjusted his frames for no reason.

Amelia stepped in, clearly developing a crush of her own in her insatiable need to be liked. She extended a hand. "Hi! I'm Amelia Davenport, Clare's granddaughter."

Marjie rolled her head slowly toward Amelia. "Who the f'k is Clare?"

"Like, only your grandmother's BFFE. Anyways, I love your hair. It's so awesome. My hair is so blah, but I did totally manage to get my ends dreaded which was way cool. I got mad props for that at my school. Danke to my Spanish roots."

Marjie stared blankly at Amelia. I read the look as one of wonder. More specifically, wondering why the hell she was speaking to her. Marjie held up a hand to Amelia's face before turning and offering her back. For the briefest moment I actually liked my sister. "Who the f'k is this annoying little twat? I can't believe I'm saying this but I like Cam so much better."

Amelia gasped. Feelings hurt. I guess I should've been sympathetic except she really was an annoying twat who I didn't actually like. She was merely a placeholder.

Marjie closed in on Wes, her chipped black polished nails grazing the visible tattoos on his arms. She lifted her sunglasses revealing the desire in her eyes. I swallowed my disgust repeatedly, trying not to show my feelings. Try as I might, I couldn't tell what he was thinking...if he liked her touch or not. But why shouldn't he? Every guy liked her. She was a *bruja malvada* who cast her wicked and sexual spell over men. Why should Wes respond any different?

"And what's the significance of these?" she asked,

rubbing her hand slowly across two cherubs that were hugging each other.

"They represent my nieces, Rebecca and Caitlin."

"Awww, aren't you so sweet?" She stepped forward, closing the gap. Biting down on her bottom lip as she looked him over, her eyes offering him her body.

I felt as though my heart had been lassoed and the rope was being tightened. Unable to handle much more, I stepped between them. "Okay, Marjie. You proved your point, you can back off now. He doesn't need you pawing all over him with your...skanky fingers."

She casually looked my way and laughed. "My *skanky fingers*? Wow, you got me with that one, sis. Did you just make that one up? Oh wait, I see what's going on here. You like him. Aww, isn't that cute. Did you f'k him yet?"

"Don't be such a child, Marjie."

"How is he supposed to know how you feel about him if you don't spread for him? Oh, but you're still a virgin, huh? Does he know? Oops, he knows now." She looked to Wes, popping her bottom lip out in feigned sympathy, then returned her focus to humiliating me. "Yeah, Javi never tapped that. Said you were scared of the D. But don't worry about it, baby sister, you weren't missing much." She ended her statement by illustrating his length between her thumb and forefinger.

I rolled my eyes, moreso to keep angry tears at bay. The worse thing you could ever do was let Marjie catch you crying. "Can you please leave, you made your point. You screwed my boyfriend – my *ex*-boyfriend – and you'll screw Wes, too. Fine, Marjie, have at it 'cause *he's* not my boyfriend. So you two can do whatever you want, except you're not interested anymore, are you? It's only fun for you if it's hurtful to someone else."

I walked away, leaving Marjie laughing hysterically. She always won. Wes called after me but I didn't stop, couldn't because the tears were building up. I had to escape. Lucy Rae trotted alongside. I was almost safe behind closed doors when Wes grabbed my arm and turned me to face him.

"What the hell was that?"

"I saw how you were looking at her."

"And what way was that?"

"The same way *every* guy looks at her. If you're interested, Wes, go for it. She'll f'k you just to get under my skin. But we're not a couple, so I don't give a shit."

Wes looked as though he'd been slapped in the face. I felt bad but I shook it off, had to. If I cared, if I *allowed* myself to care I'd only get hurt when my sister took him as her plaything. And she would if she thought for a moment it would break me.

The emotion in Wes' face took on several shapes before turning into a wall. He turned away, told the others it was time to go. Clarke and Amelia followed obediently, though Clarke still tried his best to appear impressive before Marjie.

"God, you're a bitch," Amelia said once she was a safe distance away.

"Boo," Marjie said, jumping forward and causing Amelia to scramble.

I turned my back to the scene and stomped indoors. I allowed Lucy in and watched from behind the screen as Marjie approached, slamming the door hard just as she arrived, and locking it behind me. Arms folded, I stalked across the living room and took a seat on the sofa, ignoring the banging and yelling from the back door.

Marge emerged from the half bath, drying her hands on a yellow towel.

"What in the world is all this raucous for?" she yelled, foolishly unlocking the door and allowing a livid Marjie access.

"I will *kill* you, you little bitch," she spit at me.

"Try it, slut," I yelled in return, standing up to her. Marge's living room became a bar at closing. We screamed threats and the most obscene insults we could come up with at each other, drowning out Marge's plea for peace. We didn't care. Soon, we were nose to nose, shoving one another, each trying to establish dominance over the other. I never knew how or why, despite my being bigger in stature, Marjie was stronger. Crazy people strength. She shoved me and I stumbled back into the table and fell over, banging my knee as I stood. I swallowed the pain and charged at her.

A large crash jolted us to attention. Bits and pieces of white ceramic covered the area around the coffee table. One large piece with the letters B-O-S in black caught my eye. I looked up to Marge's face, masked in rouge. Her damp eyes flicked wetness every time she blinked, an unusual sight.

"Now shut up. Shut. The f'k. Up! Both o' youse!"

I swallowed hard, releasing the flood. Took my chances. "I told you not to let her in."

"And I told you to shut the f'k up."

"You shoulda made her leave. She's nothing but trouble if you haven't noticed."

"She's ya sister."

"She's the devil. You greeted me with a shotgun barrel to my chest. You welcomed her with open arms!"

"In all due fairness, I did not know you."

"In all due fairness, you don't know her either." My eyes went to the remains of her coffee mug, one that I did not know the history behind but knew without a doubt meant something to her.

We turned at the sound of the creaking floorboard. Andie stood, watching us but saying nothing. The room fell completely and eerily silent. All I could hear besides Lucy Rae's wheezing was the ticking of the clock above the stairwell.

Andie was dressed, fully clothed in jeans, five-dollar canvas sneakers, and a misshapen white tee-shirt. Her eyes were puffy and red. She looked haggard, like she hadn't slept in days. Likely, she had not. Her bottom lip tremored but she didn't cry. Nervously, she ran her hand through her mane, pushing it back from her face, scratching slowly across her scalp. She dropped her head and moved quickly beyond us.

"Andrea," said Marge. "Andrea, where ya goin'? Ya daughters 'bout to kill each other in here. Don't you think you should deal with this? Y'know, be their *mother*."

Marge stressed the last word and I caught her meaning, recalling the fetus that my parent insisted on incubating.

"I need some air," she answered without looking back. She picked up her black purse and clutched it to her chest, held it tight like she was afraid someone would take it. She stood by the door, her eyes pointing down.

"You need some air, huh? What you *need* is to be present. You wanna be a mother, then you need to be the one that deal with ya children's issues. This ain't my duty. This ain't my mess to clean."

My mother began rocking on her heels. Her head tilting up for a moment, then down. "I need some air." She opened the door and exited, pulling it up but not closing it behind her.

"She put a gun to your chest?" Marjie asked, giggling. "That's f'kng hysterical." She jogged up the stairs. A moment later the bedroom door slammed shut, putting an end to our fight.

∻

I was sure that I'd misunderstood her when she called my cell, but when I asked that Marge repeat herself, she echoed the same words, *Your father is here.* His arrival made little sense. The last time he'd come, it was at my prompting, and I'd made it perfectly clear that if he wouldn't take Andie, he would not take me. I stood by that sentiment more than ever since giving my uncle my word the day he returned me to Fox Harbor and as part of our weekly check-ins.

So I believed there must have been some mistake except there was my dad's sedan parked right outside of Marge's house when Amelia dropped me off. I blocked her attempts to come in with me, fully aware that it was less about making sure I was okay, and all about collecting good gossip to share with Clare Bear.

"What's going on here? Dad, what are you doing here?" I asked as soon as I walked through the door.

My father stood and walked over to me, wrapping his arms around me and kissing me on the cheek. He stepped back and reclaimed his seat on the edge of the sofa, his brown Kangol between his fingertips. "Get your things together, Bunny. We're going home."

"Dad, I told you already, I'm not leaving without

Mom. You shouldn't have come."

I looked to Marge for some assistance but she looked anywhere but at me. She sat on a stool in grungy coveralls, fresh from having been knee-deep in soil. Her legs were crossed, the top one shaking obsessively, a cigarette burning between her lips.

"I called your dad." My head jerked in the direction of the creaky floorboard that announced my mother just before her words cut off my father. "I'm ready. Meg, how quickly can you get your stuff together so we can get out of here?"

I looked between the two of them, waiting for someone to tell me I was being pranked. No one did, their faces were serious. It was true, I was going home. I smiled, I couldn't help myself. It was like I'd been holding my breath for a month and a half and I'd been given permission to breathe.

"Home?" I asked.

My dad nodded, smiling. "Home. Now go ahead and get your things."

"I'm ready." I bounded over to my duffle bag, haphazardly stuffing clothes back inside, then realized I now had more than could fit. I consulted Marge to see if she had a bag I could use. Without looking my way, she informed me that there was a suitcase in Cal's closet that I could take.

I eyed her curiously. We were leaving, going home.

Once we were gone, Marjie would surely follow as she'd have no reason to stay. Marge would have her house back. She'd be restored to her previous life of monotony and meaninglessness but somehow, she did not look very pleased about it. I shook it off, not my concern, and ran upstairs slipping quietly into my former guest room and aiming straight for the closet as quickly as possible.

"What the shit? Why are you in here?" my sister mumbled, sounding every bit of a dragon waking from it's slumber. The irony wasn't lost.

"Nothing. I left something in here. Go back to sleep." I moved fast, removing the case as discreetly as possible. I didn't know if Lyle knew Marjie was there but I was certain Marjie didn't know about Lyle's presence, and I wanted it to remain that way.

I slipped out, closing the door softly behind me and heading downstairs to pack. Tension blanketed the space. My parents stood, poised and ready, waiting for me. Marge, who I'd rarely seen smoke more than a half a cigarette at a time, whipped out another one after barely smashing the first one out.

"What you expect me to do 'bout the other one?" she asked in a low voice, still refusing to look our way.

Mom didn't answer, just stared blankly at the door. My eyes shot to my father. I tried to determine whether he caught Marge's meaning. He didn't seem to notice but not wanting to take a chance of any drama unfolding, I intervened. "Why don't you guys just wait in the car? I'm almost done here. I'll meet you out there in a minute."

"Don't you need help with carrying–," my dad started.

"Nope...nope, I'm good."

Clearly anxious to be free of Marge's silent judgement, Dad happily took my advice and aimed for the door. "C'mon, Andie. Nice seeing you again, Marge."

As if on cue, the sound of metal pounded through the ceiling. My father stopped in his tracks. He looked about, agitated, his mouth agape but his words not yet figured out. I moved my hands faster.

"Is that...?" He leaned forward, conspiratorially and whispered, "Is Marjorie here?"

Mom addressed me, her tone impatient. "Hurry, Bunny. We need to go."

I moved as fast as I could then stopped, deciding that if I didn't have it, I didn't need it. We could just go as is. I closed the zipper as the growling vocals of *Sadistic Embodiment* became clearer. I knew the song, we all knew the song, because it was Marjie's favorite to drive all of us insane with. It was her theme song.

I awkwardly lifted the luggage, rushing toward my parents. "I'm ready, I'm ready. Let's get outta here. Bye Marge, it was...nice...meeting you."

My hand was pressed firm against my father's back, pushing him toward the door when the sound of my life being ruined, yet again, bounded down the steps.

"Uhm, what's going on?" Marjie asked confused, first, then enlightened. "Wait – are you guys *leaving*?"

"Marjie, please," I said.

My sister strutted across the room in a cutoff top and black lace panties. "Lyle, baby. You traveled all this way and you weren't even going to say hi?" She squealed, practically jumping into my father's arms. He caught her beneath her pits and held her at a distance, like she was contaminated. She was.

Marge looked our way, finally. With her cigarette dangling dangerously loose from her lips, she was between my sibling and parental figure, pushing them apart.

"Marjorie, go put some damn clothes on," she scolded.

"Marjorie's not here right now," she answered calmly, that creepy shadow coming over her face when she claims an alter is in control. "Name's Atika, old bitch. Nice to meet you."

"Excuse me?"

I growled loudly, demanding attention. "Mom. Dad. What are we waiting for? Let's go."

"Go?" Atika/Marjorie's eyes shifted to my bags. She looked back to Mom, fully dressed and saddled with her own bag, standing quietly. As unhelpful as always. "Go. So you were just gonna leave me here? Lyle, baby, you were gonna leave me behind? Your widdle cinnamon bun...you were going to take *them* and leave me in this fuckhole of a place with that ornery old bat?"

"Go on, nah, Marjorie," said Dad, helping Marge to push her hands away.

"I thought you f'kng loved me," she screamed, sounding every bit of the devil I believed her to be. "Guess you only love me when your cock is in my mouth. You'll take your precious Bunny but you were just going to leave *me*? You'll drive all this way for my bitch of a mother, who's carrying some other man's bastard child by the way, but *I* get left behind."

Confusion clouded my dad's face. He turned to Mom so fast I thought he must have hurt himself. Marjie had blind-sided him with the big *other man's bastard child* reveal. Hell, she blind-sided me considering I didn't even know that she knew about it. Marge and I had taken such lengths to keep it from her.

I grabbed my father's hand, using all of my strength to try and edge him forward. "Dad, don't listen to her. She doesn't know what she's talking about. Let's go."

His brow furrowed as he tried to look into my mother's face, which she kept hidden from him. "What she talkin' about, some other man's baby? That's some crazy Atika Dangerfield talk...right?"

"Of course it is, Dad," I interjected. "It's Marjie, what do you think?"

"Andie?"

Mom's eyes locked onto the floor. She took a breath,

then looked up to him. "I'm pregnant, Lyle. Now let's go. We can talk about it at home."

"You what now?"

I cut in. "She's going to get an abortion, Dad. It's not a big deal."

Mom looked to me with chagrin, shaking her head. "I'm not getting an abortion, how many times do I have to say it."

"Yes, Mom. Yes, you are."

Losing her temper, she burst into a white hot flame and screamed at me, "I am *not* getting an abortion! Listen to me very carefully because this will be *thee* last time I say this – I will not kill this baby. Got it? I didn't kill you. I didn't kill your sister – though maybe I should have. I won't kill this baby either!"

The room fell silent around Marjie's erratic giggles. Marge snatched the insignificant remainder of her cigarette from between her lips and stomped away, smashing it with unnecessary force. She pulled out another, fumbling with the lighter for a moment. Frustrated, she slammed both down and walked toward our dysfunctional nuclear family...then fell back. We were poison, get too close and it could kill you.

"You want that baby, Andie...ya keepin' it? But ya ain't right in the head. You know it but you won't take your meds. You got this first one runnin' around just like you, unmedicated and from what I can tell, undiagnosed.

Now she done been raped by your husband here for God knows how long–"

"Whoa, now what?" I yelled.

"Now wait a minute," said Dad. "You just wait one goddamn minute. Ain't nobody rape that girl. She's a goddamn legal, consenting adult."

Marge teleported to my father, a finger to his nose. "With a goddamn undocumented, but clearly visible, mental *goddamn* illness and you know it. Ya took care o' Andie all them years, you know what this disease look like. You shoulda got her treatment. Instead, you gave her your old tired ass erection. That's as good as rape where I come from."

Marjie's chest heaved and tears streamed. My sister didn't cry, it wasn't her thing. She made fun of you if you cried. So to see her in such a state, I was almost concerned. "F'k *you*, f'k all of you. There isn't shit wrong with me. Nothing! I *know* who I am. I am just fine," said the girl with the alternate personality.

Marge, calm restored now that she got what was on her mind off her chest, faced Marjie. "Yes, honey, there is plenty wrong, but nothin' that can't be dealt with."

"What the f'k ever. What do you know? You don't know me. Where the hell have you been all my life? But you got a diagnosis? Get the f'k outta here."

My father removed himself from my grasp, throwing his arms in the air in defeat. He looked from Andie's Mom to Andie. "Fine. I'll admit that maybe I shouldn't have... maybe I shouldn't have been with her. That's what you wanna hear? But you know it ain't incest, and it for sure ain't rape. I can't handle this drama. My sugar high, my blood pressure high..."

"I haven't accused you of anything, Lyle. Let's just go," Mom said, fear evident in her eyes. "I just want to go home."

"I'm an old man, Andie," he continued. "An old man that ain't got it in him to raise another man's baby. Not again. You come home, you take your medication, you terminate that pregnancy. You can't do that, you don't come home."

Although my mother's body was turned toward her not-husband her gaze fell elsewhere. "Don't do this, Lyle," she whispered.

"I ain't doin' it, Andie. I'm giving you a choice."

She stood a beat longer, looking down. Gradually, she released the floor from her visual hold, bringing her bejeweled eyes to me. She shook her head sadly and mouthed the words, *I tried*, before dropping her bag and disappearing up the stairs.

I dropped my duffel beside hers and ran after her. Catching up, I tugged at her and begged...pleaded for her to not let things end this way. Tried to convince her that she couldn't sacrifice everything for some unknown man's unborn kid, a kid who inevitably would be born to suffer unduly like the rest of us. It wasn't fair.

"Stop it, Meg, stop it. Just stop! I won't change my mind." She entered her room and closed the door, hard, in my face. I staggered backwards and returned downstairs, drenched in sadness.

Marjie stepped uncomfortably close to me. "Awww, the widdle baby's crying. Mommy hurt her precious Bunny's feelings. Now you know what it's been like to be me all these years."

I shoved her as hard as I could. "I hate you, I hate you, I hate you! You ruin *everything*! Just die already!" My outburst only made her laugh harder.

"Bunny, I'm so sorry," Dad said. He looked to Marjie and shook his head forlornly, then turned his eyes to me. "Last chance. When I leave, I'm not coming back."

My emotions were piling on top of one another, restricting my airway. I struggled for oxygen as I choked on my own tears. I looked at Marjorie, wishing she had never existed. I hated her. I gulped for air. Dad – Lyle – offered assistance, patted my back. I jerked free. I looked down at my packed luggage...the suitcase, my duffel, then walked beyond my father and out of the house. I jogged down the steps and turned outside the gate. Ignoring the sound of my sperm donor calling after me, I took off running. I ran until my legs grew weary and I could hardly catch my breath.

Finally, I slowed to a stop, gasping for air. My heartbeat gradually returned to its normal pace. I reached into my back pocket and pulled my cellphone out, accessing Wes' phone number and dialed. I listened, impatient, as it rang, waiting for him to answer, holding in my tears when he did.

"Can you come get me. Please."

day #fifty-five.

The white mist of fog surrounded me. I couldn't see anything beyond it. I continued forward, the cloud dissipating, gradually, as my mind became alert though my eyes refused to open. I stretched and adjusted slightly, rubbed the base of my palms aggressively against my lids. I tried, again, to lift them but couldn't.

The unexpected sensation of warm breath against the back of my neck gave me the shove I needed to escape the cloud of sleep. The weight of an arm around my waist made clear I was not alone. And although I was on a sofa, it wasn't Marge's and it wasn't my own, a fact which the early a.m. boner against my ass confirmed.

I pried my eyelids apart and took in the sight of the faded rose-colored hand attached to the ink decorated wrist that dangled across my body. I didn't move, wasn't yet ready to disturb him.

My eyes scanned the room for a clue...some reason for me to be there, in The Woods, with Wes wrapped around me. I couldn't move my head, not without moving him. I looked across the dirty and dusty wood plank floor to the stone fireplace that hadn't been used for its intended purpose in ages and was filled with trash.

The bright light of a new day broke through the leaves of the trees outside the window and fell in patterns across the thick layer of dirt. I felt foggy and strange but mostly bothered about my lack of understanding as to the how and why I was there.

A small rustling sound caught my ears and aroused my awareness. My eyes roamed, looking for who else was with us but I couldn't see anyone. The old abandoned cabin was small so there really wasn't any place one could be except perfectly placed on either side of my head or feet, which was unlikely.

The rustling continued, beckoning for me to focus on the trash bin of a fireplace. I squinted and leaned forward slightly. An old McDonald's bag fell and the items around it rustled as something I couldn't see darted through. Forgetting about Wes, I squealed and jumped, pulling my legs in tight and backing into him as far as I could manage. Wes stirred behind me, reclaiming his arm. He struggled a bit, trying to sit up.

"What's wrong? What is happening?" he asked in a

thick morning voice.

"Something moved," I answered breathless from panic. I pointed. "Something's in there."

He chuckled, brushing my hair from my forehead. "You're scared of a little rat?"

"A rat?" I screamed, jumping up even tighter.

He yawned. "Yeah, probably. Or a squirrel. Whatever it is, or was, I'm sure you scared it off."

I cut my eyes up to him, confused and appalled that I slept in a place where rats made themselves at home. I leaned forward, trying to get a closer look but all was still. I unfolded my body and cautiously sat upright. I looked around three-hundred-sixty degrees, confirming that we were indeed alone.

"Where's everyone else?"

He dropped his head and scratched the back of his scalp. He spoke through an extended yawn, "Who?"

"Melia, Alli, Maxey, Clarke, Dob..."

Wes shrugged. "Home, I guess."

"When did they leave?"

He paused and looked at me curiously before reaching for his beanie and easing it onto his head. "They were never here. Remember? You called me to come get you. You wanted to be alone so I brought you here."

I held my breath in anticipation as he climbed over me and jumped, barefoot, to the floor. I remembered the dust and cringed. I didn't remember much else. There was a vague recollection of calling him but beyond that was mostly fog where there should've been memory.

I moved deeper into the sofa, then jumped, putting my hands to my breasts and squeezed. My girls were hanging out, no bra. I looked to Wes' backside as he sat on the edge of the old sofa putting on his socks and shoes. Nervously, I opened my mouth to speak but closed it for a moment...fearful of what answer my question may receive.

"Did we...? Uhm, what did we do last night?" I asked.

He shrugged. "Not much. Chilled. Talked. You were pretty upset when I got you so I gave you a Xaney so you could relax."

"A Xaney?" I asked, in shock.

He looked back to me. "Yeah, you know, Xanex. It's a prescription pill for–"

"I know what it is, silly. Why did you give it to me?"

"You were real upset when I got you. Crying practically nonstop."

"Why?"

He shrugged his shoulders. "No idea. You said you didn't want to talk about it. Only that your sister...that you wished she would have stayed gone. That's about it. You wouldn't say much else. Look, you were really upset about whatever happened so I brought you here and gave you a Xaney to help you relax. I'm sorry if I did the wrong thing. I was just trying to help."

I closed my eyes tight, massaging my temples. I tried my best to pull something through. I recalled some of it, calling him after I ran away from Marge's...Marge. She accused my dad of being a rapist. My blood warmed. Bitch. Lyle had been pervy, inappropriate, disrespectful, but I couldn't support him being labeled a rapist. She was Crazy Lady Who Put Shotgun To Grandkid's Chest And Welcomed Devil Into Home, so who was she to judge?

"No...no, you didn't. Thanks," I mumbled. "But did we...you know?"

He chuckled. "No. What?"

"*You know.*"

"Ahh," he laughed. "No, we didn't. Why, do you wanna?"

I dropped my head, hiding the rouge in my cheeks. "No, but are you sure we didn't?"

Wes nodded firmly, pointing to the space between his thighs. "Believe me, I'm sure."

"Then where's my bra?" I asked, tentatively.

"Oh, that." He smiled devilishly. He dropped to his knees and moved toward me without taking his eyes off of mine. He leaned low and angled, then sat up, my hot pink bra hanging from the tip of his finger. I snatched it, clutching it to me.

"Oh my god, Wes, what did we do?"

He laughed and stood, dusting off his jeans. "Nothing. We didn't do anything. You started getting sleepy after awhile and your bra had you pretty p.o.'d, so you snatched it off."

"Oh," I laughed.

"You want...you want to talk about it? Whatever had you so upset last night?"

I bit down on the corner of my lip and glanced up at the window, staring out for a moment. I shook my head and looked to him again. He was beautiful. His smile and the way his eyes danced...he moved me. "Thanks, but no thanks. No way you want all that drama dumped on you. I appreciate it though, I really do. And if I didn't say so yesterday, thanks for coming for me."

"Sure. Hey, sorry to cut this short but I got work today. Mind if I take you home now?"

I smiled at him as he handed me my shoes.

The town was quiet, peaceful so early in the morning. No one was out and about. Nothing like back home. I glanced at the side of Wes' face. His blond sideburns shimmered in the light, making him that much more attractive. He had come for me, come when I called. I wondered whether it meant anything...whether it meant he liked me. I mean, like me-liked me. I hoped so because I found I was starting to like-like him.

Not wanting to be too obvious, I redirected my focus to the passenger side window. As he drove, I remembered more...remembered Lyle. He had come courtesy of Andie's beckoning, had her back the way Wes had mine. He came to take us home but Marjie told him about the baby...the baby that Andie refused to abort and so he refused her passage out of Fox Harbor. But Andie's pregnancy was his fault. All that had happened since we left home, my father was to blame and yet, at each opportunity to take responsibility for his and the resulting action, he declined.

It was all on him for choosing to sleep with Marjie, who Marge believed to be suffering from the same illness Andie suffered. But because our mother was sick didn't mean that Marjie was. *I* had turned out perfectly fine. *She* was a spiteful and hateful person who ruined everything. But, she was *not* a crazy person and my father was no f'king rapist.

The car slowed to a stop outside of Andie's Mom's house. I peeped her sitting on the ledge smoking and drinking her morning coffee. I rolled my eyes and turned to face Wes.

"Thanks, again, for coming for me."

"Anytime." He eyed me, licking his lips slowly. He moved forward an inch. Breathless and nervous I followed his lead, continuing until our lips were locked. The moisture on the soft pocket of flesh chilled me. He pulled back a little, sucking my full bottom lip into his mouth. His tongue grazed my dual piercing. He nibbled gently before freeing me. I gasped. "I'll call you later."

I nodded dumbly and exited the car. I stood, watching as Wes pulled away, feeling Marge's eyes on my back. I sighed heavily and turned toward the house, surprised to not see her sitting on the ledge. I climbed the stairs slowly. Lucy Rae trotted to me when I entered. I caressed the top of her head, watching Marge watch me, as she poured herself a fresh mug.

"Got something hangin' out ya pocket." I looked down and saw the bright pink strap of my bra. I pushed it in deeper. "You want to spend the night out with boys or run on back home, I don't care much. I reckon you old enough to make those choices for y'self, but what I would appreciate is at least a heads up about it."

"I didn't...I just fell asleep." I felt bad, at first, but reminded myself that I had nothing to feel bad about. Who was she? Where had she been for my sixteen and a half years of life? "What difference does it make to you anyhow?"

She stopped moving. Stared at me. Her shoulders dropped. She looked defeated. She was likely to blame for all of this anyhow. All of it. Not Lyle, *her*. Everything that had gone wrong to this point, for having been a shitty mother forty-two years ago.

She grabbed a pack of cigarettes and returned to the ledge, taking a seat. "Guess you right. No difference."

She drank from a new mug since breaking her favorite one during Marjie's and my fight, a chipped one with a smiling reindeer and colorful snowflakes. She sat it down, pulled out a cigarette and lit it, blowing smoke out of the open window.

Something about her movements, her gestures...the casual way she blew smoke from her lungs, it offended me. All of it. "You know, my father may be a lot of things but he's not a rapist so f'k you very much for saying that."

Her eyes lolled to the side of her head in my direction. She rolled the smoke around in her mouth while she eyed me. Finally, she looked away, exhaling it while dumping ashes into her sawed can. "That make you feel better 'bout yourself? Cussin' an old lady. "

"F'k you, *old lady*. God, I can't wait to get out of this place. Every time I think that maybe, just maybe you're not the old cunt that I pegged you to be you go and ruin it."

Marge smashed her cigarette as she stood, and I panicked but steadied my breathing so she wouldn't notice. "Well la-di-f'king-da, I'm so sorry I let you down. Ya ain't much less cunt-like ya damn self. I didn't ask for this – any of this trouble and yet I let each and every one of ya lay your burdens down here. What I get in return? Disrespect. From you, your mammy, and that bat shit crazy ass sister of yourn whose biggest trouble is ain't nobody thought enough of her to get her the help she need."

"You don't even know what you're talking about. Marjie isn't crazy, she's just spoiled."

"No chile, *you* the one that's spoiled. Smart mouth,

know it all, needs a good switch to your hide, pain in my ass, brat. That other one ain't right. That first one ain't spoiled, she ignored. She need therapy or a good cocktail of medication, but probably both. And my daughter know it and so do your father, but he slept with her anyhow. You call that what you want, but I call it ain't right."

I stood there, limp and unresponsive. How was I to follow that up? I'd spent all sixteen and a half years of my life being tormented by an older sister that I always assumed was most upset by no longer being the only child. And here was the mother of *our* mother implying there was more to it than that.

What if she was right? What if Marjie *had* been suffering from the same affliction as Andie, or even something different, and what if Lyle had been aware? He knew the signs and symptoms. I didn't because they shielded it from me, but certainly he did. And he slept with her anyhow, so what *did* that make him? Certainly not a rapist, but what? But Marge...she had been around Marjie for such a short time. What if she was wrong?

My mind was in a whirlwind. I was in a maze. I didn't know what to think. The pounding started small and dull, progressing slowly. I didn't know what to make of my family, how to handle the multitude of secrets being revealed. All I knew in the moment was that I'd spent the night in a dirty, rat infested cabin that the local kids dubbed *The Woods* and I needed a shower.

"I'll be in the bathroom in case you're concerned that

you can't find me." I turned toward the stairwell as Marge once again took her seat upon the ledge.

"Yeah, well before you do that, your *not-a-rapist* daddy just pulled up outside."

"What?" I turned and rushed towards the door. Remembering the bra in my pocket, I snatched it out and tossed it onto the couch. My dad was already outside of his car, standing just inside of the open door. We watched one another across the spans. He looked tired and aged. I felt conflicted. He had made a mistake, a really unfortunate one. But he was my dad.

He waved me over and eased back behind the wheel. I took to the pavement and joined him inside our family vehicle. Coolness lingered inside from the air conditioning. He turned the engine over, allowing the cool flow of air to pick up.

"I thought you already headed home," I said.

He hunched his shoulders. "I wasn't sure if you wanted to go with me or not. Staying with your momma is one thing, but you don't owe Marjie nothing."

I nodded and looked to the house. Saw Marge taking another drag, looking into the distance...pretending to not be watching us. "Dad, is Marjie like Mom?"

"How's that now?"

I turned toward him. "I mean, is she bipolar, too?"

He dropped his eyes. "Well, you know, when it come to mental illness issues, it can be really complicated–"

"Don't bullshit me, Dad...please."

His lips pursed in contemplation, then he looked away. "I don't know, maybe. Probably."

I exhaled heavily. "So what Marge said about you being a rapist–"

He turned sharply to face me. His eyes grabbing mine and pulling them in tight. "I ain't rape nobody. She was a consenting–"

"Dad...Dad, I know. I just think she means that maybe you took advantage. And I want her to be wrong – so badly I want her to be wrong but... I just don't know what to think." A tear trailed my cheek, itching the flesh. I swiped it quickly away.

He sighed. "I suggested to Andie...when Marjie was younger I suggested she take her to see someone. She showed signs. But beyond that, she had other issues developed long before we met. She had behavioral issues...always had 'em."

I waited for more but he went silent. "And? What happened?"

"She said no. Your momma said no. She said Marjorie was fine, just called her her *Wild Child*. Said she had an assertive personality, free-spirited. Didn't want nobody labeling her or treating her different just 'cause they didn't understand her."

"So you *did* know something was wrong and you...you slept with..."

"Like I said, your momma wouldn't allow—"

"But you *knew*. Dad, you knew it wasn't just an assertive personality. You've known her almost all of her life, you *knew*." Tears pooled around my chin. I wiped them away with my sleeve. "So it *is* like...you took advantage."

"Bunny, now wait one minute. Your sister may be a few filaments short of a bulb, and some lithium of her own might serve her well, but she ain't outright crazy. She knows exactly what she's doing when she flounces around the house in them tiny little boy panties and them half a shirts with holes all cut through 'em so you can practically see all her girl parts. She means to work me over. I'm a man—"

"Stop."

"She's a beautiful young woman—"

"Oh my god, gross. Stop!" I laughed, cynically. Dark and disturbed to match our conversation. "Wow, Lyle. And to think, you almost won me over."

"Come on, Bunny."

"Dad, what the f'k?"

"Now, Megan, I have talked to you about your language when you address me—"

"Do you hear yourself? Do you hear the ridiculous, perverse, bullshit – you know what, Dad...just go. Please... just leave. I'm not going back with you. I can't even look at you."

I jumped from the car, slamming the door hard behind me. I still didn't think of my dad as a rapist, but I knew that something was terribly wrong in his brain. I no longer knew who he was and wondered if I'd ever really known him. How much of what I'd believed about my father was a lie. He called me by my childhood name once...twice. I turned to face him. He stood inside the drivers side door.

"Bunny, I won't come back. You know that."

I nodded. "Yeah, I know."

His head dropped for a moment and when he looked up again his eyes were reddening and wet with tears. It was the first time, after all that happened, that my father, Lyle Blakely, actually showed a sign of remorse.

"I'm sorry, Megan. For all of it. I truly am." An apology, deep and sincere.

"Yeah, Dad...me too." I turned away and headed back up the steps to the house, the sound of my forever changed relationship with my father fading into the distance.

day #sixty.

I missed Wes something terrible despite having been with him every day since our post rescue kiss. I couldn't get enough of him. I smelled his scent and felt his presence whenever I closed my eyes. Home consumed less of my thoughts since Wes began filling my days, figuratively and literally. I was deep in fantasy when Marjie emerged and began actively sucking whatever joy existed in Marge's household, out of it. I retreated to the porch, Lucy Rae and me, texting Cam and Wes to pass time.

Thurs, Jul 28, 3:16 PM

Meg: I can't take her! She won't leave. She disappears lots like Andie used to and I hope she gets lost but she always find her way back.

Cam: You know how she is.

Meg: Exactly! Das why i want her to get lost!

Cam: And your grams won't make her leave?

Meg: Marge and NO! Her belated Andie-guilt won't allow it.

Cam: LOL! Wassup with that boy you like? He's a distraction, right

Meg: At work. UGH! Off at 5. Waiting for him to get me the hell away from here.

Cam: You give him some yet?

Meg: Of course not! It's not even like that. Were getting to know each other.

Cam: Bro, summers almost done. Ya better get on that D!

Meg: Perv but you right you right

Meg: You talk to Shonie yet, btw?

Cam: 👎

Meg: Damn. She'll come around doe.

Cam: Hope you're right.

A lull in the text convo reminded me that I'd not heard from Wes in awhile, too long for my liking. I checked his name just to be sure I hadn't missed a response to my latest message. I hadn't.

"Bump it," I said to myself, jumping to my feet.

I made the walk into downtown Fox Harbor. I was anxious to see Wes. One could even call it thirsty – hella, I can admit it. I was Desperate Girl Who Pined For Cute Boy and since I couldn't wait for him to get off work and come to me, I went to him. Grown woman shit.

I approached his store, but my pride had beat me there. It stood out front, arms folded, looking at me through a disapproving lens. Shamed. I pulled my cell from my back pocket, sending a quick text to let him know that I would maybe conveniently be in the area soon and he could find me outside of Armie's when he was off. I waited, seated in an uncomfortable green metal chair at a small matching table, nibbling a muffin between sipping my refreshing caffeinated beverage. I ignored time by observing the occasional passerby and making up stories about their lives.

"Meg?"

I looked up into a vaguely familiar face. A cute rose-tinged girl with long brown hair and a big, brown, doe-eyed expression stared back. Bambi. "Yes?"

"Hi! Oh my god, it's so cool to officially meet you," she said, excitedly, extending her small hand. I took it despite my confusion. "I'm Ness. Vanessa, Wesley's sister. We kinda met once before when my daughter, Rebecca—"

"Chocolate ice cream," I exclaimed.

She blushed and nodded slowly. "Chocolate ice cream. Again, I am so sorry about that. She can be pretty much a terror. You know how that is, the terrible twos."

I nodded, taking her at her word. I did not know how it was, although I'd heard. I had no little people experience and was less than interested in having them around anytime soon. That would all change in a few months.

"Well, anyway," she continued, "I was in the store and Wes told me I might find you here. I just really wanted to meet the girl that's occupying all of my brothers limited brainpower."

I laughed awkwardly and so did she. "Well, uhm, wanna have a seat?" I offered.

"Sure, if you don't mind. I was just about to head back home, but I can use a break from the girls. They're with my mom. You should totally come by the house some time." Her perfectly circular eyes became even wider with her epiphany. "Our mom would love to meet you. God, Wes talks about you all the time."

I blushed. "He does? All good I hope."

"Oh, he thinks the world of you. He likes how different you are. Not like the girls from The Sticks or The Skirts. Not even the Townie Girls. Guess it's being from a big city and all. Plus, it doesn't hurt that you're really f'king pretty."

"Oh...thanks!"

We chatted and I learned I liked Ness almost as much as her younger brother, despite her kid wrecking a perfectly good pair of shorts. They were genuine and down to earth, the only ones that weren't hating on me or out to one up me in some way. We were getting along brilliantly. But the trouble with small town living was the likelihood of running into the same small townie peeps whether you wanted to see them or not.

"Wow, look who made herself a new loser friend." Alli strutted in our direction, her feathery blonde mane concealing one gray eye. Her tatted arms exposed. Maxey followed, head down, lighting a cigarette. She glanced at me, offered a wink and a smile. "Guess being Amelia's flunky wasn't enough for you."

"You know what—" I began.

"Allison," Ness exclaimed in a cheerful voice, cutting me off. "How're you feeling? I've been meaning to check on you. Figured you were pretty down since realizing that not only does my brother not want you anymore, but he found someone who's better than you in every conceivable way."

Alli's face fell before she could stop it. Her attempt at a quick and graceful recovery was a miss, I'd noticed and was pretty sure Ness had as well. "Eat ass, loser."

"Aww, is someone's feelings hurt?"

I laughed openly. Maxey chuckled. Alli's eyes became gray steel as she looked between the three of us.

"Come on, Maxey, let's get out of here." She took a step forward but paused thoughtfully, and stepped back. "Ness, by the way, next time you talk to Wyatt, do me a favor and ask him if he found the panties that I left at his house last night. They were pink."

My laughter ceased as I looked to gauge Ness' reaction, but by the time my eyes reached her, she'd sprung into unexpected and violent activity. She held a fistful of blonde locs and punched wildly against the back of Alli's head. The two struggled, with Ness maintaining dominance and sending Alli crashing into my small table. I jumped out of harms way, snatching my drink just in time. Maxey leapt onto a chair beside me, a look that could only be described as sheer pleasure on her face as she screamed encouragement.

I didn't know what to do – standby, intervene, or go get help. I was from a major city, used to major city ways. This was certainly not something that I had anticipated seeing in a small town like Fox Harbor and honestly, it intrigued me.

Alli's arms swung wildly until she managed her own fist of hair, turning it from a cat fight into a tug-of-war. I watched, fascinated and becoming increasingly oblivious to my surroundings. This was why I hadn't noticed that Maxey had moved until my cup of iced drink was snatched from my grasp. Before I could react, she'd taken off, peeled the lid away, and thrown the contents forcefully into Ness' face, causing her to gasp and lose her grip, thereby losing the upper hand.

"Shit," I mumbled. I moved in slow motion, debating whether or not I was required to offer Ness assistance. Before I could draw a conclusion, the store owner and two patrons hurried past me, cutting me off, struggling to keep the two girls apart. As a young guy in a pharmacy coat managed to get a firm hold on Ness' arms, holding her at bay, a partially free Allison landed a blow hard to the center of her face.

Startled and feeling that the time had come for me to take action, if only for brownie points with Wes, I ran between the two girls. One, jerking wildly and yelling insults, while the other caught the blood that trickled from her nose into her palm.

"Get on back, gal," the clerk barked at me. "Ain't gonna be no more of this here ruckus outside my store, y'hear? I'll call up the sheriff if I have to."

"I'm not doing anything, just trying to help," I responded, as I stood in between like a buffoon because some weird sense of loyalty told me I needed to. The two spat threats past me. Maxey, disinterested now that things were under control, stepped away and took to nursing a cigarette between her lips and laughing into her cell phone.

"Hey...hey! What's going on here?" I turned at the sound of Wes' voice, inappropriately smiling at the sight of him, then remembering the fight and shifting to solemnity. "What happened? Sis, you okay?"

The clerk answered, "Your sister and your girlfriend—"

"She's *not* my girlfriend."

"Do I look like I care? I bust these two again, you gonna be bailin' 'em out of jail. Now you got this one?" He asked passing Ness into her brother's care. "Allison, Maxine, get on now. I don't want no mo' trouble outta you two."

"You can't tell me what to do. You're not my father," Alli complained.

"Praise our Lord and Savior Jesus Christ for that one, 'cause with the way your momma got around...anyhow, I do know your father and I won't hesitate to get him on the phone...let him know how you out here behaving."

It was the second time that day I saw the crack in Alli's façade, and it pleased me. Had it not been for the sucker punch she managed at the end of the fight, this would've been a relatively flawless experience.

Alli backed away, her eyes roving between Wes and Ness a few times and for good measure, landing on me. She and Maxey continued down the street, glancing back occasionally but not stopping.

"You make that the last time, Vanessa," the store clerk threatened, as he turned toward his shop. "I like you, and your momma, Bev, is a good woman but I ain't gonna keep on tolerating it. You're smarter than this. Now you and that troublemaker want to keep on about who the hell knows, take it down the street to Bud shop. Let someone else deal wit'cha."

"Sorry, Mr. Crowley," Ness called as she shimmied from her brothers grasp. She took a seat in one of the green steel chairs, holding her head back. Her wet shirt stuck to her skin.

"Dammit, Sis, your f'king nose is bleeding," Wes said.

"Oh crap, that's what that liquid is running down my face. I thought it was just raining in one spot."

"Asshole." Wes smiled, grabbing a pile of napkins and handing them to her. "You're f'kn soaked. What happened this time?"

"Does it matter?"

"You got to stop letting her get to you, Sis. You know how she is, she does this on purpose." Wes looked to me, checking me over and offering a subtle smile. "How about you? You okay?"

I nodded. "I'm fine. It all just happened so fast I didn't really know what I should do."

He chuckled. "The best thing you can do is stay out of it. This war has been raging for almost a year now, with no sign of letting up."

Ness struggled slightly to get back to her feet, holding the bloody napkins to her nose. "She's a skunt who cheated on Wes with Becca and Caitlin's dad, and I f'king despise her so, no, there is no sign of letting up. Ugh. I'm done. I'm going home now. Was nice meeting you, Meg. Sorry you had to see that."

I waved, offered my pleasantries. "For what it's worth, you kicked her ass. She just got lucky at the end."

Ness stopped and looked at me, then turned to Wes. "I *really* like her."

Wes blushed, then said, "You're not walking like this."

"Dude, Meg walked all the way from Schofield's to see you. I'll be fine."

Wes turned my way, his eyes already pleading and making me feel guilty. All day I'd been looking forward to spending the afternoon with him. I was craving his touch and now he was asking me with a look to forfeit that.

I was sad when I lied and answered, "No worries."

"Hey! Oww..." Ness started, "I have a great idea. Why don't you just come with? Yeah, bro, just bring her by the house and let Mom meet her."

Wes shook his head. "That's *not* a great idea. No way I'm not gonna put her through Mom's shit."

"Oh, it won't be so bad. Mom will actually like her. She's nothing like that bitch, Allison."

I smiled, hopeful, though trying to look like it was all no big deal. Truthfully, I really didn't want to not be with him, but I didn't want him to know that. Wes approached me, the silver of the gauge in his left ear sparkling in the sunlight. He stopped in front of me, looking into my eyes, smiling softly. He grazed his finger across my jawline. The feathery softness of the motion sent a bolt of electricity straight to my core. He bit down on his lip and licked slowly as he leaned closer. I stopped breathing.

"My moms a pest," he spoke into my mouth, "but she's nice. You can come if you don't mind being asked a bunch of nosy questions."

He eased back, locking his eyes onto mine. With his

thumb, he brushed a few strands of hair aside. I bit my lip, craving more. I wasn't ready to not be with him. I answered, "I don't mind."

He nodded, jerking his head in a gesture for us to follow.

Ness said, "Oh my god, you guys are so adorable. Ow!"

≈

"Well, aren't you just about all smiles and warm apple pie around here," said Clare from her seat at Marge's kitchen island. I walked past, phone to my ear, opening the refrigerator to pour myself another tall, cool glass of day-old lemonade. I hadn't noticed how much I'd been smiling, or even that my cheeks kind of ached until she said something.

I guess one could say that I was happy-*ish*. About as happy as one could be under the circumstances. I was making the most out of a difficult situation. Far from home. Depressed mom. Ignored by best friend. Residing in a proverbial stranger's house and sleeping night after night on a couch because Evil Sibling destroyed life as I'd known it, and kicked me out of my guest room for good measure. Such a Marjie thing to do.

But now I had Wes. I didn't know what we were to each other, not really, but I knew that I liked him...a lot. I couldn't catch my breath when he was near, his voice made my heart skip, his touch gave me butterflies, yadda, yadda, and other seriously corny shit. I'd liked Javi since freshman year but I couldn't recall him ever making me feel the way that Wes did. So if you're going to be stuck in a small town, in a land far, far away, with divided parental units, a crazy sister, and a grandparent you're only just beginning to tolerate, this seemed to be the best way.

I was on a cloud, so high that I actually offered Clare her own, personal smile as I made my way past the BFF's. I strolled in slow motion, feeling every bit of sex kitten, as I headed back to snuggle into the sofa, pretending I was in Wes' arms. I laughed at a joke he made, not too much but not too mildly. Seductively. My head hung low off the cushion, my feet were crossed at the ankles high on the sofa back.

The moment of romantic pleasure met an abrupt end when Marjie shoved through the front door, slamming it behind her with force.

"Damn, rude much," I commented, raising my body to seated.

She turned at me sharply, a look in her eyes like I hadn't seen before. I recoiled, actually afraid to challenge her. Marge stood, clearly not getting the same memo I got regarding *F'k with Marjie Day*. Lucy Rae jumped to her owners defense but heeled when Marge snapped.

"Now that's enough, Marjorie. Enough! I'm gettin' a little fed up with your attitude and ya nasty-isms. Don't slam my door *no* mo'. Now you gone continue to be here, you gone learn something Andie clearly ain't been too keen on teachin'.'"

Marge and Marjie, the named and the namesake, locked into a battle of wills. So much for being happy-*ish*. Marjie tilted her head and methodically lifted her middle finger. "Blow me," she said, before turning away and pounding her way across the living room and toward the steps.

"That girl, *that girl*! I'm tryin' but I don't think I can do it no mo'," Marge complained to Clare. "Andie wanna do thangs in her own time but I'm old, I can't take too much more of this. And don't you start in wit' that I told you so," she ended, pointing to me.

I gave her a look that said it for me.

I glanced toward the stairwell and wondered what could've happened to completely alter my siblings mood so drastically, before returning my undivided to my call and yeah, well...love interest. I apologized to Wes for the interruption. We'd barely begun to carry on with our conversation when a series of bumps and thumps from above created a new distraction.

I looked to Clare and Marge, then all eyes moved to the ceiling. I put Wes on hold, waiting with bated breath as all went quiet...then, just as quickly, erupted again.

"I'll call you back," I said, ending our most pleasant engagement and tossing my phone onto the cushion. I charged toward the stairs. Muffled, angry voices became more prominent. I had hardly taken three steps when I was nearly knocked over as Andie came charging past. I stumbled off to the side moments before a belligerent Marjorie appeared.

Andie, tight-faced and cloaked in a winter blanket on yet another blazing hot summer day, stomped into the kitchen, flipping on the faucet.

"What is going on here?" Marge cried out.

"Get your shit together," Marjie screamed. "I played your little game but I won't do it anymore. I want to go home!"

"Why?" Mom asked. "Somebody hurt your delicate feelings today? Let me guess, some asshole chose his *wife* over you?"

"Not the point. Doesn't matter, it's time to go."

My mom leaned heavily against the edge of the sink, her back to her ranting daughter. "Then leave, Marjorie. You weren't invited to come and you certainly don't have to stay," she answered with a calm voice.

"You think you can just get away from me? From us?" Marjie laughed, walking in circles. "You tried that already, remember? *Remember?* Cause I sure f'k do. I wasn't invited, huh? You knew I would come for you. You had to know."

Mom leaned lower over the sink, the blanket rising and falling on her shoulders. She raised her hand, began running her fingers aggressively across her scalp.

I stepped to Marjie. "Look, why don't you back off?

We're fine here if this is what Mom needs after the stunt you and Dad pulled. And she's right, nobody asked you to come, so if you don't wanna be here, you can do us all a favor and leave, especially considering all of this is your fault anyway."

She turned to face me, the word *Surprise* in italics spelled out across her forehead. It was as though she had no idea what I was talking about. "My fault? Are you kidding me? Grow up, kid. This is your asshole father's fault. I'm just trying to put an end to the bullshit so we can get on with life. Andie, make the call, buy the tickets, whatever you need to make it happen to get me the f'k out of Deliveranceville – *I want to go home!*"

Andie snatched a drinking glass, held it above her head and brought it down with force. She faced Marjie, pointing an accusing finger, causing the blanket to slip to the floor. "Then go home!! *Get out!* You want to give me grief over the past...make me suffer eternal for all the many ways I hurt you? You want me to tell you I was wrong, I messed up? I was, Marjie, and I did but that was a long time ago. A long goddamn time ago so *you* grow the f'k up!"

"I won't let you just abandon me like you've always done. Sorry Mom, not happenin'."

"That isn't...that's not what this is about. You hurt me. Don't you get that? Why can't you get that? You took from me, you *always* take from me." My mother's voice was raw, red, and bruised. Thick and watery. Her hair stuck to the side of her damp face.

"Okay, that's quite enough from you two." Marge stepped between them, holding a hand up requesting peace she was not going to receive. The other she used to keep her agitated pup at ease.

"Mom," Marjie said in a low, cracked voice, destroyed from yelling, "I'm not staying here any longer and neither are you. Because if you do, I will make your life hell. Every...single...goddamn one of you. Count on it."

Marge stepped away shaking her head, appearing defeated. "You gonna have to go." Curiously the statement was not directed at my sister, but instead, my mother.

Andie was stunned, a look of shock and horror lighting her eyes. "What? You're being ridiculous."

I actually reciprocated the feeling. I mean, yes, I wanted to go from the very moment I arrived but I agreed to stay to the end of summer...I was mentally prepared. I had Wes now. The idea of being forced out early...losing time with him when we already had so little time...

"You can't just do that," I exclaimed before I could manage to stop myself. "That isn't fair."

"Shut the f'k up, Meg," Marjie spat at me. "You only wanna stay 'cause you wanna keep cock teasing that boy you're too scared to actually bone."

I gave her the finger but kept my focus on Andie and her mom who, not surprisingly, didn't acknowledge me.

"Momma?" said Andie.

Marge shook her head firmly. Mind made up. "Andrea, you got to get the hell outta my house. I done had 'bout all I can take. Lessen you get back on your meds so you can deal with your own children, 'cause I won't do it no longer. You wanna stay, stay, but only – and I do mean this with every fiber of my being, Andie – *only* iffen you get back on ya medication, y'hear me? *Do you hear me?*"

"Yes," she answered hardly above a whisper, nodding repeatedly.

"As for you, young lady," Marge began, finger pointed at Marjie, her anger and voice rising. "You done. You need help, probably the same kind as ya momma–"

"Oh, f'k you. I'm nothing like her. You don't know anything."

"You gone get out or I'm gonna put you out, I know that."

Marge cemented herself. Marjie laughed, thought of it as a joke. But I recalled Big Loubelle and knew without a doubt, it wasn't. I knew Marge in a way that my sister did not. She was Crazy Lady Who Put Shotgun To Chest, Challenged Bears Twice Her Size, and Threw Boulders Through Windows. She was *not* Lady To Be F'kd With.

Andie grabbed another glass and filled it with faucet water, guzzling it. She smeared away the wetness with the back of her hand before she spoke in a quiet voice. "Leave, Marjorie. You only came here to cause trouble and you did that. So, just leave. Go."

Marjie stepped closer, ignoring the teeth bearing Lucy Rae that Marge held at bay and the shards of glass scattered across the tile. "When you leave, I'll leave."

"Marjie–"

"Old lady wants to kick me out, same as she did when I was a little brown baby, screwing up her snow white lineage. Are you gonna protect me now, *Mother*? Or will you just let whatever happen? You thought you could just leave me behind while you left your mind, and everything would be as it was when you chose to come back."

My mom's head dropped and she shook it side to side. Her eyes closed, the overflow of tears spilling forward. "Please leave..."

"Why? So you can forget about me, about us? Remember *Uncle* Windell. I do. He wasn't my uncle, he wasn't even related to me but his wife, she thought I was pretty. She liked to pretend I was their daughter, but for a fake mother, she was just as shitty. But at least she was there. Unlike you."

Marge and Clare looked to me but I could offer nothing more than a shrug. I had no idea what this conversation was about, who these people were, what Marjie wanted our mother to remember nor why that memory was relevant.

Mom wept. "I'm sorry about that, sweetheart. God knows, I am so, so sorry," Andie whispered. "But I can't change the past, and I'm not going...and you can't stay."

Marjie's fist landed so hard against the island counter, I winced in the pain I assumed she felt. But if she felt anything, it didn't show. She was on Andie, practically nose to nose, glass crunching beneath her shoes.

Clare Bear courageously stepped forward, attempting to separate them. "Marjie, that's enough now. Your mother's pregnant and frankly she don't need all this stress. It isn't healthy for the baby."

The shadow of hatred covered my sister. She glared at Clare as she mumbled words I couldn't quite catch. Marjie turned back to face our mother. She yelled, her words punctuated by her balled fist pounding against the countertop that Andie was pressed into. "F'k her and that baby! She cares more about her other babies than she *ever* did me. All I *ever* wanted from you was love. The same love you had for Lyle. The same love you have for Meg. But you can't give me that because you *don't* love me...you never did. Oh my god, I can't believe I never realized it before now. You *never* loved me!"

"Marjie, that is just not true, you *know* that is not true," Mom insisted, fear in her eyes as a waterfall of tears poured down her face.

"Marjie's not home."

I didn't know what happened. Marjie had hardly moved in any remarkable fashion. But Mom stumbled off to the side, clutching her belly and Lucy Rae attacked, sinking her teeth into my sister's leg. Startled, she yelled and began pummeling the dog. I rushed forward, trying to use my relationship with Lucy Rae to save my sibling but to no avail.

The sound of Marge's shotgun cocking preceded the order for Lucy Rae to heel and Marjorie to get the hell off of her dog.

Clare gasped. "Oh my god. She stabbed her."

"What?" Marge asked, for clarity I supposed.

"She stabbed her. Call the ambulance, Marjie stabbed her mother."

Our mother sat in a heap on the floor, her back pressed against the cabinet, her hands clutched to her belly. Tears created pathways down her face. Clare held her, offering comfort as Marge made the emergency phone call.

I swooned. "What did you do? Why would you−" Then I saw it, the paring knife that no one noticed Marjie swipe from the table. She'd dropped it when Lucy bit her. I gasped, "Marjie..."

"Atika," she responded, snatching up the knife and slicing it across her wrist before I could do anything to stop her.

day #seventy-five.

"You're still cold?" Wes asked as though it were a surprising and ridiculous notion.

"Duh. Yeah," I answered, full body shivering for added effect. We laid together in his bed, chilling, while on-again/off-again watching a streaming original comic series. He'd seen it before. I hadn't heard of if it, couldn't be sure my recollection of its title was accurate, and was too focused on being with Wes to even know what the point was.

I pulled the old, flimsy blanket that, prior to my arrival rested at the foot of his bed, tighter to my chin, then settled deeper into his arms with my head resting against his chest.

It was a hot, humid day, well over 80 degrees. The

kind of day where a tornado seemed to be looming in the distance, taunting. The gray and cloudy skies, occasionally illuminated by the crackling of lightning strikes. Rain pounded hard against the homes rooftop. Despite the heat and threat of destruction occurring outdoors, inside the Mason home the air was cranked to Antarctica, and all were at ease.

The juxtaposition was a mirror held up against my life; quietude versus dissonance. Summer was quickly coming to a close. The sweet freedom that I'd craved for months was suddenly mine for the taking, but in opposition sat heavy, like a crushing weight pressing against my chest. I tried to block those thoughts, the ones where Wesley Mason was no longer a presence. Focus on the here and now.

But when I lay in bed at night, in the old twin in Uncle Cal's room, I often couldn't sleep for the wonder of what awaited me back home. Everything in my world had changed. I had changed. How could I not be made different knowing the things that I now knew of my mother's illness, my parents sham of a marriage, my experience with Marge, my falling out with Shonie, and my once-and-for-all breakup with Javi?

And then there was Marjie.

I hadn't before considered that Marjie's issues could stem from anything more than her role as a spoiled and selfish bitch. And the idea that Atika Dangerfield could somehow be real, felt like a joke – sounded like a joke.

Not that I was necessarily sold that it wasn't just that, but I couldn't deny that in the name of Atika she'd taken a blade across our mother's pregnant belly and made an attempt on her own life.

Their wounds were by no means innocent, but they weren't life threatening. Thankfully my sister proved incompetent on the matter of murder and suicide attempts, but it begged the question of whether the efforts were real, or yet another stunt in her quest to satiate her unquenchable thirst for attention.

Whatever Marjie's objective, whichever personality was truly in charge, the fact that the ordeal prompted Andie's decision to get back on her meds made my sibling a sort of savior. Although to my dismay, our mother remained insistent on bringing this new baby into the equation, she worked willingly with Dr. Van Aalsburg on getting the right dosage that would return her to her right state of mind. A good mother who made the right decision to do what was best for her child.

But were any of Andie's choices about what was best for her children? There was the possibility that Marjie's actions had been fueled by a mental disorder...a pus-filled disease that had been allowed to fester and grow from neglect – or shame. How could she be trusted to not emotionally damage another child? Andie and Lyle, together, turned my whole world inside-out in a matter of weeks....her first-born was locked away in the mental health ward of a hospital on suicide watch. But rather than face up to her past mistakes and deal with the daughters she'd created and destroyed, she preferred the idea of this pregnancy as her chance to start over...*get it right*. At least, that is how it seemed to me.

Focus. Here and now.

I snuggled more firmly against Wes' body, directed my mind to what was on the mid-sized television screen before me. "Okay, so who's that guy?" I asked.

"Ohmagod, seriously, dude?" Wes laughed.

"What?" I said, shyly.

"Are you paying attention at all?"

"Yeah...kinda..."

He kissed my forehead then answered, "That's Luke Cage."

"And what's so special about him again? I mean, besides being hot?"

His head dropped to the side, shaking in disappoinment. "You're kidding me, right?"

I laughed. "I am. He's got unbreakable skin or some shit, and he's super freaking strong."

"You remembered."

"Of course, I remember. I'm a smart girl, you know."

"I know. And smart girls get rewarded." He leaned down, pressing his lips firmly to mine.

"Ahem."

Wes sighed, gently banging his forehead against my own. "Whaaat," he growled.

Ness entered the room fully, smiling shyly, while looking a mix of embarrassed and stressed. Her eyes were shadowed with dark circles, and her long brown ponytail was a frazzled mess.

"I'm sorry guys but I can't find Becca's binky. Mom and I looked everywhere and you know she won't go to sleep without it."

"Maybe she's not tired," Wes suggested, hopeful. The two fell silent, Ness looking at Wes looking at me. He cried out in feigned frustration. "Fine, I'll take care of it. Uncky Wes to the rescue," he said, pecking me on the lips before jumping up and gently pushing past his sister.

"Thank you, little brother," she called after him. Ness turned and smiled at me before taking a seat on the edge of the bed. "He's so good with the girls, he's gonna be such an awesome dad someday. Way better than ours was. There's only one way she'll go to sleep without her binky, and that's if *Uncky Wes* reads her a story. I don't know what I'd do without his help."

Pride filled my chest. "That's so sweet. Wish me and *my* sister had that kind of relationship. But, that's family. Can't always be perfect, I suppose."

"True. So how much longer before you go home?"

"Not long," I sighed, my eyes dropping to my nails. "Couple weeks."

Ness cringed as she stood. "So soon. Poor Wes, he's gonna be crushed when you leave. That's too bad, but I'm sure you guys'll work out the long distance thing. And of course you'll be back next summer."

"Yeah...yeah, next summer."

"Guess I should go check on his progress."

She left me alone with her hand delivered sadness. Thanks, Vanessa. Poor Wes? Poor Megan. For as much as I wanted to be home, surrounded by familiarity, in my own room with Flaca and my stuffed bunny rabbits, with Cam and working things out with Shonie, prepping for my last year of high school...I didn't want to have all of that and not have him. We hadn't discussed long distance. I hadn't considered returning to Fox Harbor. But I was falling for him. Maybe falling in–

"She's asleep, finally. Now where were we?" Wes pushed the door closed behind him with his heel as he ran to the bed, diving in like it was a pool. I squealed and rolled away. He caught me, pulling me to him, slipping beneath the blanket and bringing our bodies closer together. His hand gripped my side, his fingers sliding underneath my shirt and whispering across my flesh. My thighs clenched. My head fell away as the moist warmth of his breath enveloped my neck.

A loud far-away thump snatched me from my lust-induced trance, jolting me to reality. I froze, remembering Vanessa and the toddler Becca...recalling his mother.

"Wes," I whispered, my voice hoarse and broken in

half. "What about your mom?"

His face came up to meet mine. "Shut the f'k up," he spoke into my mouth. I submitted as his tongue wrestled mine for dominance. His hand trailing higher up the side of my body. I instinctively eased deeper into him, and yet still did not feel that I was close enough. His erection pressed the material of his silver and blue basketball shorts against me. I struggled between feelings of shyness and an intense desire to experience him.

His hands slipped quietly around to my back and his fingers easily undid the clasp of my bra. My breath caught in the top of my chest. I'd never been naked with a guy before. Javi and I had made out plenty, he squeezed my boobs and pushed my bra up so he could put his mouth on them, but he always managed to ruin the mood before things went further.

Wes guided the strap from my shoulder and, though we were beneath a blanket with one strap still in tact and my tank top still securely around my neck, I felt exposed… vulnerable. But I was okay with that. My hand began its unsteady descent into the space between his thighs but stopped just shy, fearful of touching it.

"It's okay," he whispered, taking my hand and placing it firmly against his hardness.

"Wes is about to get some pussy!"

I jumped at the sound of the voice. I didn't realize how close I was to the edge until my head banged against the night stand. I cursed out loud, caressing the quickly forming knot at the top of my head while trying to cover my exposed tits with the aroused nips.

Wes moved in a swift motion, grabbing a pillow and flinging it across the room. "Cody, get the f'k out of here," he ordered in a deep and gritty voice.

"No way! It's my room, too. Go bone Alli someplace else."

I paused, momentarily distracted from fixing my clothes, and glared at him from beneath the covers.

"Dude, shut the f'k up. You don't know what you're talking about. It's not Alli, her name is Meg. Dickwad."

I dragged the blanket slowly from my head, revealing how much I was not Alli. I waved my hand to the side. "Hi."

A pre-pubescent boy, skinny with dirty blond hair, bright blue eyes and little resemblance to Wes and Ness, stared back. "Wow...she's f'kn hot," he said. I blushed.

"I know, so get out."

"Hell no. It's my room, too. We can share, though," he said in a salacious tone much too advanced for his age.

"Ewww, no thanks, kid," I answered on my own behalf.

"I bet I can show you how much I'm not a kid." He grabbed the space between his legs, jerking up and down.

"Cody," Wes yelled.

"Thanks, but no," I answered.

"Suit yourself," he spoke in that inconsistent voice boys develop when they finally grow their first pubic hair. He turned and left the shared bedroom, yelling, "Mom! Wes is f'king some girl in your house!"

Wes' cheeks were flushed from embarrassment when he turned to face me. I could only imagine mine were tinted as well.

"You mind if we go someplace else? Someplace we can have some privacy? I mean, if you still want..."

I considered for a moment the mention of Alli, wondering why Cody would assume I was her. Wondered if maybe something was indeed still going on between them. But to be begrudge him would mean going back to Marge's and I wanted to be with him more than I wanted to be mad at him.

I nodded. "Sure. Let's get out of here."

❧

The rain slowed but didn't stop. The overbearing nimbostratus cloud, gray and looming, sprinkled droplets on Wes and me, as we walked the short distance from his car to the abandoned cabin. I stopped short of the door. He stepped around and, taking my hand, led me inside. My nerves paralyzed me, not from what I suspected was about to happen, but moreso from the idea of it happening there. Who knew what could've been lurking in the corners of the dusty and musty place.

I couldn't dwell long. We were barely inside before Wes was hovering above me, pressing my body backward against the wall. His arms locked me in on either side. Our tongues slipped into a gentle embrace. I forgot where we were, about dust and creepy creatures. Okay, so I didn't forget but I didn't care where we were. We were alone, that was what mattered most. Wes grabbed the edge of my shirt, pulling it roughly above my head... tossed it. I ran my hands up and over his chest and shoulders, landing my arms around his slender neck. My fingertips gripped his black beanie and pulled it from his head, dropping it at our feet, so I could caresses the silky strands of his short hair.

His hands traveled a path leading to the button on my shorts. He flipped it open, then slowly tugged on the zipper and inserted his slender fingers, touching the damp spot on my panties. I jumped back, embarrassed.

"What's wrong?"

"Sorry. I...I don't..."

"Meg, I'm sorry...I just thought..."

"I...yeah, yeah, I do. It's just..."

For a moment I felt like I couldn't breathe, like I wouldn't ever breathe again. My eyes dropped, skimming past the boner raging in his shorts, and suddenly I felt more apprehensive than I ever had in my life.

"Are you...was your sister right? Are you a virgin?"

My eyes began to sting but I didn't know why. I was a

virgin, so what. We were all virgins at some point. Is that such a crime? Still, I was humiliated when I whispered, "I'm sorry."

"Hey. Hey." He lifted my chin so that our eyes met. "It's cool, really. We don't have to. You're young, I know. It's just the girls here...well, there ain't much to do so, you know, they find something to do. I just didn't realize..."

"No, I want to. I want...you." With caution I looked up to see his reaction. He looked more surprised than anything. "Unless you don't want–"

"Of course, of...yeah. I totally want...you know, if you're okay with it."

I swallowed hard and nodded, chuckling. "Yeah, I'm okay."

He smiled. Looked shy himself. "Stay right here," he said, rushing back out into the rain that was now coming down harder. I stood just inside the door watching as he ran to the car and popped the trunk, blocking my view of him. A moment later he slammed it shut, running for cover inside, carrying a blanket in his arms. He walked to the dirty red sofa, the lone piece of furniture, and spread the blanket across, covering it completely. He gestured for me to join him there. Nervously, I allowed him to guide me onto my back.

I laid still, rendered helpless in my inexperience while he removed my shorts. Pulled gradually into the quicksand of awkward affectivity, I wished that at the very least I'd worn matching undergarments. His eyes traveled my frame. My arms shifted unconsciously covering me in patches as though that would somehow make me feel less exposed. To my advantage, the cabin was beginning to darken as evening began to overcome the already dark sky.

Wes plucked his shirt from overhead revealing a slender, toned chest and a huge, beautiful, albeit illegible, tatt up the side of his body. I kept my eyes there, trying to focus on making it out as a means of taking my mind off what was about to happen – what I'd decided would happen. And it worked until he pushed his shorts and underwear beyond his waistline.

I looked away, stared at the ceiling. I left my body and focused on the rain's pounding against the roof. I felt his heat before the touch of his flesh. His finger stroked the thin piece of material between my thighs. I closed my eyes and swallowed my fear, urged myself to relax as he separated me from my underwear.

His body fit between mine, perfectly, as though we were designed for each other specifically. Totally naked, except for my bra, which I refused to allow him to remove. I needed some sense of security no matter how small.

"You okay?" He whispered, pressing deeper so that all of his stiffness could be felt against me. I bit my lip and nodded, closing my eyes and trying my best to still my nerves and steady my breathing. His hand went down between us and shifted around until...

I yelped and tensed as he entered me. My breathing

became more shallow and laborious as my body became more rigid. He stopped moving. Fearful that I'd done something wrong, maybe offended him somehow or turned him off, I opened my eyes. His face was close to mine, centimeters away.

"Relax. Just relax. There you go. See? Not so bad, huh? Feel that? Yes...," he answered his own questions on my behalf. "You're okay. You just have to let your body relax and enjoy it. Good. Mm... Does that feel good to you?"

I nodded but I wasn't sure what I was feeling. Not good, but not bad either. It didn't hurt, not really. I just felt...*it*. There it was, inside me. This was sex. This was, okay. I supposed it wasn't...not bad, a little better than when it began. But this was sex. That thing I'd waited just shy of seventeen years to try. It was *deep inhale*...okay *heavy exhale*...

There was no concept of time, no value of thrusts Wes made before his face balled into a tight fist as his body shook and deep, guttural sounds escaped preceding his collapse. His weight was heavy on top of me although somehow, not uncomfortably so.

We laid there awhile, him still inside...me being fascinated by the feeling of the girth of his manhood diminishing. I opened my mouth to speak, but didn't know what I should say. Thank you? I bit my lip, kept my eyes to the ceiling and my ears on the beating rain, listening to it slow, mimicking my heart rate. Trying not to wonder if I was...*good?*

Wes lifted his hips, prying himself free. My being recoiled from the discomfort of separation and what I assumed to be what one felt when a flaccid penis purged itself from the body. He reached down, removed his condom...a condom that I hadn't realized he put on.

My eyes flooded as an ocean of awareness overcame me, more powerful than I could comprehend. I was startled by my own reaction but I could do nothing to stop it. Not only had I not noticed that he'd put a condom on, it hadn't even occurred to me to ask! How could I not have known? How could I not have asked?

Wes drew back from me. I could just make out the concern in his face in the dying light. He wiped the wetness from my cheeks, pressing firmly with the base of his palm. He whispered to me that it was all okay, that I was okay. Said it in the manner a parent says to a child having a tantrum in the grocery store. He asked if I wanted to talk about it. I didn't so he rolled over, landing behind me ...wrapped his arms around me. Held me while I bawled.

Despite the onslaught of teardrops, I was not actually sad. I didn't know what I was. I garbled out a lame apology for my behavior. He told me this kinda thing was normal. Horrified by the prospect that this was somehow true, I cried harder.

I closed my eyes, darkness covering darkness, and held his arm tight. Nails digging in. The rhythmic sound of nature had a calming effect and began to goad me into unconsciousness. I found myself on the edge of a dream where Cam and Shonie were helping me pick out baby clothes. Every item displayed an illustration of Babe the Blue Ox. In my hand was a baby bottle filled with lithium. When I looked down, I saw my belly protruding from beneath my pink tank top. I gasped, frightened and questioning who the father was – Wes or Javi? I heard my name and looked up to see Marjie standing there, aiming Marge's shotgun at my pregnant belly. My body shook fiercely. Marjie was saying my name repeatedly but it wasn't her voice. The voice belonged to Wes.

"Megan, wake up. Someone's here."

"What?" I rubbed my eyes hard, trying to force the fog away.

"Someone is here," he stressed.

I paused a beat, then realized what he'd said. "Shit. Shit! I can't see!" I jumped to my feet, scrambling about in the darkness. Wes tossed my underwear at me and I quickly shimmied into them, nearly tipping over as I reached to grab my shorts from the arm of the couch. I zipped and buttoned.

"Where's my shirt?" I yelled, frantic.

"What?"

"My shirt, Wes! Where is it?"

"I dunno! I put it with your shorts."

I hurried back to the couch, using the light on my cell

and feeling around until I caught a glimpse of it on the floor. I grabbed it, quickly slipping it over my head just as the LED light of a portable lantern lit the space.

I turned sharply to see Clarke, followed by Dob, standing in the open doorway. I imagined myself to be the literal definition of Deer Caught In Headlights. Clarke's eyes widened with recognition. His jaw dropped as he watched Wes, who was pulling his own shirt back over his head.

"Dude, f'k me." He dropped low, bent knees. His eyes glued to Wes, laughter filling the stuffy space. "Did you two just...?"

"Mind your own business, okay," Wes answered.

"Dude, Alli's right behind us. I can't believe you f'kd her *here*, of all places."

"Clarke, shut the f'k up. Asshole."

Humiliated, I shrank into the background, trying foolishly to go unnoticed. I had lost my virginity in a dirty, abandoned cabin, and I hadn't even a chance to process how I felt about it before news of my little indiscretion became word on the street. Maxey stumbled in, obliviously pushing past Clarke and his standoff with Wes.

"Why are you two dillwads eye-humping each...other. Oh shit!" Maxey laughed, then ceased abruptly, covering her mouth. She looked back and forth between Wes and me before asking, "You two did not?"

Wes turned slightly, glancing at me with an embarrassed expression and sad eyes. "Guys, can you just drop it, okay? It's none of your business."

Footsteps crushing gravel became louder and I sucked in my breath. I didn't need this...I just wanted to be back at Marge's. It was the first time that I'd ever longed to be at Marge's with a mug of coffee...the scent of cigarette smoke. Alli came into view, her ever-present scowl clearly visible. "What the shit, you guys? Why are you assholes just blocking the door? Go in already, I'm getting wet."

Alli shoved Clarke forcefully aside, hardly acknowledging Wes but stopping once she noticed me attempting to fade into the shadows. She leaned in, looking closer at me and then turned to Wes. The squint in her eyes rounding out, her chest rising and falling higher and faster.

"Allison—" Wes began.

"Did you just f'k her?" Not giving him a chance to respond, she directed her line of questioning to me. "Did you f'k him? Did you just f'k my boyfriend, you f'king slut! *I WILL KILL YOU!*"

Alli lunged for me. I let out a small shriek and backed away, anticipating the same type of blow that Ness took to the face not all that long ago. I was not ready to deal with this. I was not emotionally prepared to defend myself against her wrath. Wes grabbed her before she could reach me, held her by the waist and pulled her back as she launched promises of major bodily harm at me.

"Back off, Alli," he yelled, jerking her around so that she would face him instead of me. "You're not going to touch her. Do you really think I'd let you put your hands on her?"

"How could you? After all these years, after everything we've been through you screw me over for some skunt who's probably already giving blowies to some guy back wherever the f'k hole she slithered out of?"

"Oh my god, Alli, do you hear yourself? I didn't screw us, Al, you did when you slept with my sister's boyfriend. The father of her kids, for crissakes."

"We weren't together when that happened. And I told you I was sorry. I've tried to make it up to you so many times but—"

"No shit we weren't together, just like we're not together now, so you have no say in what I do. We're over, Allison. Done. Forever. When are you gonna get that?"

"You don't mean that." She shook her head, vehemently. "You know you don't mean that. You say that and then you come back, Wes. You always come back."

"Not anymore, Alli. Not anymore."

Alli snatched free. She glared at me but she backed away as she did so. She laughed, despite herself, biting the side of her lip and shaking her head. "Y'know, the summer's almost over. Pretend all you want but we both know who's panties you'll be sniffing around once your pretty little black whore is gone for good."

Alli turned sharply, practically mowing Amelia down in the process. She caught her footing and eyed me, shooting daggers my way as though *she* were somehow personally offended and impacted by my actions. I swiped away the stray tears that lingered beneath my eyes. I adjusted my expression, offering my very best in *I-don't-giva-a-f'k* looks. She turned away, following Alli back out into the rainy evening.

Maxey stood alongside Dob, a small smile on her face, pleased. Alli bellowed in the distance. Maxey smiled full-on, offering me a meaningful head nod and thumbs up before following as ordered.

అ

"If I was a bird I'd fly away..." The lyrics to one of my favorite songs by one of my favorite singers, played over and over in my mind.

My forehead pressed against the cool glass of the passenger window. I didn't know what to think or how I should feel about the evening. Less than romantic, that was a start. Wes hadn't said a word to me during the drive to Marge's. To be fair, we weren't alone and he hadn't uttered a single word to our companions, Clarke and Dob, either. As a matter of fact, the only sound in the car was that of their incessant jabbering from the backseat.

The car began to roll to a stop but my door was already open and my feet on the pavement. I slammed the door hard behind me.

"Bye, Meg," Dob called out the window in his thick, hairy-pawed voice.

"Yeah, later, Meg. Hope you won't be too mad at Wes now that you know what a dickhole he really is," Clarke laughed as he climbed out the car and walked around to claim my abandoned seat.

I waved limply, completely missing his humor.

"Meg. Meg," Wes called, jogging after me. I turned to face him, trying hard to not cry again. "I'm sorry about that with Alli...you didn't deserve that."

I nodded and exhaled heavily. I tilted my head back slightly to stave off the tears, whispering, "It's okay. It's not your fault."

But it wasn't okay. I didn't know what was between Alli and Wes, but between Cody's assumption and Alli's reaction, there was clearly more to it than he let on. I felt duped. I'd made an important life decision without having all the facts. We eyed one another timidly. Something had changed in our relationship. And while I didn't know exactly what that was, I could feel that there had been irreparable damage and that realization caused me to physically ache on the inside.

He leaned forward, kissed my lips gently. I hoped that he wouldn't stop, didn't want him to stop. I wanted so badly for him to hold me again. For him to look at me with the kindness and warmth that he had earlier in the evening, before everything went wrong. What I wanted most was a do-over. A do-over with no Clarke or Dob, no

Maxey or Amelia, and certainly not Insane Ex-Girlfriend Who Couldn't Let Go.

But to my dismay it did end, and abruptly. "I'll call you," he said, almost robotic. He returned to his running car and jumped into the drivers seat. Took off without once looking back. I looked up into the dark, wet sky, hoping for more rain. I turned to the house and jogged up the steps wondering how something so beautiful turned so ugly so fast.

"You know, Meg, that was really lame what you did."

I jumped so hard, I thought my heart had shot out of my chest. I turned around and found Amelia standing just outside of the gate. "What the hell, Amelia? Are you stalking me?"

"I thought you were a better person. You knew that sleeping with him would hurt her and you did it anyway. How could you do something so...so ratchet? She loves him...you know that? She really loves him."

"Did I hurt her, or I did I hurt you because I can't tell the difference."

"It's not about me and you know that."

"Do I? Because you get all butt hurt every time I'm with him. Why is that, Amelia? Could it be because you wanted to sleep with him, but you couldn't have him so you're mad that he chose me?"

Amelia jerked her head, appearing to be appalled by my assertion. "I can't believe you're like, such a complete and total biatch."

I took a couple steps in her direction, halfway down the staircase. "You know she doesn't even like you. She has no respect for you, she just uses you. Both of them, Alli and Maxey, and you just take it. Desperate, pathetic little Amelia with no friends, who looks forward to coming back to this shit town every year so she can hang with the pop kids and feel special. Well guess what, you're not special and neither are they. You're f'king ordinary with your white entitled, culturally appropriating ass."

I hadn't intended to take my aggression out on Amelia. Maybe she didn't deserve it...maybe she did. Who cares, it didn't matter. I felt better. Alli had gotten the better of me because her timing was perfect, so finally placing Amelia was the least that I deserved. She looked like she might cry and for the first time in months, I actually felt like my old self.

"F'k you, Meg. And just so you know, we are no longer friends." She turned away, stomping back toward Clare-Bear and Confederate Grandpa's place.

"News flash, dumb ass, we never were!"

My phone rang inside my back pocket. My heart jumped into my throat and I prayed that it was Wes. It wasn't.

"Shonie? My god, is it really you? I've been calling you for weeks. I'm so sorry," I blurted out before she could speak.

She sighed. "I know and I know. But just so *you* know, this ain't no social call. I'm just calling to let you know that I'm *almost* ready to forgive you. We sisters so... y'know."

I smiled hard. Cheesed, really. "So relieved to hear that cuz I have something to tell you. I'm not a virgin anymore. There's this guy–"

"Megan...Megz. Not yet. Did you miss the part about this *not* being a social call? I'm comin' around to it but we ain't there yet, okay?"

"Yeah, yeah, my bad. Okay. Take all the time you need." I said it, but I didn't mean it.

"Aiight then. Well, that's all I wanted say so...I'll holla."

She hung up before I could try to stop her.

day #eighty-three.

I felt sick. Heartache was likely the diagnosis.

Uncle Cal confirmed that he and the family would be to get me the very next evening. The start of senior year was just a week away and who didn't anticipate their last year of high school? I was finally, officially returning home. I would get to be with my friends and work on having my life back. My seventeenth birthday was a mere three weeks away. I should've been thrilled. I could've, at least, been okay but, instead, I felt sick.

I sat on the edge of a stool. My elbows pressed against the island counter, hands up, palms open, acting as a brace for my forehead. My cell sat before me. I raised my head and peeked at it, trying to will it to ring again. The last call, the one that left me nauseous, was from Ness asking if she'd see me that night. I doubted it, I hadn't heard from Wes all week. And the last time we saw each other it was courtesy of some lame excuse I made to go into town and visit his store. He was busy, conveniently so. Out of the ordinary busy. No doubt once I was gone, his sudden surge in retail responsibility slowed.

"I think you should come out," she'd said.

"Really? I guess you hate me just as much as everyone else in this town."

She laughed. "On the contrary. I hate that bitch, Alli and I hate that she ruins everything good. Wes likes you, Meg, likes you a lot. Maybe even loves you."

Now I laughed. "Yeah, well he has an interesting way of showing it."

"Did you hear what I said, Megz? He *loves* you. My brother is in love with you."

My lashes splashed against wetness. "Your point, Ness?"

"He loves you and you're leaving him. You're going back home soon and he just couldn't...he can't deal. I think he figured if he just backed off it would be easier, y'know?"

"Easier for who?" I cried, the tears burning my eyes and anger burning my cheeks.

"He's a boy, boys are dumb. That's why I think you should come out tonight. At the end of summer every year, before the high school kids go back, the Duggan brothers throw a big party in one of their family's barns. It's always a total blast. Booze, drugs, games, and best of all, no adult supervision. I think you should come...talk to Wes. Don't let that asshole get away with it." She chuckled awkwardly. "I'll pick you up at 6, okay?"

I sighed...considered rejecting her offer. "What about Alli and those guys? If it's a big townie event, I gotta assume they'll all be there."

"F'k 'em. I can't wait to see the look on their stupid faces when you walk in there tonight."

I agreed, reluctantly, so who was the stupid one? But Ness was right, I didn't want to leave without seeing him and telling him how I felt about his bullshit behavior. It wasn't as though I didn't understand...being upset and hurt because we'd gotten close and then would be pulled apart, but the problem was that it was always going to happen that way. There was never a chance of me staying in Fox Harbor. We would both be hurt but that was why it was so important that we spend as much time together as we could.

Turns out Wes was selfish, surprisingly so. Hurting me as a way to spare himself was some f'kd shit of Marjie proportions.

"What's the matter with you?"

I looked up. Marge was entering from the garden with dirty knees, pulling her large, thick gloves from her hand and slamming them on the counter, Loyal Lucy in tow as usual.

I rolled my eyes as more of a reflex than anything else. "As if you care."

She shrugged. "Suit ya'self." She washed her hands at the sink and began prep work on a fresh pot of coffee.

"Sorry," I mumbled. "I didn't mean to...do you mind telling me what happened? Why Andie left home with Marjie? Did you really put her out because Marjie was... y'know..."

"Cause she was black? No." Marge locked the filter in place and pushed the switch, before taking a seat across from me. "Believe it or not, I ack'shally remember the day little Marjie was born. Cal was gone off to do his service so we set up the corner of his room as a nursery, that way Andie could still have some independence. I had Andrea's old crib, and Cutter went out and bought a buncha butterfly decals – pink decals – to put on the wall."

"That explains the random wing by the window," I chuckled.

She nodded. "If you'da seen my six-foot-fo' husband in Gertie's Shop for New Momma's pickin' up pink and purple butterflies."

The pot sounded and she poured herself a mug. She told me the story from the beginning. How an ill and under-medicated Andie, in an effort to attract attention – the wrong attention – spent her summer after high school hanging in bars across The Line. No one of a certain generation, on either side, the whites nor the blacks, were accepting of *'mixing the races'* back then.

Andie was, by Marge's assessment, more interested in making trouble than social progression. And so my mother supposedly took up with a married man of color, and carried on until she could have the joy of saying she was carrying a mixed-race child.

Admittedly they were none too happy about what Mom had done but when my sister was born, I'm told my grandfather, Gene "Cutter" Schofield, fell in love. Andie always claimed her parents had kicked her out when she revealed herself to be pregnant, but this new version of the tale has Marjie as the center of our grandfather's world for six entire months. Right up until a large and loud, fair-skinned Black woman showed up on their doorstep with a narrow man half her size and several shades darker, threatening to sue for custody if Marjie was indeed the small man's child.

If I chose to believe Marge over Mom, Andie was not ejected for having gotten herself knocked up by a black man. Threats of having their grandchild taken, a child her husband adored, caused Marge to threaten to put her out if she couldn't get it together. Andie answered by packing up Marjie and disappearing, never to return with said baby until...well, now. I wasn't sure what to believe.

"I'm gonna show you something." Marge set her mug on the counter and walked to an old brown cabinet. She knelt down and sifted through a few moments until she found what she was looking for. She handed me a framed photo. "After Cutter passed and I finally had it in me to clean out his things, hidden in there among the work shirts he chose from everyday, I found that. It meant a great deal to him, so I framed it. Kept it on my side of the bed for years until one day I got up and looked at it – I mean, really looked at it. Couldn't take it. Reminded me of all I lost, so I tucked it away."

I looked over the photo, one taken from a distance by a terrible photographer. It was dark and sorta blurry, though clear enough for me to make out the old man, large, with shaggy white hair, oversized eyeglasses, and a full white beard and mustache. He was seated in the very same recliner I'd sat in over the summer, feet up. In his arm he held a baby. Tiny and wearing yellow footy pajamas. Marjie. In his other hand he held a mug. I looked closer. World's Greatest Boss.

"So he loved Marjie," I stated.

She chuckled. "Understatement. He'd a loved you, too. Better than I know how to love you girls. But it ain't 'bout ya color. He was a good husband and a great father. Much better than me. When she left and took his grandchild away, she broke his heart. She'd call, promise to come by and bring the baby for a visit but she never did. She hurt him somethin' terrible. And I know she was sick, but he always been good to her...he ain't deserve that kind of hurt." Sadness covered my grandmother's face but she didn't cry. My grandmother.

"Wes hasn't called," I shared. "I lost my...I haven't seen him since...it's been over a week."

"Ah, so that what got yo' face all screwed up."

I nodded and spun my empty mug in a circle. "His sister says it's his way of dealing with me leaving. I think that's dumb. It'll be tough on us both, but we had this time and he wasted it. So she's taking me to a party later. He's gonna be there."

"You alright with that?"

I pondered the question. "I honestly don't know."

"Well," she began, taking our mugs to the sink and rinsing them out, "you could always head into town with Clare and me instead. She be here for me probably about another 15...20 minutes."

"Yeah, thanks, but no. Me and Amelia didn't end on the greatest terms. Might be kinda awkward."

Marge laughed. I eyed her strangely. I swore it was the first time she'd actually laughed since I'd been there. "Yeah I heard about that. Sound like you were pretty hard on the gal."

I blushed. "Yea, probably."

"Eh. I say it serves that needy little social climber but, you might be right. Clare ain't too keen on you right now. Right for ain't too keen on me neither since you my granddaughter, but I stand by you. Don't make me no nevermind. She got but one friend 'sides me and his name Biscuit."

I joined her in laughter. It felt nice and if I wasn't mistaken, Marge had actually acknowledged me aloud as her grandchild, and not in a cynical way. Until that moment I hadn't realized I cared.

☙

I was wrapped in rope and cable, knotted and wound up tight. Nerves were shot. Processing why I had agreed to do something so foolish. I didn't know where we were. Ness picking me up meant sweet talking some guy *friend* into a detour to my part of The Skirts. A prehistoric caveman who didn't speak outside of the occasional series of grunts. And a string of well-placed grunts made it evident he wasn't very pleased about the third-wheel sitch.

A thirty minute drive landed us on a farm with, I could only assume, every resident dependant in the town of Fox Harbor and its surrounding areas. Unfamiliar music themed the party. A group gathered around a keg filling up cups and laughing. A game of beer pong was well underway, and a couple ran past wearing bathing suits covered in mud, nearly bumping into me.

The entrance to the converted barn had all the makings of a hillbilly hip hop video, shrouded in marijuana smoke and saggy jeans. I followed Ness through the crowd of Snoop Doggy Dogg worshipers – *fa' shizzle* – trying to stick close despite the short leash Grunting Ass had her on. Kids were everywhere, some paired off, others in groups, some making out, a few dancing.

We made a pit stop at two large vats, one labeled Hooch and the other, Sweet Tea. Ass Grunt ladled up a cup of each and handed one to Ness. Not wanting to be drunk in foreign territory, I opted for the Sweet Tea.

I followed my guides diligently, taking a swallow of my drink. A ball of flames scorched a path down my esophagus, and I struggled to catch my breath while coughing. I gasped loudly, my eyes watering. So much for being low key. Ness wrapped an arm around me and took the cup from my hand.

"That is not tea," I exclaimed.

She laughed, shaking her head. "So sorry. I should've warned you."

"What the hell is it?"

Ness shrugged. "Tea is one of the ingredients, at least. Hey, you gonna be okay if me and Phillip sneak off for a minute? Or five," she giggled while Ass Grunt became Ass Grinder.

"Yeah, sure. I'll be fine," I lied.

"I'll find you," she called out as she was pulled deeper into the party. I rolled my eyes and observed my surroundings. Stupid mistake going there. To cope with my bad decision I headed back to the vats and chose Hooch instead, more for something to do with my hands than for something to drink. I leaned against a pillar hoping to blend into it, but the only attendee with melanin at a party in a wide-open structure has little luck of being inconspicuous. I peeked around occasionally and cautiously, hoping to see Wes, while hoping not to.

"Wow, you made it." Clark approached me from behind. "Ballsy. You're not so bad, Meg."

"Clarke, don't. I'm really not in the mood."

"Hey, you don't gotta worry about me," he held his hands up defensively, waving a lit cigarette between his fingers. His eyes were bloodshot and his speech unsteady. He pressed his glasses higher onto his nose. "Between you and me, I think everybody likes you and Wes way f'kn better than Wes and Alli. But you don't have to live in this shit hole."

I read Clark's face. He seemed sincere enough. "Thanks...I guess."

"You tell her I said that shit, I'll deny it. That bitch is crazy." Clarke stumbled away, squeezing a girl's boob as he passed her by. She squealed and shoved him. He looked satisfied despite losing his footing.

I turned away and did a double-take as my eyes met with Wes' in the distance. My stomach bottomed out and my heart sped up. He watched me as he turned up a cup and guzzled it. I battled mentally, trying to make a decision on what to do. Should I go to him or make him come to me? But hadn't I gone to him over and over and been ignored? Even taking the risk of coming to a total stranger's party in a strange town with total strangers. We were locked in a standoff. Silence fell around us, the barn was suddenly empty. There was only the two of us, just like the last time we were together on a rainy day in The Woods. I watched as recognition lit his eyes and knew he'd had the same thought. My heart ran faster as I watched and waited.

His name was called and he looked away. He turned back to me with a cold, glazed over stare before walking off. The urge to cry overwhelmed me but I refused. No more of this weepy, Fox Harbor version of self. I turned away and left the barn. I would wait outside until Ness and her f'k buddy, Ass Grunt, were available to take me home but first – I needed a drink...a strong one. I ladled up another cup of whatever the hell was being peddled as Sweet Tea, but this time paced myself.

I found a bench and claimed it. People gathered around and moved on. One kid vomited on his shoes but I remained. I couldn't handle seeing Wes again. I was livid but if I saw him I wouldn't stand up for myself, I'd only cry. I was behaving as Andie behaved when Lyle or Marjie did some f'kd shit. Falling down rather than standing up. It was official. I was ready, again, to go home.

"There you are," Ness stumbled my way, a red Solo cup in hand. "Wes is in there, y'know. Why are you out here?"

"I saw him. He didn't want to talk."

"Then make him."

"I tried," I lied, my face contorting into one big scowl. "Sooo, you and Ass F'k about ready to go?"

"Ass what? And why, we barely just got here?"

"Because I'm not having any fun. I should've never come with you."

She looked me over once, then grabbed my hand. "Come on."

"No."

"Yes. You two are gonna talk about this."

"He doesn't want to talk to me."

"Forget what he wants. He's a guy, he doesn't know what he wants. Come on."

I allowed her to, yet again, have her way despite my better judgment. The party had somehow gotten bigger without my noticing. My feet weren't steady on the ground and I was surprised to discover I wasn't actually sober. Ness, unapologetically, shoved people aside, clearing a direct path. I saw him, leaning against a short wooden gate where pigs or chickens should have been. He was not alone. Juicy Jenna was there and so was Clark and Dob.

And Allison.

She sat on top of the gate, straddling him from behind while taking a deep hit from a small bong. I stopped abruptly, watching him smile and laugh as she exhaled the smoke purposely around his head. My heart thumped faster and harder, but this time for a much different reason. I continued forward, walking faster...my absence of sobriety making me much f'king angrier. I stopped in front of him. He looked wasted, not present. Alli snarled at me, trading the bong for a plastic cup and a skinny joint.

"Can I talk to you?" I asked through gritted teeth.

"Does he look like he wants to talk to you?" Alli asked in a taunting tone as she seductively slid a hand down his chest, passing him her joint.

I rolled my eyes from her and addressed him again. "Wes. Wes, f'k. I'm leaving in a couple days. Can we just talk?"

He shrugged his shoulders up and stuck there a moment. "What's there to talk about?"

"I'm leaving in a couple days—"

"Bingo."

"What does that even mean?"

"You're leaving. So leave."

A punch to the gut could not have hurt more.

The sting of saltwater knocked me off balance. "I don't understand. I was always going to leave...from the very beginning I was always going to leave."

With a hooked index finger he summoned me closer. I obliged. He leaned in so close that his lips touched my ear and I involuntarily shuddered. "But I didn't always know I was gonna love you."

I turned slowly, looking him in the eyes. "Wes, I..."

He leaned back but stayed close, his eyes locked on

mine. I lost my battle and the tears flowed. He continued, "I'm here. Stuck here. Never leaving. For me, this *is* home."

"Aww, baby's crying cause her hick boyfriend f'ked her and f'ked her over," Alli taunted, laughing and high-fiving her friend.

"Shut the f'k up, Allison," Ness stepped in, defending me.

I shook my head, holding my hand up to stop her, then sidestepped Wes. The way he handled things? A mess. But I knew the truth. He loved me. Not her, but me.

"Jealous much? Mad because now he sees you for exactly what you are? A substanceless f'k-hole with daddy issues, who tries to hide her insecurities by being a bitch to everyone she comes in contact with. You're nothing, Alli. Nothing but a f'king worthless burnout. You ain't shit, ain't about shit...hell, you ain't gonna be shit. Without Wes, what do you even have to look forward to, huh? Top stripper at The Cubbyhole? Maybe you can be someone's sorry ass sister-wife. But you know what your real problem is, Alli?"

She scoffed and glanced around, shrinking beneath the weight of all judgemental eyes on her. "No, but since you think you're so much better than all of us, I'm sure you'll tell me."

"Your biggest problem is that you're salts because you've always known Wes could do better, and now that he actually did, you don't stand a chance in hell of competing. So f'k you, you pathetic inbred bitch."

Silence fell around us. At first I thought it was my imagination again, but I could hear little short of the music in the background and my heartbeat in the foreground.

I sympathized with Ness when cold beer splashed against my face and I gasped for air. The foam tickled my nose and officially made me wet T-shirt material.

I shook in violent anger, though less from taking Alli's beer to the face in the center of an observant crowd who no longer saw me as a badass, but rather a laughingstock. I was most enraged because, after all of that, Wes just stood there. Useless and pathetic.

Ness, however, did not remain idle. "What the hell is wrong with you?" she screamed at her brother, right before grabbing a handful of golden locs and jerking Alli from her post. This fight, I knew exactly what to do, and I wasn't sticking around. I stomped out, drenched and humiliated with all eyes and pointing fingers on me, with no idea how I would get home. Surprisingly, it was not long before a wild-eyed Ness caught up to me, dangling Wes' keys.

"Come on. I'll take you home."

∂

I let Ness ramble on about how happy she was that I'd let Allison have it and how good it felt for her to win this fight. How every other girl in town was afraid of Alli, and she was glad someone else had the balls to stand up to her. I had very little to add to the convo. I was pissed. I had more pressing concerns in my life and I'd allowed myself to be distracted by some stupid boy who I would likely never see again.

The house was brightly lit when we pulled up, the door half open and a loud voice yelled indecipherable words. I scrunched my face trying to make sense of it. Who would be creating trouble? Marjie was detained, I didn't see my father's car so that wasn't the issue, and Andie was back on her meds and had been perfectly calm and balanced...practically back to her old self.

Ness looked curiously toward the house. "Is everything okay?"

"I don't know."

There was a loud bang which caused us to jump from the car quickly and run up the stairs as fast as we could. I pushed the door open wider, stepping inside with Ness close on my heels. My mother stood with the look of having seen a ghost, plastered onto her face. I stepped deeper indoors, turning toward the spot her eyes were trained. Noticing my presence, she yelled at me to leave but it was too late. I stopped so short that Ness bumped into me.

"Marjie, what the hell!" I stumbled back.

"Oh my god," Ness said when she saw the shotgun that was aimed at my mother, the one being controlled by my sister.

"What are you doing?" I asked dumbly. "Why aren't you in the hospital?"

"Sister! Great, the gangs all here. Now all we need is Dad but hey, this'll do."

"Marjie, c'mon. Put the gun down."

"You know why they put her in the hospital, Meg... had her locked up like some psychopath? Because they think she's crazy just because *she* is." Marjie nodded sharply toward our mother.

"In all due fairness, who's holding the gun?" I queried sarcastically before realizing my double entendre, and asked, cautiously, "Atika?"

She smiled at me, looked relieved. Like a weight had been lifted. She was acknowledged without needing to announce herself.

Ness backed away, chuckled awkwardly. "This looks like a family matter, so I'm—"

Atika/Marjie backed up, kicking the door closed. "Atika. Atika *f'king* Dangerfield. And do you know why? Because *she* would leave her, all the time, with strange women and men who we didn't know and Marjie was scared, she was always scared."

I looked to my mom, shivering and raking her nails hard across her scalp. Wondered what this was all about, what other family secrets were being revealed. I turned to Marge who stood aside with her face red and tied into a knot, soothing Lucy Rae – or maybe her own self. I wondered what I'd missed, how this setting came to be. But it didn't matter. Only I could put a stop to it. "*Atika*, please just put the gun down. You can tell us everything Andie did wrong without a gun."

She didn't react. "Uncle Windell...he loved that old comedian, somebody Dangerfield. He watched him while he raped her. In that little dark room, upstairs. The one at the end of the hall. You remember, Mom. Anyway, he had a VCR – a f'kng VCR – and he would play these old VHS tapes. Not sure why he decided to double down on the perv factor. Maybe the humor let him believe what he was doing was all in good fun. He named her *Atika* Dangerfield, because he said it was part of the game...part of playing pretend. That's all they were doing, playing pretend. Playing...House."

I turned sharply toward my mother, horrified. Wondering if it could be true. She gasped, but didn't question the validity of the recollection. "Mom...that didn't...was she...?"

Marjie continued, "He gave her candy after. That was always strange, too. Like, why candy? But I suppose it made it nice. Laughter and sweets, it couldn't all be bad. No one gives me candy anymore. Sometimes I wish they did. But people just take and then leave me all alone to pick up the pieces of myself...by myself."

Tears rained from Mom's eyes. "You never told me."

"You were never there! And when you were...you

weren't. We were in that house because you said we had nowhere else to go. You said it was Grandma's fault. Remember that? You used to always tell me that...when I wanted something and couldn't have it, or if I was sad or upset, you'd say, *Marjie, I'm sorry. It's your grandmother's fault for putting us out.*"

"Oh, Andie," Marge lamented, shaking her head.

"I was sick," Mom explained. "I don't remember any of that."

My sister shook her head vehemently. "Oh my god, don't lie to me! You were always running...always avoiding responsibility. Even now. Even with Lyle. You knew it was going on, you had to know. But you didn't protect me, you didn't defend me. You just left me there! And came here of all places! All she wanted was to be with you, but you were *never* there."

"I didn't know, Marjie, I didn't. And you made that choice to be with Lyle...to be with *my husband* – you! *That* didn't have to happen. You didn't want my protection, didn't need it because your aim was to hurt me. And you did that. I won't be blamed for that one, but for the past...I was sick," Mom said, forceful. "I was young and I was ill. I needed medication that I didn't have, couldn't afford. I didn't know."

"Poor little Marjorie. She was so scared. I protected her. Me. Not you. *I* did."

My mother groveled through her thick, mucus tears. All of the lies, the withholding of information.

Manipulation of history. My mind was reeling, wondering if maybe Marge was wrong. Despite her pointing a gun at our mother, maybe Marjie wasn't mentally ill after all. Could it be that I'd been mistaken and she wasn't spoiled *or* a brat? Maybe Marjie was just traumatized by the abuse she suffered from the neglect of an unstable parent. And somehow Andie thought it wise to have another baby? What would become of that child if no one was around to make her take her pills? What might have happened to me?

"My god, Andrea," Marge said. "It didn't need to be that way. You know it didn't need to be that way."

"I'm sorry, Momma," my mother blubbered, "but you don't understand, none of you understand what it's like! People shaming you...judging you...calling you *crazy* because of something you can't control."

"But that's just it, that's the issue," Marge continued. "You *can* control it. You made a choice."

"I didn't have a choice! People pointing fingers, teasing me. They called me *Crazy* Andie-Pandy. And when I took the meds...when I tried to do what I was supposed to so I could be...*normal*, I just...I didn't know who I was when I was on them." She faced Marjie again. "I was sick, honey. I was young, I didn't know any better."

Marjie appeared unaffected by our mother's version of an admission of guilt. "Well, now we're here. Remember, Andie, it was Grandma's fault, that's what you told her. That's what you *always* told her and then you bring her here–"

"I didn't bring–"

"–to Grandma's house. You abandoned her over and over and over and now...you leave her again at a time she needed you most. You could have, *for once*, done the right thing but instead you bring her here, to Grandma's house. And suddenly she's dubbed crazy and gets psych eval'd, and that's Grandma's fault, too, I suppose but where were you?"

"In the hospital myself, remember. You put me there," Mom spat in retaliation.

"Why weren't you there for her? *Where the f'k were you?*"

Andie dropped hard to her knees, sobbing, smearing water and ooze. Repeating her reasoning rather than accepting responsibility. "I was just a kid, a sick kid. You can't blame me, honey. You can't blame me for that."

"Oh, I don't. I blame her." Atika/Marjie shifted the barrel from Andie to Marge. Recklessly, I jumped in front, blocking her. My sister and I hadn't ever gotten along but I needed to stop her from potentially making a huge mistake. Whatever she called herself, whatever PTSD-fueled identity she claimed, I would not allow my sister to destroy her life by killing our grandmother.

"Whoa, Marjie, it's not what–"

A punch to the gut could not have hurt more.

I'd thought that being rejected by Wes was the worst

pain I could ever endure. But a cute boy breaking your heart could never compare to being shot in the chest by your sister.

I gasped for air but there was none. The sounds around me...the vicious bark of Lucy Rae, Marge's command for me to stay with her, Marjie's emphatic apologies and insistence that she hadn't meant to, Mom's wails and Ness' repeated cries to God...it all sounded far away. In a tunnel...in the distance.

The heat that summer had been incessant. But as the cold crept over me, I longed for it. If I survived, I would never complain again, not about anything. I would forgive my father. Everyone had a story. I would learn what Lyle's was and then I would forgive him.

I would graduate from high school, walk across the stage. I'd take pics with Cam and Shonie, hashtag best of class. I would forgive Wes and make him do right by me. I would come back to Fox Harbor, spend the summer before college in love. I'd convince him to come with me to California or Massachusetts, depending on which school accepted me. I'd graduate early at the top of my class and be highly sought after in my career, the breadwinner. Wes would be a wonderful stay-at-home dad.

And Flaca...I wouldn't need Lyle to feed Flaca because Wes would do it.

The sounds faded further as did the world around me. I struggled to remember something important. What was it? Uncle Cal was coming. I hoped he wouldn't be too upset about the wasted trip. No, that wasn't it. Something else...something important. Marge...my grandmother.... something she said. She told me to hold on. Hold on. Just...hold on...

"*Buuuunnnnnnyyyy!!!*"

epilogue.

I hate Fox Harbor.

I wasn't born here. I was born in a major city – meant to be in a major city. A big city girl through and through, and all I want is to go home. To be with my best friends, Cam and Shonie, graduate high school and move toward my destiny. I want nothing more than to put my summer of heartache and heartbreak behind me, and create new and happier memories to replace them with.

Instead, I died in this piece of shit place, Fox Harbor. Eternally trapped in this back woods, *Village of the Damned*, insult to all that is good, beauteous, and meaningful about American civilization. Fox Harbor. Where there is no actual harbor and the local kids call a dilapidated cabin *The Woods*. Brillz.

I will forevermore be a Harborite thanks to Marjie's alleged split personality, Atika Dangerfield. I said alleged and I maintain alleged because, although it was in the name of Atika that my older sibling aimed a gun at my grandmother but wound up shooting me, it was Marjie that held my hand and begged me not to die. It was Marjie that apologized profusely while insisting that she hadn't meant to do it, that it was an accident. While I lay on Marge's living room floor, gushing blood from the newly formed cavity in my chest, there was no Atika. There was only the broken spirit of a damaged girl who, if she hadn't needed help before, certainly would now.

And it was ironic, really. The one person who seemed to make it her life's mission to take *everything* from me... literally did just that. Now that's some real f'kd shit.

But who is really to blame for it? Marjie for pulling the trigger? Or Dad for sleeping with her and sending her off the rails to begin with? Maybe my blood is on Andie's hands for her refusal to do what was necessary to get well sooner. For not being a better parental figure to her first-born and getting her the help she needed – or maybe, simply giving her the attention she craved.

What does it matter if the tragic loss of my life could've been prevented? It wasn't. There is no going back...no undoing what has been done. So all that I hope for is that my death is met with some purpose. I hope that losing me will illustrate to my mother the importance of staying on her meds so that she can raise her new baby better than she did her first two. I hope that taking my life will force Marjie to finally get the help that she desperately needs.

It's funny how being in the throes of posthumous-self reflection provides one with profound perspective. Although this, by far, is not the ending that I would have written for my life, it is what it is. Eternity is such a long time, so I suppose I cannot begrudge my family...I love them too much. And so I forgive them all their trespasses against me, I really do. All the secrets and lies and dangerous concealment of pre-disposition to mental illness. And though it may be hard for some to believe, I even forgive my sister for accidentally murdering me. I hope that they know this and find it in them to forgive themselves and each other.

People make mistakes. During my short life, I made my fair share and had I survived, I'd have made plenty more. I can't eternally begrudge them because I love them and I wish them well. Even Crazy Lady Who Put Shotgun To My Chest But At Least Didn't Kill Me.

I should go now. Eternity waits. But before I do, I hope you'll do me a favor. If you see Lyle, be kind. I don't know what will become of my dad and that's the one worry that I carry to the other side with me. Certainly he blames himself. Had he not succumbed to the temptation of Scuzzy Stepdaughter Who Aimed To Hurt Mother, I would very likely be alive and well today. I don't blame him, but surely this has destroyed him. Now that I'm gone, hopefully there is someone there to hold his hand, dry his tears, and give him cause to carry on.

Shit. If Dad is as much of a catastrophe as I think he is, now who'll feed Flaca???

꩜

In Memoriam

Shonie: Today was the first day of school. I can't believe I even went since we just buried yo ass last thursday. Momma told me not to go but I just couldn't be at the crib just thinkin bout you all day. Cam ain't go. I don't blame her. For awhile it was nice. We had a rando assembly and peeps that knew you got to get together and talk about you and share stories and shit. You wouldn't believe all the fools that came out the woodwork talm bout dey yo friend. Lbvs! Some niggas is just thirsty for attention doe. Girl I miss you sooo much. So fkn much. I can't even believe this shit is real. I don't even know why i'm texting like you gone hit me back or sumthin.

Mon, Aug 29, 2:23 PM

Shonie: Smh. I just can't stop crying and feeling like shit for getting mad and not speaking to you all summer on some dummy. You did what you had to do to get through what you was going through. I was foul Megz. Not you, me. You know I got control issues doe. And I guess I just ain't like you goin to somebody else over me, even if it is the mutual homegirl. I am so sorry. I love you, Meggy-Megz. You my sistr 4 always. RIH

Mon, Aug 29, 11:17 PM

Cam: Meg...I don't even know what to say. Shonie said that Andie kept your phone on so we can text you but what the fk for?!! Fkn Marjie how could she?!! I miss you so bad, bro. It hurts so bad sometimes I can't even breathe.

Tue, Aug 30, 4:10 PM

Shonie: Hey girl. Ohmagawd! Cam is like straight up losing it since you gone. I'm so worried about her I don't know what to do. Even Marcus say she drinking too much. Marcus girl! Lol! Miss you...

Wes: I'm sorry. I was such an ass to you. I wish I could take it back. I'm real sorry.

Shonie: Omg guess who I got for Advanced Cal, bruh. Dr. Pasternak. Yasss gurl! It's phenna be interesting. Love you. Miss you!

Shonie: I saw Javi today. He is messed up over this. I can't blame him. We all are. Me and that fool ain't never really got along but I was there for him today. It felt good to have somebody to talk to since Cam shut the world out. I feel like Im all by myself now. I know you watching over me though.

Javi: Damn Megz. Dis shit fkd up for real doe. like I just cant even believe you aint here. I cant even sleep last night Das why i'm texting you so early cause I'm going to mass with my moms. you know the last time anigga been to mass? i bet yo ass laughing up in heaven at this shit! I hope so. I miss you girl. you was my first love for real even doe i ain't act like it. RIH Megz.

Ness: Hi Meg. This is Vanessa, Wesley's sister. I'm sorry about what happened to you and that I couldn't help you. I'm just now starting to sleep. That night keeps playing over and over in my head. I just want you to know that I'm sorry. I wish that didn't happen to you. You were such a nice girl. My brother left town. After it happened he quit his job and spent all his time at the woods by himself. About a week ago Cody found a note that said he needed to breathe so he was leaving for a while. I hope he's okay and comes home soon. I probably won't write again. I just wanted to say I'm sorry.

Shonie: HAPPY BORNDAY!!!!!!! You woulda been 17 years old today! We was gone straight kick it. But I'mma turn the hell up in your honor! Hope you gettin' LIVE in heaven!!!

Cam: Happy birthday Megz. I miss you.

Unk: OMG! I was totes super sad when I heard what happened! So sorry I yelled and ended our friendship but I was so mad that day! You were so awful to Alli. Anywayz, your bday came up in my phone. I guess it's not really happy but I hope you went to heaven instead of y'know. So at least today can be okay. ~Amelia

Aunt Julia: Happy Birthday, Bunny. Your Uncle Calvin, the boys and I miss you something terrible. Love you loads, Auntie J.

Wes: Happy birthday. I love you.

Cam: Fk you for dying! I'm so mad! Why didn't you try harder to live? You're supposed to be here right now! It's your birthday We're supposed to spend it with YOU

Cam: Ay Meg. Dis Marcus. Cam drunk ass shit man. She ain't copin. RIP my nigga.

Shonie: Hey girl. I know I ain't texted in awhile but you know I be talking to you ALL the time. It's just that today is 6 months from the day. I been handling it but today was just really hard. And me and Cam don't get down no more so I don't really have anybody that understand so... I saw your Pops the other day. He ain't lookin too good. Not at all. I didn't wanna be cryin and shit so I crossed the street before he saw me. I know. Real fkd up. Im sorry about that. I know you would want me to check on him. Next time I got you. And I heard your bitch sister got 15. That ain't shit. That bitch need life! Well let me get to this homework. Pasternak ain't no joke. Love you and miss you always!

Unk: Hi sister. Marjie here. I'm writing you because they say Mom never turned your phone off and my counselor thought it would help me if I sorta talked to you. So this is her cell I'm using. Smh. I think it's sorta silly. It isn't like you'll write back and say you forgive me. Look, whatever. I'm sorry. I swear I didn't mean to shoot that gun. I was so mad at mom and at that bitch Marge for locking me up. I just wanted to scare her. I swear. Then you jumped all in the way and I don't know what happened. It just went off. But you gotta believe me I wouldve never done that on purpose. I used to always say stupid stuff but I loved you baby sis. I still love you. I'm sorry. Please forgive me.

Cam: I don't know if this phone is still on but today is the anniversary of your death and I just need to talk to you. You died today, bro. How crazy is that? I lost my shit when I found out. I guess I was always kinda on the verge ever since my dad walked out. But I had you and Shonie and that helped me to kind of hold it together. And then I got this call from Shonie saying that your dad called her and said you died and I just bugged out, y'know. Now what? It's been a year and I miss you so bad. But I'm working through. Sho went to college. She got accepted at Spelman. I fkd up senior year so I'm picking up the pieces. I hope you knew how much I loved you and that I miss you. Goodbye.

~

2 Years Later

Mom: Megan, this is Mom. I'm not sure what to write. Maybe this is just silly but I left your phone on for a reason. So I could feel like you were still with me. Every time it vibrated because one of your friends sent you a message, it made me smile. Those have been pretty tough to come by since you've been gone. It's been more than 2 years! God, I can't believe it. You would have been 19 years old today. I remember the day you were born. I was in labor for 27 hours because you refused to come out! You were stubborn from the onset! That's why I know that if there was anyway for you to survive that bullet, you would have. I'm sorry, Bunny. I should've gotten Marjorie some help a long time ago. I just didn't want to believe that there could be anything wrong with my beautiful and perfect child. I didn't want her to suffer the same embarrassment that I did. Stupid huh? I so wish I could have a do over. I pray for it every night. I go to church now. After you died and Marjie was sentenced, I just couldn't cope. I had a new baby and I was so scared I would destroy his life too. You have a little brother by the way. Teagan Michael Schofield. I gave custody of him to my brother Cal. He and Jules can give him a much better life. Marge lives with them now so she helps. I ran for awhile but I wasn't getting anywhere. I finally realized that this was the cycle of my life. The hamster wheel. I met my new husband Garrick - my actual husband :) and he introduced me to the church. Showed me the unfailing love of Jesus Christ. I'm a certified counselor now and I got a job in the church helping people deal with issues like anxiety and depression. Can you believe it?! I'm actually helping other people! I heard that 1 in 5 people suffer with mental illness every year so I'm trying to do my part. I'm trying to heal Bunny. I swear it. I plan to do better by Teagan, even if I'm only in the background of his life. I owe it to him and I owe it to you girls to do right by him. And in the spirit of healing, I suppose this will be the last text to this number. Your dad thought I was crazy for keeping it on this long anyway. Maybe he's right. Who knows! I love you Bunny, your dad and me both. I can't wait to see you again and I promise you, I will. Bye for now. Mom.

final thoughts.

For the record, I didn't set out to write a book about mental illness. And honestly, I don't know if that's actually what this story is even about. But if it is or isn't, that wasn't my goal. It is merely the recollection of a dream that felt more like a movie than a construct of my imagination.

But though it was never a goal to tackle the topic of mental illness, for whatever I've done, I hope I did it justice. For my baby brother, Christopher, who was diagnosed with Bipolar Disorder and Schizophrenia in 2005. And for my mom who has been a caregiver for diagnosed relatives for countless years.

I asked Chris, if there is one message he wanted me to get across, what would it be? He replied, *Be a hero.* The hardest part about this illness, from his perspective, is being ignored and disregarded because you are thought to be crazy. But according to the National Alliance on Mental Illness website, approximately 1 in 5 adults in the U.S. experiences mental illness in a given year and 2.6% of adults in the U.S. live with bipolar disorder.

If you believe you or someone you know is struggling with a mental disorder, please talk to your physician about treatment. For more information on mental illness, please visit **http://www.nami.org**.

Turn the page to read an excerpt from **Miki Starr's** acclaimed novel...

Zella Dora

a fictitious memoir

Prélude

Those were the sounds which defined my existence.

The rhythm of life. That pounding, smacking, contact of sweaty flesh upon sweaty flesh. The hissing and moaning and beautiful profanity that was the theme music of my days of youth. Others may have thought it retched… a child subjected to such sonnets, but they knew nothing of beauty.

In those sounds – love. In that cadence – music. So long as that undeniable pleasure of my parents existed, my mother's wails and demands upon my father's continence, assured that we'd be a happy family for many years to come.

My mother never shielded her tone. I was never certain whether her openness was based upon her intentions all along or rather an inability to contain the carnal affinity which my father aroused in her. Either way, I was raised on their vibrations. Fed it like a hearty bowl of grain on a cold winter morning. Their prose awakened my soul most everyday (oft times more frequent than once) and brought a smile to my face and glint to my eyes.

I missed those sounds when I went away to college and had to rather settle on incarnate poetry of my own. There were several with whom I shared my bed, and although every experience was rich and fulfilling, bold and beautiful, never once had I matched the ethereal lilt of my parents.

I smeared away the tears that trailed the side of my face as my eyes remained deadlocked on the ceiling. I swallowed hard and smiled a bit though my soul was heavy and emotion was creeping slowly, threatening to take hold of my being and pull me inside.

The apartments were small and the walls like paper. They'd only recently moved into the unit next door, maybe it'd been three weeks... possibly less but I couldn't recall. They made love often. I knew this because their bedroom was on the other side of mine. When I could, I listened and with eyes closed experienced the joy he must have afflicted upon her body. He was an aggressive lover. I could tell by the solos on the wall. I guess she liked it rough.

But tonight...

Tonight was different. Something happened earlier. There were muffled voices which carried across the room. A coherent word or two speckled about was not enough to decipher the scenario. I'd fallen asleep. I couldn't recall when.

Thump.

Thump.

Thump.

The sound was steady, vastly different from the normal *th-wap, th-wap, th-wap* that typically struck in uncertain rhythm. My lids were heavy, and though initially I was unaware as to what had wakened me, the gentle taps against the wall behind my bed soon clued me in. I was suddenly fully awake for I recognized the rhythm. It was familiar and a feeling not unlike panic though much more positive by definition overcame me. I searched for the remote and switched my television off. I must've fallen asleep to its tenor.

Thump.

Thump.

Thump.

Something was missing, somehow the scenario incomplete. Frantically I searched the room. The window! Unnecessary ambience. Without haste, I moved across the room and pulled the frame down swift and firm. I returned to my temporary resting spot, on my back, eyes to the ceiling, breath on inhale… and out easy and as hushed as possible.

I listened carefully.

Her prose came to me. Muffled moans and staggered breath becoming louder as he stroked deeper. She called out, and I imagined his flesh beneath her nails. I'd never met them; I hadn't seen her as far as I was aware. So I only imagined… imagined her face brown like my own. Her mane thick and course with sweat like hers was, like my mother's was, the morning after. Her legs luscious and firm and wrapped around his waist, locking him there and insisting by their mere presence that he go deeper, further within.

I envisioned his face brown like my father's. His back strong and masculine, muscles flexing as he stroked. Sweat dripping from his brow… to her… further connecting the two.

I fantasized that they were them. That my neighbors were them. That they were my parents. My parents before she died. Before my mother fell ill and died, leaving my father alone and helpless. In my mind, in that moment, I was twelve, one of the last few years those sounds existed in my household and that impetuous call to God above was that of my mother.

I was pleased though my pleasure birthed no physical arousal. To do so would be utterly incongruous for in my mental these were the sounds of God and Earth, my own personal God and Earth eternally blessed Mother and Father.

It'd been nearly a year, the time that I'd been gone from Jacob and Zahrah's nest, since I'd ceased mourning the loss of Zahrah…my matriarch. My mother. I hadn't released her but rather only stopped. Simply stopped. No closure, no moving on. It was now my time to purge. I sensed it creeping, its presence hovering above me, breathing down my neck. I listened to her who was now Zahrah and his grunts which had become Jacob's promises to love and cherish her for all of her days…a promise he kept and continued even in her passing.

They were beside me now. I could smell her ambrosial scent and hear her weeps and moans and sighs. I could feel her mane, thick and coarse yet feathery soft; sweep the side of my face.

"Jacob," she whispered. *"Oh Jacob… I love you."*

I listened to every syllable, noun, pronoun, every adjective and verb. The thumping from behind the wall had ceased and was replaced by the thumping of my heart. My body shook as hers vibrated. It shook, and my palms locked across my abdomen as her legs locked around his waist. A painful wail escaped my frame as a guttural moan escaped her lips. My eyes closed tight in a failed attempt to dam the salty flow as her eyes widened to connect with his as she reached her apex and I, mine.

"Oh Jacob!" she cried.

"Mommy!" I wailed.

The thumping from behind had ceased long ago. My heart's pounding continued as I sat upright with a start. Frantically I sought their presence, but I was alone. I felt my bed around me… it was cold. The room was dark and silent. My forehead fell against my palm, and I shook my head from one side to the other and back. I reached to scratch the back of my scalp; my lioness mane had come undone. I inhaled deeply then slowly pushed from the size bed fit for a Queen, fit for me, Zella Dora Robeson. Named by my mother. Zella for my maternal great-grandmother and Dora for my aunt who passed only months prior to my birth. My surname evidently inherited from being a descendent of the late actor, athlete, and *'faiseur de tout'* Paul Robeson.

I staggered across the hardwood floor of my one room apartment to the bathroom. I shielded my just-brown eyes with the embedded golden embers from the light as I flicked the switch up. Stiff with layers of old paint, I offered more effort than one should have for such a simple task. I stood before the mirror, removing my hand from my face. I looked at my reflection looking back at me. My face was drenched from tears. I studied my features and saw hers staring back.

I chuckled. I sniffed and chuckled.

I sniffed and smiled and chuckled.

It was over and I knew it. I loved her in life, and I knew she'd be with me in death every time I passed a mirror or spoke a word. Every time I laughed or flashed a smile, she was there.

My matriarch.

My mother.

And now after six long years, I could move on. I was ready.

1 *Chapitre Un*

The telephone ringing vibrated inside my mind.

In moments like this, I wished that I'd taken the Illinois Bell sales assistant up on the offer to add voicemail to my phone plan. For an additional couple bucks per month, I'd be able to ride this out for maybe one... two rings longer before I could roll over, snuggle my head deeper into my pillow and return to a peaceful slumber. But I hadn't. No, I decided it wasn't worth dipping into my monthly Starbucks stipend for someone to verbalize what standard Caller ID would digitize. Too bad I didn't have that either.

I thought I could wait it out. Eventually they'd have to hang up; it couldn't possibly be someone important. I owned a cell phone. It wasn't anything fancy, an outdated Nokia that took up an excess amount of space in my bag. It was one of those pay-as-you-go plans. Its purpose was to keep me available to my dad. I needed for him to reach me whenever, wherever. If it were him, the Basie tune I downloaded would be pleasantly lulling me into consciousness rather than the pesky ring-ring-ring of my landline. For a fleeting moment, I thought it could be Ayinde or Darwin, but they, too, knew the best method of reaching me in an emergency.

The ringing persisted. I buried my face deep in my pillows and let out a fierce growl. My fingers somehow managed to find their way through my tangled locs of hair to massage my scalp. I sent a silent prayer for peace. It'd been a long night, and the last thing I wanted was to desert my current position.

But… the ringing persisted.

"Alright, alright, alright!" I rose from my bed, pillow in hand as though keeping that object near my side didn't make it so. As though holding on to a part of my slumber could somehow keep me in that state.

"This better be good," I grumbled as I sat upright, slamming my bare feet to the wood floor. I stood and crept across my studio apartment to the recliner chair, the one my dad had for years until Mommy, on the twentieth anniversary of their union, bought him the one he presently watches his shows in.

I sat and stared at the phone, an old thing with a rotary dial. For how old it was, I was in awe that it found the energy to screech so loudly. I stared down at the ringing phone sitting there on the cute little oak table I'd found at Goodwill a few months earlier.

"Robeson residence," I spoke in my most business-like manner, more than prepared to tell the person on the other end of the line as professionally as possible to *"f'k off"*. However there was no immediate response to my greeting. "Hello? Robeson residence."

Now my face was becoming warm. I was prepared to

hang up and in a state of pisstivity, return to my bed when a small voice came through.

"He's seeing someone else."

The voice was so small, so distant, I couldn't make out who it belonged to. "Excuse me?"

"I don't know what I'm going to do."

"Ayinde?"

"He's killing me, destroying me from the inside out."

"Ayinde, is that you? What are you saying? Is this about Marcus?"

"Zella."

"Yes?"

Silence.

I waited but there were no words following, only the sound of heartbreak. I was fully awake now; there'd be no more slumber on this day, not before long past the time where the sun would sink below the Earth. I gave another moment for her to offer up something more. She did not.

"Ayinde!"

"Huh?"

I tugged my hair in frustration. "What's going on? Where's Marcus?"

"He left."

"What do you mean he left? You two broke up... again?"

"No."

More silence.

"Ayinde!"

"Huh?"

I tossed my head back, blinking my eyes at the ceiling, counting backwards from three. I had a sudden and incredible urge to relieve my bladder. I took the phone by its handle, the receiver cradled in the crook of my neck. The telephone cord was a hundred-footer, long enough that my old rotary could act as an awkward portable. I carried it across the room to the bathroom. I pushed my panties to my ankles and sat before I spoke again.

My tone was soft when I addressed my friend. "Ayinde, have you been drinking?"

Her tone was innocent when she replied, "Yes."

"Baby, what time is it?"

"I don't know, maybe eight."

I let the phone slip from my ear but caught it before it could fall. I took in a fresh batch of oxygen and withheld any desire to curse. Replacing the phone to my ear, I spoke, "Hold on."

I stood, wiped, and flushed, then carried the phone to my bed. "Yinde, are you still there?"

"Uh huh."

I opened the drawer of the table at my bedside and sifted through. I really needed a drag. I found the Ziploc bag in the back with four joints left inside. I pulled one out, lit it, and sucked long and hard.

"Did you and Marcus get into a fight this morning?" I asked while managing to hold the smoke in my mouth, allowing it to slowly leak into my lungs.

"No, he went to work. He *said* he was going to work."

"So how did you decide he was cheating?"

"I didn't decide it, Zella!"

I let out an exasperated sigh. "Fine, how do you *know* he's cheating?"

"Evidence. What do you think? I found evidence. You don't believe me."

Oh, I believed her. "I'm not saying that I don't believe you."

"You think I'm making it up. Everyone's not so perfect like you."

"I didn't say - okay, Yinde, how much have you had to drink?"

"I'm not drunk."

I picked up my watch and checked the time; it was 7:48 am. Doesn't make one much value sobriety either, but I knew Ayinde was fragile and when dealing with her one had to form their sentences carefully.

"Sweetie, what have you been drinking?"

"Vodka."

My eyes grew large as saucers but I shook it off. "Straight?"

"Not at first."

"I'm coming over, okay?"

"Okay."

She hung up before I could make another utterance. I sat, my eyes on the receiver, my joint burning between my fingers. I hung up the phone and took another hit.

AYINDE DOMONIQUE PHELAN

Ayinde was one of my closest friends. I knew a lot of people but had only a couple friends. She was four years my junior and regarded me as more of a big sister. I was honored to be that to her.

Yinde was a freaking blast to be around; she was funny and outgoing, unique and spontaneous. But she was troubled, deeply so. She was an experiment gone too far. The daughter of a White mother who had an extramarital affair with a Black man ten years into her marriage and two Caucasian children later. The step-daughter of a White man who despite all his efforts could never seem to escape the reality that her brown skin tone was a constant reminder of his wife's infidelity. The young sibling of the two White children who didn't understand how to dismiss what her flesh tone and kinky hair represented to the family, not to mention the stigma resulting from being the kids with the *"whore mother and nigger sister."*

Granddaughter of established racists who could never quite seem to remember her name but rather referred to her as *"the brown one."* A young woman with no identity, no culture, no love, no home. No self esteem. The only blood tie she had was her baby brother Josiah, born five years after the melee. The only Phelan family member with enough courage to love her as she was. Unfortunately, his love alone wasn't enough.

At sixteen, she escaped her lily White neighborhood and landed on her father's doorstep where she spent one tumultuous year trying hard to fit in with her new, colorful surroundings and a father that drank too much, while doing her best to escape his incestuous advances. He was shot and killed in a bar brawl over a five dollar bet. She never mourned his death.

A month later, she legally became Ayinde, the name of her father's sister, an aunt she'd heard about but hadn't ever met. She never told me her birth name. She'll never tell anyone.

She'd been with Marcus for two years. In that time, he's gotten one woman pregnant (abortion), left her twice, and cheated on countless occasions. He's no good for her, he keeps her buried, but he tells her he loves her because he knows that is what she craves. No one can convince her to leave him because she loves him, or at least she thinks she does, and chooses to believe that he feels the same way. It scares me when these things occur. My friend is a wounded animal, starved for attention and negative is how it best resonates with her.

I sat the phone along the bedside and again rose to my feet. She'd drink herself into a coma if I didn't stop her, all so that Marcus would come to her bedside and hold her hand. So he'd promise to be there for her and swear to her that an act such as this would never happen again. She wouldn't want him to say he was sorry. She needed him to show it. Demonstrative love. My fear was that someday Marcus would decide he was over her antics and leave her to die. This struggled against my hope that he would someday leave her once and for all.

I had to pull myself together as quickly as possible; she'd already been drinking for at least an hour as far as I knew. I took a final puff on my herb before I put it out in my ashtray. I jumped from the bed, slamming my naked feet onto the faux oak, moving pointedly to the bathroom. There was no time to be thorough. Instead I adjusted the running water in my sink and took a towel from the cabinet behind me. I washed my face first, then cleared any remaining debris with a witch hazel soaked cotton ball. I pulled my underwear off and tossed them in the hamper. With my lathered towel, I took a swift bird bath or as my aunt used to call it, a hooker bath.

My cell phone cried out from the other room.

Oh now what? I thought to myself.

Quickly, I pat myself dry and rushed to my phone to see if it was Ayinde calling again. It was Darwin.

"Good morning."

"Hey, what's up, D?" I grabbed a fresh pair of undies from the drawer and performing a balancing act, held onto my phone and pulled the fabric over my buttocks.

"Nothing, chillin'."

"Are you at work?"

"Of course, but I just got the strangest call a minute ago."

"Ayinde?"

"I guess you've already talked to her."

"A few minutes ago." I took this call as my cue to move faster. I held the phone between my ear and shoulder as I tried to dance into a pair of jeans. I listened to Darwin as I fumbled through my small closet for a thick enough hoodie and a pair of worn gym shoes. "Hey, what's the temp outside?"

"Uhm, it's kinda cool this morning. Probably low fifties right now, not too bad."

I nodded at the sweatshirt I'd picked out, good choice.

Darwin continued, "So what's going on with her? Did Marcus do something? She wasn't clear, she kinda just rambled on."

"Oh, she's drunk."

"She's drunk?" Darwin's voice raised with astonishment.

"Oh yeah. Drunk." I ran to the bathroom and spread toothpaste across my brush. "See wez Wakus is cheday."

"She said what was that?"

I quickly spit and rinsed. "My bad. She says Marcus is cheating. Says she has evidence, I don't know. I'm on my way over there."

"So she's drunk. From what?"

"Vodka."

There was a pause. I could hear and translate the hemming and hawing coming from Darwin's side of the conversation. "What's... Zella, it's barely after eight in the morning."

"I know."

Darwin sighed dramatically. "Well alright, keep me posted okay."

"I will. Hey, I know you gotta get back to work, so I'll make it quick. I wanna go back to school."

"Wow. So when did this life changing decision come about?" Darwin asked, a smile in his voice.

"Last night. I can't explain it to you, but... something happened. Something miraculous and freeing, and I think I'm finally ready to get back to living my own life." I stood for a moment at my doorway, keys in hand, forgetting about Ayinde and her psycho-drama and for a moment, just a selfish moment, focused on me.

"Are you thinking about leaving us and going back to London?" he asked fearfully.

"No," I reassured. "You know I can't leave my dad. But I do think I'll go up to Northwest and check out the campus."

"Hey, good for you. You know I'm proud of you, Z."

"I know. Means a lot." I snapped back to reality. "I gotta go."

"Okay, later."

I grabbed a book for the short train ride and rushed out of the door.

There was a Starbucks on the corner a block away from Ayinde's apartment. I was in a hurry. I knew she needed me, but more importantly, I knew that I'd be unable to function or be any bit of understanding had I arrived without the benefit of my morning caffeine fix. And she'd been drinking all morning; a little caffeine might be just what she needed to offset the effects alcohol may have had on her.

I could hear a loud commotion as I neared Ayinde's door. The sounds of shattering glass traveled into the hallway. Panicked, I moved my legs faster and fiercely worked the key in the lock and let myself in.

"Ayinde!" I gasped as I entered the apartment. The place was a mess. Magazines, photos, clothes, and various other items were strewn about. Menswear covered the quaint sofa. Feathers covered nearly everything in the living space. Ayinde stood wild-eyed in the middle of the kitchenette holding a glass high above her head. My jaw hinges unlatched in my amazement. I could hardly believe what I was witnessing. Carefully, I sat the drinks on top of a speaker. When I opened my mouth to address her, I was surprisingly calm.

"Yinde, put the glass down."

She glared at me but did not move. I glanced at the nearly empty Vodka bottle sitting on the counter and wondered how full it'd been when she began her binge that morning. Before I could look away, I spotted a bottle of Rum on the counter behind her, top off and at least a glass and a half shy. I returned my focus to her.

"Ayinde. Ayinde, put the got-damned glass down."

"Aargh," she screamed, slamming the glass onto the floor in front of her.

I charged at her, balancing my way around the many busted shards of glass. I grabbed her tight, using the force of all my weight to push her away from the row of dishes she'd prepared to destroy. Her back slammed hard against the refrigerator. She was a slight bigger girl than me, but I was determined not to lose the upper hand as she struggled hard against me. I pushed against her repeatedly until she finally allowed her muscles to begin to relax.

Calmness crawled slowly but steadily into her eyes, and her face went from anger to sadness. Tears welled up as she crumbled into my arms. I fell to my knees with my friend in my possession, rocking her, consoling for what I didn't really have a clue. I noticed the trail of blood running down her leg.

"Oh, Yinde," I lamented. "Let me clean this up."

"Leave it."

"You can't just leave it; you don't know how deep it is. What if it needs stitches?"

She pulled forcefully from my grasp and struggled to her feet. "What, are you deaf? I said leave it."

"Fine. Leave it. But what's Marcus going to think when he comes home and sees your leg, sees his house?"

"Hopefully, he'll feel how I feel."

I raised my body from the floor. "But what did he do?"

Seemingly excited for the opportunity to share her discovery, Ayinde's eyes lit up as she moved across the room to Marcus' workspace which seemed to be the only spot in at least this section of the apartment left unscathed. His laptop sat open on the desk. I was taken aback by the rotation of photos of Marcus and Ayinde that transitioned in and out as his screensaver.

"I'll show you."

I moved cautiously toward the computer as she jiggled the mouse and struggled to position the cursor to highlight a block of text. It was a previously sent message from an online networking account. I read softly, audible but barely.

"Damn, that new pic you put up is hot. You should email me some personal ones. When you coming to the city?" My eyes rolled the back of my head. *This* was the "evidence" that had me out of my comfy bed way too early?

"He's so stupid," Ayinde spoke. Not to me specifically, sort of thoughtlessly. "He forgot to log out. Stupid."

I stood up straight and turned to face her, my hand on my hip and my expression stern. "Yinde, you have to clean this mess before Marcus gets home." I scratched my neck uncomfortably as I glanced about.

"She's not even pretty you know. I looked at her profile. She's not even prettier than me."

"I'm sure. You have to clean this. I'll help you, but you have to clean this."

"Zella, you're not listening"

My fists clenched involuntarily. Not because I wanted to hit her, not that she maybe didn't deserve it in this moment, but out of frustration for being caught up in this. That all too familiar feeling of defeat was creeping up, frustrating me further. I didn't know what to tell her. It was a sin to suggest she leave him, but what else was there to say under such circumstances?

I exhaled patiently. "I'm gonna head over and check out the Northwest campus. You wanna go?"

Ayinde stared at me silently, her expression refusing to give way to her feelings toward me in that moment. Abruptly, she turned and grabbed a handbag and her house keys. She was already dressed, likely in what she'd worn to work the night before. She walked out the door. I grabbed our drinks and followed her lead.

The walk to the el stop was a quiet one. We walked arm in arm, less as a display of our fondness and undying affinity toward one another but more as a requirement for keeping her steady on her feet. She'd been drinking for years, even worked as a bartender four nights a week; her tolerance was high, so these occasional missteps reinforced my suspicions that she'd overdone it.

I glanced at Ayinde in the cool spring sunlight. She was one of the most beautiful women I'd ever met with her honey complexion and deep set brown eyes. Her curls were a much finer texture than my own and hung at least eight inches lower. There were pink streaks throughout the front; a month ago they were orange. The tiny stud diamond in her nose glistened in the sun. The tattoo that traveled from her forearm, across her shoulder, and ended at the base of the right side of her neck was my design.

No one knew exactly what it was, not even me. It was born in a dream, one where I was spending quality time having an inaudible conversation with my mother. It was on a wall that was behind her. For that reason it was important to me. It was abstract, but Ayinde found it beautiful enough when she saw the canvas I'd painted it on, to have it permanently adorn her person.

She sipped her coffee and likely hoped that Marcus would stay with her. I finished mine off and prayed that he'd finally go despite secretly fearing for her life if he did ultimately decide to move on. They'd met two years ago at one of the bars she worked and had a one night stand that had yet to end. Ayinde was looking for love, and she was sure she'd found it in Marcus. I don't know what he was in it for outside of an apparent great lay.

"What's with Northwest?" Ayinde asked, breaking me free from my thoughts.

"I'm going back to school," I answered while cursing silently as I watched the train pass above us.

Ayinde stopped. "Why?"

"What sort of question is that? Don't you think it's time? I've been out of school for six years because of my parents. My dad is my dad, and my mommy isn't coming back. I gotta try to move on with my life."

"I can't believe you're involving me in this." Ayinde snatched away and turned back toward her apartment. I stood, in awe, frozen as I watched her walk away from me. I shook it off and ran after her.

"Ayinde, stop!" I demanded.

She obliged and turned abruptly toward me. "What do you want?"

"Stop it, okay? You just stop it. Every time I mention school, you spaz. What's up with that? What is so bad about me finishing my education?"

"You know."

"No, I don't know, but let me tell you what I do know. What I know is I work in a print shop to supplement the minimal insurance payments I get."

"So what are you trying to say?" she asked defensively.

"I'm not trying to say anything and you know it. Nothing other than it isn't for me, it isn't how I saw my life, and now

I want to reclaim my life. You still have some good years ahead of you, but *I'm* almost thirty, and I want something more from this world."

"You're trying to leave me."

"What?"

"If you go back and finish your program, what do you think you'll do? Your little job won't be enough, your little apartment on Greenleaf won't be enough. Why would your little under-educated, underachieving friend be enough?"

"I can't believe this."

My words were directed at myself. Not knowing what to do, my hand went to my mouth, squeezing it then letting go. I stepped forward, then back, hands on hips then back down as I paced. I walked a few steps to the bus stop and took a seat on the bench beside an older gentleman who was trying hard to pretend he wasn't paying attention. Ayinde coolly moved one of her hands to her mouth and placed a black painted fingernail between her teeth and chewed, a nervous habit which resulted in the absence of nails.

I rested my forearms on my thighs, leaning forward, ringing my hands in pure frustration. I was nearing the end of my rope, and at this point, it was taking all of my inner strength to pull myself back up.

"Ayinde, I will not leave you."

"You say that now."

"You are my friend, the presence or absence of a degree does not dictate my relationships. Can you understand that?"

Ayinde was silent. Her eyes glistened, but she held her head back, refusing to allow the approaching water to create a trail. I looked away from her and into the streets. I watched students heading to classes at their respective schools and felt a pang of envy. The bus finally arrived. The old man offered me a reassuring look before climbing on board. I half-smiled in response.

I looked back at my friend, "You think if I finish school, I'll return to London."

Ayinde nodded.

And you'll be left virtually alone, I thought. "Are you hungry?"

Ayinde shook her head and smirked. "Tired."

"C'mon, my little princess. We'll go to my house and get some rest. I'm not going to leave you. I'm here for you, okay?" She tried to look away from me, but I turned her face toward mine. "Okay?"

She nodded in response.

www.ingramcontent.com/pod-product-compliance
Lightning Source LLC
Chambersburg PA
CBHW020222180626
46810CB00006B/2015